Skeleton Key 🗝

JEFF LaFERNEY

Kejthis
Adrianna,
Thanks for your interest.
Best wishes!

Jeff LaFerney

TOWER
PUBLICATIONS

SKELETON KEY

Published by
Tower Publications

DEDICATION

Two years ago, while aggressively seeking goals that were 100% my own, I finally realized that my chosen path was approximately 0% God's. He had shut door after door and frustrated my stubborn pursuits. Finally, I got the hint and plunged into my first book-writing project—except I continued to wonder if I could continue seeking my own goals at the same time. Um, no. As I stubbornly forgot the earlier lessons, God patiently put trials in my life that pointed me back to the computer and book number two. I don't know what the future holds as far as my writing "career," but I can say without hesitation that my goals have changed and I'm grateful for God's direction and patience. I didn't write this book for me, God. I wrote it for You.

JEFF LAFERNEY

ACKNOWLEDGEMENTS

Well, a second book is done and once again the greatest portion of thanks must go to the Lord. I'm extremely grateful for the ability to write and the ideas that seem to appear miraculously. It is difficult to express adequate thanks when I consider the support and encouragement from family, friends, and other readers of my first book. For those who have partnered with me in the sales and promotion of *Loving the Rain*, thank you all very much. Jennifer, Torey, and Teryn—I love you. Thank you to my wife, Jennifer, and my friend, Andrea McGlashen, for reading my manuscript for *Skeleton Key* and helping me put together my final version. Thank you Marguerite Somers for your editing skills and Dave Vinton for your cover design. Special thanks go out to Chrissy (at the Durand Depot) and Dan Brooks who helped in numerous ways answering questions about the Depot, trains, railroad jargon, the railroad tracks, and the town and its history. Dr. Brian Hunter was more than just my forensic expert. It was Dr. Hunter who gave me the idea of how to solve the mystery of Adrian Payne's death. I am extremely grateful for his help. Finally, I must give enormous props to my friend, Attorney John Folts. John answered all of my law questions, and believe me, I had a lot of them. Thank you so much, John. Your insights, knowledge, and suggestions are woven throughout the book.

CHAPTER 1

The horn sounded, and Tanner Thomas stepped onto the court as a six-foot-two-inch freshman substitute in his first University of Michigan college basketball game. He had missed the first four games because of a sprained ankle. DeMarco Newton, the senior point guard for Oakland University, grabbed Tanner by the jersey. "It's gonna be a long night, Rookie." Tanner was substituted earlier than either he or his father expected. It was a Friday in late-November and Clay Thomas, his father, was sitting in the second row of the stands next to his friend, Dr. Zander Frauss. The Michigan Wolverines' starting point guard, Darius Williams, committed an early second foul and was removed from the game.

On Tanner's first possession, he fumbled the ball for a turnover while he attempted to dribble through the lane. "Nice ball handling, Rookie," taunted Newton. "If you want to see good handles, keep an eye on *me*. Unlike *you*, I have some skills."

Tanner bit his tongue and didn't respond. After all, he *did* just make a turnover. Not a great start to his college basketball career. The Oakland player continued his smack talk as Tanner pressured him up the floor. The dribbler faked a quick crossover dribble and drove right past the U of M freshman, dishing off an easy assist on the play. Newton beat his chest and leaned against Tanner, holding onto his jersey to keep him from getting open. The inbounds passer was called for a five-second violation and Coach Beilein called a quick timeout. "You ain't no good, Rookie," Newton taunted. "You ain't ready for the big time. This ain't high school, but you still 'bout to be schooled." Tanner took a deep breath and headed for the huddle.

Coach Beilein stared at Tanner initially, but then gave him a pat on the butt and said, "Settle down and play your game. We need you out there."

As Tanner stepped back onto the court, his father yelled, "Mental toughness, Tanner…and use your head out there!"

During a short delay while a shot-clock malfunction was being serviced, Newton got in Tanner's face again. "You can't stick with me, Rookie. Won't be long and you'll be back on the bench where you belong. Gonna be a *long* night."

A frustrated Tanner had had enough of the cocky trash-talker. DeMarco Newton was about to learn a great lesson in humility. Tanner held a finger in front of Newton's eyes, moving it side to side, slowly and purposefully. "Listen! Look at me! You've just lost your confidence, Mr. Upperclassman," he said sarcastically. "Focus right here, Newton. No matter how hard you try, you *can't* keep up with me. And you *don't* wanna dribble with your left hand." With a smile, Tanner added, "Gonna be a long night."

Newton's brash angry eyes immediately took on a look of uncertainty. With the clock problem fixed, the official returned to the baseline and handed the ball to an Oakland player who passed it in to Newton. On his first dribble, Tanner reached for the ball, making a steal and dribbling the length of the floor for a lay-up. Newton was unable to catch him. After the inbounds pass, Newton bounced a left-handed dribble off his foot. Tanner recovered it and passed for a second consecutive easy basket.

Zander coolly stuffed a handful of popcorn in his mouth and chewed. He said as casually as if he were doing nothing more than watching the clouds float in the sky. "I think Tanner hypnotized him."

Clay leaned back just as nonchalantly and put his feet up on one of the empty seats in front of him. "Hmmm. And here I thought his only powers were mind-control and clairvoyance."

"Surprise, surprise. I guess he took that 'use your head out there' line kind of literally, didn't he?"

"Yep, he *does* tend to think literally."

"You have any new powers, Clay?" Zander cautiously asked as Tanner drove past Newton and sank a short jump shot.

"Mind-control, telepathy, other random extra-sensory messages. I'm starting to get the hang of telekinesis. That's a new one for me."

"Why do you hide these things from me?" Zander asked as he watched Newton pick up his left-handed dribble and have his pass deflected by Tanner for another steal. "You don't have to go through life alone, Clay. Since your wife died, you've pulled away from people. You don't need to trust only in yourself. You have friends."

"Thanks for the lecture, Doc. I'm doing just fine on my own, I think. We can talk after the game, okay?"

Clay had already said far more than Zander could usually get out of him. He much preferred to not talk about his powers *or* Tanner's at all. It was his opinion that the tragic events in his life the past year were because of the misuse of those powers. He and Tanner witnessed the murder of Jessie, Clay's wife, at the hands of a man that was seeking revenge on Clay because of how he used his power in the past. His wife's behavior at the time, Clay believed, was also his fault because his dishonesty had a harmful effect on their relationship. Professionally, Zander Frauss was determined to learn as much from Clay and Tanner as he could, but even though he was their friend, both men were cautious in their dealings with the doctor. So, while he watched his son, Clay just sat back and made small talk the rest of the game.

DeMarco Newton had a terrible first half and sat out most of the rest of the game, while Tanner continued to impress once he cured himself of his early game jitters. Michigan rolled to an easy victory. At the end, Michigan's play-by-play announcer, Matt Shepard, described Tanner's day as "an impressive debut." While shaking hands at the end of the game, Clay and Zander observed Tanner approach Newton and snap his fingers in front of the Oakland player's face, releasing him from his hypnosis. "Kind of a long night for ya, wasn't it?" Tanner quipped with a smile. "Maybe you won't be so cocky next game. Good luck the rest of the way."

***

Roberto Gomez and his wife, Stacy, walked away with their three cute girls. The two youngest were dark-haired and dark-skinned and resembled their father very much. Anna, the oldest, who had developed a very close bond with Logan Payne, was fair-skinned, blond, and blue-eyed like her mother. She had the cutest little dimple when she grinned. They waved goodbye and pulled away in their banged-up Ford pickup truck. Roberto was a railway worker at the Durand, Michigan, railway yard. He was hired shortly after his wife was hired to work for Adrian Payne and Marshall Mortonson, co-owners of the Durand Depot and the Durand Railroad. Adrian hired the long-legged buxom blond in 2001 with the intentions of getting more from her than just someone to file, answer phones, and sort the mail. Adrian Payne had a gorgeous wife, but he also had no conscience and cared little about anyone but himself. He liked it when Stacy was happy, so he hired Roberto and made it clear that he did it for her. She seemed pleased.

Erika Payne and her son, Logan, watched politely and waved as their friends drove off. "They're such nice people," Erika commented as they re-entered their home. The Gomez couple had been loading up their children and bringing the Paynes one meal a week for the past seven years—ever since Adrian's mysterious disappearance after the famous Amtrak train wreck. "Time for dinner, Logan. Set the table while I take this out of the box."

Logan was a seventeen-year-old senior who was four months shy of his eleventh birthday when his father disappeared. He had inherited his straight brown hair from his father, but he got his blue eyes from his mother. He had long bangs that hung over and hid those eyes, a hairstyle that symbolized his entire personality. Logan barely talked, had no close friends, and tended to spend more time asleep than awake. His mother was energetic, outgoing, and loving. She had remarkable patience with her son and was the only one able to get him to care about anything at all. She was a five foot three inch bundle of joy with short, curly, nearly white blond hair and the most expressive, beautiful blue eyes imaginable. She was cute *and* beautiful. She was sexy and desirable, but didn't seem to know it, and that humbleness made her even more attractive. When her husband disappeared, she seemed to become happier and more content with her life, and those that knew her husband understood completely. Logan, on the other hand, was already introverted before the disappearance, and then withdrew more after the incident.

Once in the kitchen, Erika began working on the tape that secured the box holding their meal. Logan reacted to her instructions to set the table in the normal teenager way—he didn't move a muscle. As Erika began picking at the packing tape with her perfectly manicured nails, Logan observed that she was making exactly no progress, and he was hungry. He loved Stacy Gomez's cheese tortellini with butternut squash. He pulled his jackknife from his pocket and gently touched his mother's hand—an indication that he would open the box for her. The jackknife was a gift from his father. While most teens carried a cell phone around twenty-four seven, Logan carried his jackknife. He flipped it open, sliced the tape expertly, and pulled the meal from the box. "Thank you," Erika smiled.

"Yep." No eye contact. The knife spun in his palm, clicked shut, and disappeared with the skill of a magician.

"I believe I told you to set the table."

With a subtle nod of the head, Logan did as directed, then sat at the table waiting. Erika sat across from Logan, reached for his hand, and said grace. "Lord, thank you for your love and graciousness to us. Thank you for providing this food. Help us to be your servants, and we ask that you bring someone into our lives that we can show your love to and who might love us back. Amen."

Logan squirmed. "Why do you always ask for someone to love us back?"

A question? A *whole* sentence. Wow. "We've been alone for seven years, Logan. Wouldn't it be nice to have someone that we could share our lives with?"

"We have the Gomezes, and Coach Duncan, and Morty, and Mrs. Frauss."

"Let's see…the Gomezes are a sweet *married* couple who have three small children. Dan Duncan is a stressed out egomaniac and your baseball coach when he's not too busy being a cop. Marshall Mortonson is my boss, and Dr. Frauss is your behavioral therapist. I was thinking more along the lines of a male figure in our lives whose company we can enjoy. Wouldn't you like to have a father figure around here occasionally?"

"No." And that was the end of the dinner conversation. Erika worried about her son. These years without Adrian had freed her to be happy again, but Logan seemed to live in fear of something…something he'd yet to express to a single person in seven years.

Chapter 2

Dr. Zander Frauss was a neuroscientist for the University of Michigan's Department of Psychiatric Medicine who specialized not only in the field of neuroscience but also in the field of parapsychology. He headed a parapsychology laboratory called The Division of Perceptual Studies. Except for his glasses, he looked nothing like a scientist. He dressed casually, combed his wavy blond hair stylishly, and had a strong, athletic frame. Clay and Tanner Thomas were seated in his office, patiently waiting for the good doctor as he agitatedly paced back and forth, eyeing some files he held in his hands. Zander would only glance at Clay when he was willing for Clay to receive a telepathic message. Clay heard, *"When will you trust me?...I can't help you if you won't include me...Are you ever going to trust anyone other than yourself?...When are you going to use your powers for good?"*

Clay never liked discussions about his powers with Zander, so the silence wasn't bothering him in the least—and the thoughts he was pulling from Zander's head were interesting to him. Tanner was texting and seemed oblivious to Zander's irritation. Tanner was tall, handsome, intelligent, athletic, and had a good sense of humor. His dark, sparkling eyes accented his short, dark hair and ready smile. Tanner never seemed to take his powers too seriously. He reminded his father of Johnny Storm, the Human Torch in the Fantastic Four. He *liked* that he had powers and was so good-natured about having them that Clay only worried about him doing something immature. He was wondering about the hypnosis thing that he had just witnessed, but he knew that Zander would get around to asking the questions once he stopped fretting about being left out of the loop. He was also curious about the papers that Zander kept eyeing.

Finally Zander turned to Tanner. "Since when can you hypnotize people?"

"Oh, you noticed, huh?" He turned to his father. "He was such a jerk, Dad."

Clay just rolled his eyes a bit and shrugged his shoulders. It really wasn't his business, he figured. And not Zander's either, but when Zander set his mind on something, he was difficult to be denied.

"Well?" Zander asked.

"In my psych class, we were talkin' about hypnotism. The prof had some pretty funny examples. Anyhow, I figured I'd try it and see what happened. So anyway, Big Jake from the hoops team is always comin' into our room eating our food and smellin' up the place, so I told him I was gonna hypnotize him if he'd sit still. Didn't know if I could do it or not. Told him it'd help him shoot free throws better. I grabbed a spoon—no kidding—and swung it back and forth in front of his eyes. I talked all calm and stuff. I was watchin' his eyes and his pupils dilated and started kinda bouncin' around, so I said, 'You're very, very sleepy.'" Tanner laughed. "Stupid words like that, and then I said, 'Whenever you're in our room and we say "Jake," you're gonna smell a horrible smell. So bad you can't stand it and you have to leave.' Then I told him he was a great free throw shooter. He stays out of our room now, *and* he's been makin' his throws."

Clay couldn't help but smile. "That's not what you did tonight, though. I didn't see any spoon."

"Well, once I realized that it actually worked, I did a little studying. Stage hypnotists usually use short, firm commands because their audience volunteers are already on edge. I figured it might work in front of a screaming basketball crowd too. So I got the dork's attention basically by shakin' my finger at him, gave a couple of commands, and I saw the same look that Big Jake had, so I just told him he wasn't gonna play so well anymore. You *saw* me snap him out of it at the end, right?"

Clay nodded. "Any other stories you wanna share?"

"I had Jake clucking like a chicken in practice yesterday. He was struttin' around without a care in the world. Thought Beilein was gonna have a stroke, but we were laughin' so hard he gave us a drink-break instead. Said if Jake wanted to act like a chicken, it was his business as long as he kept makin' his free throws."

Clay laughed, but Zander had other things on his mind. "Did your dad tell you that he's telekinetic?"

"Like, you can move things with your mind? Really? That's so cool, Dad! Show me."

Clay usually didn't feel very comfortable using his powers, but he figured he'd mess with Zander, just for the fun of it. The doctor had been pacing in front of his leather office couch holding what seemed to be important papers in his hands, but when Clay stood up, Zander stopped and stood facing toward Clay and away from the couch. Clay telekinetically used his right hand to start pulling his friend's file folders from his hands. Zander clearly objected and began pulling back while Clay used his left hand to slide the couch forward several inches. The doctor tightened his grip and with additional effort began pulling back. Clay simply released his "hold" on the files and Zander stumbled back, hitting his calves on the sofa, falling backward, and literally flipping over the back of the couch, papers flying every which way. Amazingly, he managed to land on his feet, his hair flopping over his eyes and his glasses hanging crazily from just one ear. Tanner's eyes got big until he saw the doc's face and then he lost it, laughing hysterically. Clay laughed, and then Zander lost all seriousness and broke out in his own laughter.

"You *have* been practicing."

"Yeah, a little," Clay wisecracked.

"How do you do that, Dad?"

Zander answered for him. "Telekinesis is the ability to move objects using the mind or thoughts. We know that energy never dies but merely changes form. We also know that one form of energy can physically move another form. Logically, then, thought waves, which are produced by the brain and are forms of energy, should be able to affect another form of energy. Your dad is just simply focusing that energy in a way that others can't, and I'm not surprised. The latest test results for both of you are pretty interesting."

"What's the news, Doc? Is that the paperwork scattered back there on the floor?"

Zander ignored the question. "Well, the brain activity for both of you has increased. It appears you're both getting smarter. Tanner, how're your classes going?"

"They're pretty easy, actually."

"How 'bout you, Clay? Anything different with you?"

"Yeah, actually. I was thinking yesterday."

"And?"

"And what? Aren't you impressed that I was *thinking*?"

Tanner started laughing again, and though he was smiling, Zander couldn't help but roll his eyes just a little. It was only about a year before that Clay and Zander had a conversation that helped Clay realize for the first time that there was actually a scientific reason for his powers and that he wasn't some sort of mutant X-Man or something. Zander explained that his patients who actually showed genuine parapsychological abilities had much more active brain activity in the medulla oblongata. In addition to regulating breathing and blood pressure, the medulla oblongata also controls such things as heart rate, perspiration, swallowing, reflexes, blinking, and even sexual arousal. The functions regulated by the medulla oblongata take place at all hours of the day without any need for input from the rest of the brain. The medulla oblongata is also involved in the *response* to certain stimuli, creating reflexive responses, which are designed to keep the body functioning. The ability to respond automatically to certain stimuli is critical to survival, as is the independent regulation of necessary functions like breathing and swallowing.

Whereas most of its actions are involuntary, some work in tandem with the conscious mind. The medulla oblongata is made up of two parts. One part is open and one part is closed. Dr. Frauss discovered that in people with special mental abilities, the closed part was at least partially open, caused generally by spinal cord trauma or some sort of trauma caused by strangulation. With both parts open, people theoretically could receive "super" autonomic functions. The doctor also explained to Clay that while most autonomic functions were involuntary, some, like breathing or blinking, could be conscious or unconscious. A person could make himself stop breathing or blinking or could hold his urine, for instance. His research seemed to indicate that persons with special mental powers were getting additional sensory information through the medulla oblongata—they experienced "super" autonomic functioning. Their brains could input data that common people could not input. But the kicker was, they were somehow able to control that input. For example, they could control objects or control thoughts of others or control what thoughts they could read. The control was what made those people special.

Both Clay and Tanner had severe trauma as a result of difficult childbirths. In both cases, they were severely strangled by their own umbilical cords at delivery and had to be resuscitated. In both cases, according to Dr. Frauss's tests, the closed parts of their medulla oblongatas were *completely* open, far more open than any other patient that he had ever tested. Both Clay and Tanner miraculously, and coincidentally, had super brain powers that seemed to be getting more powerful and more focused. They were Zander's "super patients," and they were also Zander's closest friends.

"What I was *hoping*, Clay, is that as you get smarter, you might also get wiser. Maybe you'll stop secluding yourself and listen to a voice of reason. Listen, Jessie passed away almost a year ago. Have you gone on a date since then?"

"Zander, you know I respect you and consider you to be my closest friend, but it's really not your business how long I mourn my wife's death. Especially when it was *my* fault."

"Though I don't agree it was your fault, I'll try to respect your wishes. But it's my goal to help you to move on and lead a more productive life. You'll probably be just as stubborn as you are about helping me with my research, but I don't tend to give up easily."

"So are those your research papers on the floor, Dr. Frauss?" Tanner interjected in hopes of changing the subject. His dad shot him the thought, "*Thanks.*" Tanner just nodded in reply.

"No, actually they aren't. They're some papers my wife has shared with me along with some research that I've done. Because of patient confidentiality, I can't share all the information about the patient, but my wife, Lydia, has a case in which she thinks maybe you, Clay, or you *and* Tanner could help. And there's a *very* interesting back story."

"What's up, Doc?" Clay enjoyed using those words.

"Well, there is a nice lady who works for the Durand Depot. Since you still haven't sold your house and you're still living in Flint, that's not too far away. Her husband disappeared after a train accident about seven years ago, never to be heard from again. Her son is a high school athlete—basketball and baseball. He was withdrawn *before* his father's disappearance, but he's worsened over the years. Lydia was thinking that maybe you could befriend the family and help the young man. He's a senior this year."

Clay became interested in what his friend was thinking because he sensed that Zander wasn't telling the whole story. His biggest clue was that the doctor was looking at Tanner, who couldn't read his mind, instead of Clay. "*Tell him to look at me and tell whatever it is that he's not saying, Tanner,*" Clay directed his son when they made eye contact.

Tanner got the message and relayed it to Zander, who turned uncomfortably and looked Clay in the eyes. "There's something that I'm not saying." Clay and Tanner laughed, and Zander sensed immediately that they were messing with his mind. "Okay, guys, so much for the fun and games. Jeesh! I'll tell you what's on my mind. The whole train accident is a mystery. I was actually wondering if you would be able to figure out what happened. Lydia is most interested in helping the boy, but my sense of mystery and my intuition is telling me that if you find out what happened out there, you may be able to help the boy at the same time. Besides, it'll give you something to do."

"So what do you want me to do? You want me to show up in Durand unannounced and simply start reading people's minds until I solve a mystery? What is it with you, Zander?"

"It's an adventure. A way to help someone. A way to possibly use your God-given gifts to benefit someone else. And maybe you'll learn something about yourself along the way. Use some of those new brain cells and see if you can figure out what happened," Zander smiled.

"And how do you know that I won't end up hurting someone else or getting someone else killed?" Clay asked.

"None of us knows what life has in store for us. But we continue to walk by faith. And maybe we build relationships along the way and learn to trust in someone else too. Lydia says the mother leads caving expeditions. What do think about caving with her to get to know her? You're always game for a little physical activity, and Lydia says she's quite a looker too. If I set it up, would you be willing to go?"

***

A dwarf-sized man was standing along the side of the road with his thumb extended in hopes of hitching a ride. A car whizzed by, causing the man to leap off the road's shoulder. Passengers in the car roared with laughter. While screaming endless obscenities at the driver, Jasper angrily stepped back to the side of the road. Someone had stolen or hidden his bicycle while he was in the downtown drugstore, and now another bad day was turning worse as he tried to make his way home. The car turned around on the road and headed back at breakneck speed, stereo blasting so loud that the passengers' ears might have been bleeding. The teenaged driver was speeding down the road in the wrong lane in a direct line toward the little man.

Once again, Jasper leaped out of the way to avoid being struck by the car. The knit hat that was covering Jasper's ears fell off in his headlong avoidance of death and disappeared in the weeds along the side of the road. Jasper's face reddened in anger to a shade akin to the red curls that were newly exposed on his head. The miserably dispositioned little man was about as unpopular in the town of Durand as a man could be. He felt around in the weeds for his hat while the car slowed in preparation for its third run at the helpless man. He found the hat at the same time that his hand discovered a large piece of timber, which was actually a two-and-a-half foot piece of sawed-off railroad tie. Jasper grabbed the wood rectangle and pulled, finding that he was able to move it and eventually lift it. He pulled it out to the side of the road, fully intending to hurl it into the car's windshield if the driver intended to make another pass—which actually *was* his intention.

Once at the side of the road again, Jasper noticed a crater-sized pothole in the pavement—a specialty of most Michigan roads. He also noticed that the car was turning in preparation for a third thrilling run at the hitchhiker. Jasper lay the 7 x 9-inch white-pined tie at the far side of the pothole, then stood in front of the hole to wait. As the car sped toward him, he saw police flashers light up in the distance and a siren sounded. The driver saw the police lights in his side mirror and looked into his rear-view mirror, taking his eyes temporarily off the road as he rapidly approached Jasper. The conniving dwarf jumped out of the way for the third time as the right-front tire plunged into the hole and emerged with a stunning jar, slamming first into the concrete edge and then into the railroad tie. The right-front wheel snapped off at the axle and the car skidded along the road on its frame, spinning in a nearly three-hundred-sixty-degree turn. The railroad tie flipped back into the weeds alongside the road while the tire bounced a couple of times and then made a lonesome roll down the road.

First one police car and then another braked to a stop in front of the damaged vehicle. Jasper took great pleasure in his role as eyewitness to the accident. Officers Dan Duncan and Verne Gilbert wrote up an accident report and gave tickets for speeding, reckless driving, and failure to exercise due caution to avoid colliding with a pedestrian. After Jasper told his tale to the policemen, failing, of course, to include information about the railroad tie, he accepted a ride home from Officer Gilbert and filed a police report regarding his missing bicycle.

CHAPTER 3

Zander turned and gathered up the scattered files and papers. "Have a seat at this table," he pointed. "I have some things to show you."

Clay and Tanner did as they were directed.

"In August of 2003, there was a train accident in Durand. I've found two news articles on the internet that I'd like you to see. He pulled the first article out. Clay began reading while Tanner looked over his shoulder.

Tracks Cleared After Amtrak Train Collides with Horse Trailer
August 8, 2003

Amtrak will be operating its Blue Water service to and from Durand again normally this evening. Clean up and track repairs were completed during the night after a train collided with a semi-tractor-trailer Thursday at 9:05 p.m. near the Durand Union Station. Amtrak Train 364 collided with a trailer carrying four harness-racing horses meant for delivery to Sports Creek Raceway in Swartz Creek. The semi-truck was abandoned on the tracks at the South Oak Street crossing. The train, carrying seventeen passengers, smashed into the horse trailer, destroying and setting it on fire, derailing three train cars, and causing damage to the main-line track. Eleven passengers were treated for minor injuries while the train engineer, Joseph Carrollton, was transported to Memorial Healthcare in Owosso with critical injuries. One passenger, Adrian Payne, a co-owner of the Durand Depot, has been mysteriously missing since the accident. All four of the horses were killed.

The derailment and track damage affected Friday morning Amtrak service. The main engine and two coach-cars derailed, putting the two passenger-cars on the ground and damaging the rail itself as well as the track circuitry. Track Superintendent Wilson Goodrich began supervision and direction of cleanup and repair operations within hours of the disaster. Durand area police and paramedics arrived promptly, while firefighters arrived on the scene and quickly extinguished the truck fire. Police Chief Luke Hopper identified two of the injured persons as Marshall Mortonson, co-owner of the Durand Depot, who jumped from the front of the moving train along with the engineer, and Logan Payne, son of the missing co-owner, Adrian Payne.

The truck's driver, Lawrence Maloney (38) from Louisville, Kentucky, was driven to the site via police cruiser after the collision occurred. He claimed that his rig was stolen while he was at the Durand Shell station using the restroom after refueling his truck. There is no explanation as to why it was left on the tracks or who may have stolen and abandoned it. Track Superintendent Goodrich was willing to neither estimate the cost of the damages and repairs nor speculate as to why the Amtrak engine was unable to avoid the collision. He was willing only to state, "An investigation will be made."

When the two Thomas men finished the first article, Zander slid it away and replaced it with a second. "This is the follow-up article," Zander explained. "It was printed five days later after the so-called investigation was finished. I think you'll find it interesting." Clay and Tanner began reading.

Amtrak Wreck Details Tracked Down
August 13, 2003

Just five days after the disastrous Amtrak train wreck at the South Oak Street crossing in Durand, the investigation has been concluded. Amtrak Train 364 collided with a semi-truck rig carrying four harness-racing horses meant for delivery to Sports Creek Raceway in Swartz Creek. Eleven passengers were treated for minor scrapes and bruises. Joseph Carrollton, the Amtrak train engineer from Chicago who had been rushed to Memorial Healthcare in Owosso, was tragically killed in the accident. Engineer Carrollton leaped from the moving train just before impact. The Shiawassee County Medical Examiner determined that the cause of death was impact from the overturned second car of the derailed Amtrak train. It was also determined that Carrollton's blood alcohol level was .17 percent—more than twice the legal blood alcohol limit.

Durand Police Chief Luke Hopper confirmed that the truck was stolen from the parking lot of the Shell station at the I-69 exit in Durand while the driver, Lawrence Maloney (38) of Louisville, Kentucky, was using the restroom. The four racehorses were all killed in the impact of the crash and impending fire. Track Superintendent Wilson Goodrich reported, "After the train completed the ninety-degree curve between Monroe Road and Oak Street, Engineer Carrollton was unable to bring it to a stop before it collided with the horse trailer which had been abandoned across the tracks." According to Goodrich, the train's "black box" recorder indicated that a failed attempt was made to brake the passenger train "in time to avoid the disaster."

One of the most bizarre aspects of the train wreck is the mysterious disappearance of Adrian Payne, co-owner of the Durand Depot. Railway records and various passengers have confirmed that Payne was on board the train, but since the accident, there has been no sign of his whereabouts. His wife of thirteen years, Erika Payne, and son, Logan, have yet to hear from Payne.

Board members of the Durand Union Station Michigan Railroad History Museum, in cooperation with Amtrak, have agreed to display the crashed train engine outside of the History

Museum at 200 Railroad Street in Durand. It is to be located next to the 1968 refurbished caboose that was purchased at auction from Grand Trunk Railroad and donated to the museum. In an interesting gesture, the four horses were buried Monday along the railroad tracks about fifteen hundred feet west of the South Oak Street crossing where a tombstone will be placed as a memorial. The body of Joseph Carrollton (44) of Chicago, Illinois, has been transported to Drake and Son Funeral Home on North Western Avenue in Chicago. His wife and two children survive Carrollton.

When Clay finished reading, Zander said, "So what do you think, Clay? Would you be willing to meet Erika Payne? I think you can help her with her son. Lydia has been unable to get through to Logan Payne, and he's been unwilling to talk about the accident and the loss of his father. It's just possible that if you can solve the mystery behind his father's disappearance, Lydia or Erika may be able to get through to him."

"And in the meantime, I'll get out and will begin 'moving on' with my life. That's what you're thinking, isn't it? Don't deny that's what you're thinking because I read your mind."

"I think you should do it, Dad. And I'll help in any way that I can. Go with her to the cave, and have a good time. Get your mind on something different and important. Maybe Zander's right, and this'll be good for you."

Clay stopped to consider his son's words which held more weight than Zander's. He was somehow impressed by Tanner's sincerity. "Well, I don't see how I can help them, but I have to admit, I *am* curious about what happened. I guess I'll give it a try, but don't expect too much. Tell that Erika Payne lady that I'll go caving if it's okay with her."

"Great!" Zander said enthusiastically. "I'll tell Lydia to make arrangements. I have a good feeling about all of this."

***

"Hello." Erika Payne looked at her watch as she held the phone to her ear. She'd had trouble getting Logan out of bed and now she was running late for work.

"Good morning, Mrs. Payne. This is Dr. Lydia Frauss. I was hoping to catch you before you headed to work."

"Morning. I'm running a bit late, but is there something wrong?"

"No, nothing like that. I have a favor to ask of you."

"Sure, Dr. Frauss. What is it?"

"Well, my husband is a neuroscientist at the University of Michigan. He has a friend who's been going through a tough time after the death of his wife. I've told my husband about how you're a caving guide and how you give faith lessons. He seems to think that you're just the person to help him snap out of his doldrums. Do you think I could schedule a caving expedition with you? Zander's friend has agreed to meet with you and take one of your tours."

"Well, I'm interested. Sure. But I don't know if I can just take off for the day with a complete stranger. Could you give me his name?"

"His name is Clay Thomas."

Erika got immediate goose bumps. She *knew* a Clay Thomas. What had it been? Twenty-five years? Her pulse was racing and she nearly dropped the phone. "Um, okay, what can you tell me about him?"

"Zander says he's never met a more trustworthy man. He's a baseball coach. Fortyish. Tall and handsome. Came from the Lansing area—Haslett, I believe. Now he lives in Flint while coaching the University of Michigan baseball team."

Erika felt excitement that she hadn't felt in a long time. She had grown up in Haslett, and she knew Clay Thomas. "Okay, Dr. Frauss, I'll do it. I need to get Logan to school and get to work. You can call me there, and we can exchange information. There are some things he'll need to bring to be prepared."

"Sure, Erika, I'll set everything up. Thanks. I'll talk to you later today."

CHAPTER 4

Roberto Gomez was standing in his living room with his youngest daughter in his arms. He was watching his tall, long-legged, sexy, blond wife, Stacy, jog down the street. He was waiting for her return so he could head to work. Roberto had been given his job by Adrian Payne, who hired Stacy for her looks, and then hired Roberto to impress her with his generosity. Roberto hated Adrian Payne just as much as everyone else did, probably more, but since his disappearance, the job he'd provided had supported the Gomez family. Stacy had quit sometime after she had her first child, and Marshall Mortonson, Payne's partner, had given the job to Erika so that she and her son could survive without her husband. Stacy and Roberto had been bringing meals to Erika ever since the train wreck. He often wondered if Erika was as happy that her husband was missing as everyone else was.

When Stacy entered the house, Roberto, a very handsome Hispanic man, who was three inches shorter than his wife, quickly handed over the child, grabbed up his keys and phone, and said, "Morty called. There's some kind of problem at the railroad that needs my attention. Something about brake work. Gotta run."

"I need to do some grocery shopping today, so I can make dinner," Stacy informed her husband.

"Are we going to see Logan?" Anna, their seven-year-old daughter asked.

"No, we take them meals on Thursdays. Not tonight, Honey."

Roberto gave each of the girls a hug. Stacy gave a soft kiss and ran her fingers through his long, dark hair—he loved her more than anything and would do anything to help her, provide for her, and protect her.

"Have a nice day, Robbie!" said Stacy. "Call me if you're coming home for lunch."

"I love you, Stacy. Adios."

***

When Roberto arrived, Marshall Mortonson greeted him outside the depot. Police lights were flashing and the train yard was in a moderate state of confusion. Police Chief Luke Hopper was standing outside of his vehicle talking to Officer Dan Duncan on the police radio. A cargo train was just finishing a turn on the wye track at the end of the yard where it would come to rest on the repair track. Marshall was only in his early forties, but he appeared much older because of graying, balding, and a paunchy mid-section. He explained to Roberto that his brake repair expertise was needed on the slowly moving train engine.

"Lemme get my tools, Mr. Mortonson, an' I'll get right on it. Why's 'Copper' here?" Roberto asked, using the nickname that always annoyed the Police Chief.

"Another break-in at the depot. I called it in, but it's no use. There's never anything missing and never a clue left behind."

"You *still* don't believe the ghost stories, do ya?"

"I don't believe in ghosts, Robbie, but if there *was* such a thing, my ghost is one major pain in the butt."

Chief Hopper signaled that he was off his radio and ready to take a look inside the building, so Roberto headed for his tools and Mortonson turned to lead the way.

Hopper was maybe six feet four inches tall and built kind of lean and wiry. He had curly, copper-colored hair, light blue-green eyes, and even some freckles, giving him a "can't-take-you-very-seriously" look. Because people tended to not take him very seriously, he learned to hate being called "Copper" and usually demanded that he be called a proper name. "Sorry for the wait, Morty. Dan stopped a semi-truck that we were keepin' an eye out for. He made an arrest and impounded the truck. Anyway, we can head to your offices now. Same as before?" What Hopper was alluding to was that he'd investigated over a dozen break-ins the past six years or so. There was always an appearance of a break-in but never anything missing. There was never any evidence as to how the vandal broke in either, nor was there any physical evidence left behind. Whoever it was seemed impossible to catch and whatever he or she was looking for obviously still hadn't been found. Chief Hopper tended to side with Roberto on *this* particular case. The best explanation was a ghost. It was kind of tough to write that up in a police report, however, so once again he was prepared to go through the motions of making an investigation and filling out the paperwork. Every cop in Durand would've volunteered to do the fruitless work at the depot just to get a glimpse of Erika Payne, but Hopper was the boss and he pulled rank and made the "ghost break-ins" his personal case.

Walking into Marshall Mortonson's office was like déjà vu. Every "break-in" was eerily similar. Mortonson's desk nameplate was always turned face down. Desk drawers and file cabinet drawers were always open and papers were always scattered on the desk and floor, giving the appearance that the intruder was looking for something in particular, but Mortonson could never discern that anything was actually missing. The break-ins simply made him feel violated; they were an invasion of his privacy. The desk and furniture were always rearranged in the same general disorderly way. When Marshall worked, he would sit at his desk with his back to the window and face the doorway, but after the break-ins, the desk was always turned the opposite way so that the desk chair had a view of the railroad tracks through the office window.

The strangest but most consistent change was that a silver shovel would always be found lying on top of the desk. When the depot broke new ground, laying some new track and building a couple of new buildings on the grounds about nine years earlier, two silver shovels were purchased and used by Marshall and Adrian Payne to officially make the first two ground-breaking scoops. Marshall's shovel, no matter where he stored it or hid it, always ended up lying on top of his desk.

While Chief Hopper was going through the motions, once again, of filing the report, Erika Payne poked her head into the office. "Hey, Morty. Hi, Copper," she said with a flirty smile.

"Chief *Hopper*, Erika."

"Ooh, you must be on duty. No funny business this morning?" Then she noticed the office in its state of disarray. "Is it another break-in?" As she asked the question, the hair on her arms rose. Every time Marshall's office was invaded, so was hers.

"Erika, look around. Does any of this mean anything to you?" asked Hopper. "Everything is always so similar."

"I don't know. The thief must've liked the way Adrian decorated his office because the furniture is always moved like Adrian liked it." She smiled, but the break-ins really weren't funny.

As she started to head for her own office, she nearly ran into Officer Duncan. "Whoa, excuse me, Erika." He stared at her speechlessly for a second, just as nearly everyone did, but then he regained his composure and asked Chief Hopper, "Is there anything I can do?"

"What're you doing here, Dan? I thought you were impounding the truck you just seized."

"Yeah, I was driving it over to the impound lot, but wanted to check things out here too." He had several reasons for driving the truck to the depot. Like everyone else, he was hoping to run into Erika, which he *literally* almost just did, and he also was more than curious about the ghost that was rumored to haunt the depot offices. In addition, Dan happened to be the kind of person that liked to show off by driving *anything* that was not his own. He possessed every kind of license—boat, motorcycle, operator, commercial, taxi—so he drove the truck to the depot just so people could see him drive it.

He followed Erika into her office, and observed her perfect figure with curiosity as she repositioned a picture of Logan and her that had been tipped over. The family picture on her wall had been removed and was face down on the floor. Erika replaced it. Duncan was a short, stocky, barrel-chested man. His thick neck, shoulders, arms, and chest were ample proof of a lot of time working out in the gym. But except for his obvious crush on Erika, Duncan was a hard man to figure. He acted the part of the tough guy with precision—cockiness, vanity, and all—but he was a bird watcher and a frequent community service volunteer who was always looking for ways to relieve the constant stress he felt. He used to play softball at a very competitive level, but after Adrian Payne disappeared, he began coaching instead and took a lot of interest in Logan Payne—he always made sure Logan was on any team he coached, and that included the high school team. He was a decent police officer, who sometimes wore his badge a bit too proudly, but he seemed to actually have more interest in big trucks, fast cars, and dirt bikes than in his career. Many years earlier, his tobacco chewing led to some lip cancer, so most times over the last decade, he could be seen chewing huge wads of gum or, even more regularly, handfuls of sunflower seeds. Duncan had some seeds to spit, so he headed for Erika's wastebasket where he noticed a couple of woodcarvings had been tossed. After considering spitting the seeds anyway, he wisely grabbed a disposable plastic cup instead. Erika noticed the "trash" and removed it. After expertly spitting his shells, he asked, "Why would a thief throw your son's carvings away?"

Erika seemed a little agitated when she answered, "I don't know, Dan, but every time there's one of these break-ins, I find some personal items of Logan's—usually the carvings since he's started doing them—thrown in the wastebasket. I don't understand."

"What if it really is a ghost?"

Erika felt a chill of cold air on her skin before she answered. "Still wouldn't explain what it has against my son's personal things."

As Chief Hopper arrived to finish his investigation, Dan excused himself and Erika's phone rang. It was Lydia Frauss with the arrangements they had discussed earlier in the morning. Erika left instructions for Clay Thomas. She was told that he would pick her up so they could drive together to the cave in Indiana.

CHAPTER 5

Erika drove Logan to school earlier in the morning and was waiting nervously for the arrival of Clay Thomas. She knew Clay from Haslett, Michigan, where she went to high school before moving to Durand her senior year. After twenty-five years, he certainly would have changed, but she couldn't keep herself from being excited to see him. Marshall Mortonson would pick up Logan after early season basketball practice at school. He would take her son to get something to eat and then drop him off at Dan Duncan's when his shift ended, where they would play video games and watch some college basketball. Erika was grateful for help from her friends because she was unwilling to leave Logan home alone. His depression was such a concern that she worried he might do something desperate.

Clay was a few minutes late, so she gathered her gear in a pile and then headed for the bathroom to touch up her makeup again. As she was perfecting her blue eye shadow, the doorbell rang and her pulse started racing. She walked to the doorway as casually as she could and excitedly opened the door. Clay Thomas had barely changed from high school. "Hi, I'm Clay. Sorry I'm a few minutes late, but I was stopped by a train." Same grin. Same smiling eyes. Erika was a year older than Clay, which meant he was forty-one years old, yet he was as fit looking as ever. His brown hair showed no signs of graying or balding. His dark brown eyes were just as she remembered. He was tall and athletic looking, but what she remembered most about him was that he was nice—somewhat shy, but always nice.

"Happens all the time around here. I'm Erika," she replied politely, nervous that he might not remember her as fondly as she remembered him.

Clay's smiling eyes turned curious, and then he recalled how he knew Erika from his past. "Erika? Erika Baring...Payne? Baring-Payne? Now there's an interesting married name."

"Great...I haven't seen you for twenty-five years and the first thing you do is make fun of my name? I've heard it before, Clay." She smiled.

Clay thought it was a wonderful smile. She was just as beautiful as he remembered her from high school. The smile was the same; the gorgeous blue eyes sparkled just the same; the good humor was just as evident. Her hair was shorter and not quite as curly, but it was the same deep, nearly white blond that captured his attention in school. She was stunning, and it made Clay instantly sad. Erika noticed the sadness immediately, but she knew they had a twelve-hour round trip to get reacquainted. Her goal was to help him along his road to recovery from the loss of his wife and to help him snap out of the "doldrums" that Lydia Frauss expressed. She reverted to small talk as they loaded Clay's car with her gear and she closed up her house for the day. It was going to be an interesting trip.

***

Logan Payne's first hour class was the only class he actually enjoyed and it was probably the only reason that his mother was able to get him out of bed in the morning. It was a woodshop class. Logan's latest project was a small storage chest. He was attaching the hinges when his teacher, Mr. Jorgenson, stopped to look at his work. Mr. Jorgenson's jaw dropped as he looked at the cover that was lying on Logan's worktable. On it was a remarkable carving of a horse. The detail was exquisite. The horse was lying on the ground next to some railroad tracks, apparently lifeless but nonetheless beautiful. "You did this?" he asked in amazement.

"Yes." That was all that Logan said while he continued to work.

"How? When?"

"Knife. Home."

"You're kidding. You carved it with your jackknife?"

"Yes." Logan was well known for his monosyllabic answers.

"This is amazing. Do you have other carvings?"

"Yes."

"Could I see them?"

Shrug of the shoulders.

"Well, if you don't mind, I'd love to see some of them. You're really talented, Logan."

Another shrug of the shoulders. His hair was hanging over his eyes and he never even gave his favorite teacher any eye contact. "Thanks."

***

After Erika meticulously checked her supplies and loaded the car, the two old friends drove off and did a little catching up. Erika's father took a job at J & R Machinery Engineers and moved the family to Durand for her senior year. When he retired, her parents moved to Tampa, Florida. After high school, Erika headed off to Michigan State University to be a cheerleader. First she got mono, and then she had an emergency appendectomy. She managed to catch up on one semester, but dropped out and headed home during semester two. She never finished college and eventually married Adrian Payne, who was on a fast track, no pun intended, to success in the train business. His best friend, Marshall Mortonson, and Adrian partnered to take over the Durand Depot and Railway. It wasn't long and he'd finagled business contracts with various shipping companies, putting a local trucking company out of business.

"Maybe this is too much information, but he was a terrible husband and a worse father. When he disappeared after the train wreck in 2003, my life improved drastically, simply because he wasn't in it." After she explained about the train wreck and her husband's mysterious disappearance, she went on to explain that

Adrian and Mortonson had a partnership contract. The partners had voting shares in the company that did not pass to heirs upon a death of a partner. The heirs would be able to own part of the business, but they'd have no say in how it was run. So even if Adrian was declared dead, which he had never been because there had never been any evidence of his passing, she would have no control over the business. Their partnership agreement *did* stipulate, however, that if a partner passed away or decided to sell, the other partner either had to purchase his partner's shares or agree to sell as well. Because Adrian wasn't declared dead, Mortonson kept the company and had complete control of it as well. Erika was left out in the cold, except that Marshall Mortonson hired her as an employee and she'd earned small capital gains over the years. She had no other work experience, education, or training. Her son, Logan, was only ten years old when the accident occurred. Erika was trapped in Durand with no other real options, as far as she could see.

Eventually Clay explained that after high school, he attended Eastern Michigan University on a football scholarship, but after being red-shirted his freshman year and only making the playing field a handful of times his sophomore year, he quit the football team, got a teaching degree, and began a teaching and coaching career. "About eight years ago, I took a job at Mott Community College, teaching math and coaching the varsity baseball team." He then explained how he had met his wife, Jessie, got married, and had one son, Tanner. He outlined briefly how his wife had been murdered about eleven months before. He finished by telling that Tanner was at the University of Michigan on a basketball scholarship and that he'd been hired as the head coach of the Michigan baseball team but that he'd been unable to sell his house, so he was living alone in Flint.

Both stories seemed kind of tragic, and there was a long pause in the conversation, neither person knowing what to say next, but both knowing exactly what they wanted to talk about. Finally it was Erika that broke the silence. "I had a huge crush on you in high school."

"I had a crush on you too."

"I don't know why I broke up with you."

Before Clay could stop himself he blurted out, "I told you too."

"No, you didn't. The way I remember it, I was totally acting like a fool and then all of a sudden, I decided that I just wanted to be friends."

Clay had been hiding his powers of mind-control his entire life and it made him an unhappy person. His dishonesty, he believed, played a major role in his wife's death, and he was determined to be honest with people, so he took a deep breath and explained to Erika what had actually happened. "You might not believe what I'm about to say, but I have a medical condition which gives me the ability to control minds. When I look into people's eyes, I can influence their thoughts as well as their memories. I was a sophomore. You were the cutest, nicest girl in the school— everyone wanted to go out with you. I told you to like me, and you did—except you went a little overboard. You were smothering me with affection, and I knew that the only reason you were doing it was because I told you to. After the first few days when everyone thought I was 'the man,' I realized it was just a farce. I had taken away your choice and I got no pleasure from that, so I got back in your head and told you to tell me that you just wanted to be friends. You broke up with me, and that was that. It was the right thing for me to do because I had taken away your choice. I'm sorry, Erika. Please forgive me."

Erika looked somewhat confused. "I honestly don't understand what you mean by 'mind-control,' but before you explain, do you remember when I was in eighth grade and you were in seventh and we had a drama class together?"

"Yeah, Mrs. Jackson hated me. Always gave me embarrassing things to do, and the class was filled with popular eighth grade girls. It was humiliating."

"No, Mrs. Jackson didn't hate you. She thought you were just as cute as the rest of us. Practically every girl in the class had a crush on you, but most of them got over it once they got into high school. I never got over it. I always liked you."

"But in tenth grade, I told you to like me."

"Well, if that mind-control is real, that explains my obsessive behavior my junior year. But the way I saw it, it was the first time you actually paid any attention to *me*. Telling you that I just wanted to be friends has haunted me my whole life. I'm sorry that I said that to you because it wasn't what I wanted. And, Clay, I've always been a very affectionate person. My affection was genuine."

Clay's mind was whirling. It seemed to him that every time he controlled someone's mind, he made a complete mess of things. Clay proceeded to tell Erika about how he messed with a rival in high school, bringing chaos to his life, and how his powers affected his relationship with his wife and son. He told how he hid his powers and vowed to not use them, but nearly every time he *did* use them, it came back to haunt him. He told about how Tanner began developing his own powers, and then he told about how unhappy and lonely he was that he couldn't have a proper relationship with his wife or son. It led to the murder of his wife, and he felt responsible. When Erika suggested that he was gifted, he responded that he felt it was more of a curse than some sort of blessing. Erika listened intently. She knew that she was supposed to be helping Clay, and she was trying to determine what it was that he really needed—what it was that was his *real* problem. Clay was talking about it; that was a first step in a faith lesson. He was trusting her with his pain and his secrets. But once they reached the cave, the real lessons would begin.

***

With Erika gone for the day, Marshall Mortonson, walked to the 'attic' door at the end of the upstairs hallway of the Depot. Mortonson had taken to occasionally pulling out his old account books and reminiscing about his past as he spent more and more time, of late, thinking about his future. It was actually an unfinished storage room—the actual attic was above the second floor—but the real attic was rarely accessed and the storage room became known as the attic, mostly because that is exactly what it looked like. The historical building had managed to keep its original design even after over a hundred years of wear and restorations. The door to the storage room attic was no exception and was still unlocked by one of two skeleton keys that Mortonson carried. Marshall kept his account books locked inside a Sentry fireproof safe inside the attic. The electronic keypad was long since inoperable, but the safe could be opened via a backup system by using a skeleton key. Marshall Mortonson was the only person who had copies of each key.

Marshall was a numbers geek. He'd always kept the books for the business while Adrian Payne took care of sales. Approximately four years into the partnership, the Durand Depot was turning a tidy profit and looked to be on the verge of an even brighter future. Adrian had worked a deal with the shipping industry, which would soon put a profitable local trucking company out of business. Marshall wasn't too thrilled about how the backdoor deal was negotiated, but it was to be a very profitable enterprise. With dollar signs in his eyes, Marshall was persuaded to invest money that he didn't have in a real estate deal in Palm Springs, Florida. It would be his vacation home until retirement. So Mortonson embezzled twenty thousand of the business's dollars for the initial investment. His plan was to keep the books secret from Adrian until he figured out a way to pay the money back or "cook" the books to make the transaction disappear. However, Marshall Mortonson eventually learned that his money was stolen in a scam. He had lost the entire twenty grand, and then Adrian discovered his partner's financial ledger. One day, Marshall entered his office to find Adrian sitting in his desk chair. Desk and file drawers were opened and papers were scattered all over the desk and floor. It looked like the office had been ransacked. Adrian's face was red with anger.

"What happened?" Marshall asked. But he was more concerned with Adrian's anger than he was with the mess in his office.

"I've been reading the company's books. Are you keeping any secrets from me, Morty?"

Marshall saw his account ledgers in Adrian's hand, and he knew he had been caught, so he confessed. As Marshall spoke, Adrian's temper died down, and eventually he began to smile. Then he said, "You need to take care of this, Morty. What you've done is a crime. I could turn you in, and push you out of the business. Probably I'd bankrupt you, and possibly you could end up in jail. You and I are supposed to be *partners*. I won't forget what you've done."

Over the next many years, Marshall began embezzling from the company a little at a time—stealing money from the business—and then showing Adrian how he was "repaying" the large amount he had originally stolen. He began keeping two completely different sets of books. One set was legitimate, and one set of books was a masterpiece in creativity. However, trouble was just beginning for Marshall. Adrian had begun the process of legitimately *spending* the company into debt. Whenever he was approached by Marshall about his exorbitant spending, Adrian would say, "Have I done anything *illegal*, Morty? Stealing is more *your* cup of tea, I've noticed. You'll have to take care of it, won't you?"

Marshall Mortonson, who was stealing money to pay back the money *he* had previously embezzled, was additionally being forced to figure out ways to cover the debt that his partner was creating. He began to underreport earnings and cheat on the company taxes. He was creating false vendor accounts and creating phantom employees who he then paid with false payroll checks. Adrian was enjoying life while he was basically blackmailing his partner into a life of crime. Occasionally, Marshall would sneak back into the depot "attic," take another look at his duel set of books, and give thanks that Adrian Payne had been missing from his life for so many years. He had built the business back up once Adrian disappeared, and it was doing a profitable business once again. Still, he feared that someday his dirty deeds would be discovered. The consequences of that would be devastating.

CHAPTER 6

Clay donned what looked to him like a miner's cap, headlamp and all, and stood before Erika feeling kind of silly. Clay decided that Erika was the sexiest woman—even at 42 years of age— that he had ever seen. She was already making him smile and feel like a kid every time he looked at her. From the moment she'd opened her door, he could see that she had a zest for living that was missing in his own life. He, on the other hand, had spent the past year in near seclusion. She smiled a perfect smile and claimed to Clay that she was a speleologist. Clueless as to whether there was really such a thing, Clay cared only that he was actually very much looking forward to spending more time with her. They were standing at the mouth of Doghill-Donahue Cave in Bedford, Indiana.

A pried-open, grill-like filter spanned a huge drainage pipe that lay beneath a four-lane highway. It was through that drainage pipe that the couple would access the cave. It was a cold, blustery day. Erika told Clay that they would spend the next couple of hours spelunking, which meant they would be exploring the cave together. Clay anxiously had visions of Tom Sawyer trapped in the cave with Injun Joe, but decided to trust that Erika knew what she was doing if for no other reason than he was looking forward to the zest and the perfect smile.

Prior to their entry, she was meticulously checking supplies for the second time since they initially left Michigan. Headlamps, flashlights, ropes, and first-aid supplies were rechecked. At a shapely, sexy 110 pounds, she looked more like a woman about to head to the mall than someone about to embark on a journey through a dark, wet, muddy cave. Clay stared at the blue eyeliner that accented her sparkling eyes and wondered how someone so beautiful could be so adventurous, tough, and fearless. "You remembered to dress appropriately, right?" she asked.

"Yep, polypro from neck to toes. Long johns, long sleeve undershirt, socks, hiking boots, everything. I've been sweating like a pig. Is it gonna be cold in there?"

"The cave'll be cool, but the polypro is mostly for when you get wet. Cotton'd be cold and miserable...polypro'll keep you warm." Erika paused and asked the question that Clay had been expecting ever since he told her in the car that he had the ability to control minds. "So if you look me in the eyes, you can control my mind?"

"Yeah, and since high school, I've learned to read minds too."

"You're looking at my eyes right now."

"But I'm just admiring, not controlling. Sorry, I can't help but look," Clay smiled and even blushed a bit.

"Well, get a good look because in just a few minutes we'll be engulfed in darkness and you'll have no control over me." She smiled a flirty smile. "As a matter of fact, you'd better do just as I say 'cause I'm the only one here who knows what to do once we get in there. Do you trust me?"

"You make it sound kinda scary, but yeah, I trust you...I think."

"You don't sound so sure. Follow me." Smiling, as she always seemed to do, she turned on her flashlight and entered through the grating to start through the pipe. Clay eyed her perfect behind before inhaling a deep breath, letting out a long, satisfied sigh, and following her in.

Within a few steps into the drainage pipe, light became scarce so Erika switched the light switch on her helmet to the "on" position. Clay did likewise and flashlights were clicked off to save battery power. When they exited the pipe just seconds later, they were in the cave. Sculpted walls rose as much as thirty to forty feet overhead. A glance up revealed stalactites reaching down from the ceiling. It was cool inside the cave and no light was revealed at all, save the light from their helmets. It was dark and spooky. *"How will she know where to go...and how to get back out?"* Clay wondered.

"You wanna know how I'm gonna keep from getting lost, don't ya?"

"What? Are you reading *my* mind?"

"No," she laughed. "That's what *I* would be thinking, so why wouldn't you? Would it bother you if I *could* read your mind?"

"It doesn't bother me for you to know that I'd rather not get lost, but if you knew what I was thinking while I followed you through the drainage pipe, *that* might be a little embarrassing."

"I *do* give quite a view from behind, don't I?" she giggled as Clay's mouth gaped open a bit. "See? I knew what you were thinking *then* too. All I had to do was deduce that *you* are a man, and that I look good in these jeans, and I kind of put 'two and two together.'"

Clay laughed. "So you don't mind that I can read and control minds?"

"I can see how it could be a problem, unless you happen to be a trustworthy person. I mean, if I trusted you, and you *talked* to me, I think it's something I could live with. I'd probably invest in a pair of dark sunglasses to put on when I planned to hide something from you," she joked. "But I don't think your problem is that you have a gift, Clay. I think you're a person who lacks faith."

"Faith?"

"Faith is the substance of things hoped for...the evidence of things unseen. You don't seem to believe that God gave you your gifts for a reason, and you aren't able to trust Him because you lack faith in what you can't see. And you don't trust that people in your life were put there for a purpose too. You try to make it through life all on your own, trusting only in yourself."

Those were some pretty harsh words coming from someone that didn't really know him, but it actually rang pretty true, and

Clay didn't seem to mind hearing it from Erika, so he decided not to try to defend himself.

They walked a short time in silence while they were making their way deeper into the cave. Finally Clay asked, "What makes you so sure?" The cave floor had been sloping downward, yet the impressive walls somehow seemed to be shrinking in size. The temperature was cooling a bit, but Clay was getting more of a chill from the conversation. What was Erika getting at?

"You told me about your mind powers as we drove here. I said you were gifted, but you said you were cursed. A person of faith would believe there is a reason or purpose for his powers. Don't you believe there is a way to use this gift for good?" While she was speaking, she began pulling rope from the bag she was carrying. They were approaching a twelve-foot barrier of solid rock. Erika instructed Clay to boost her to the top of the wall. Once she grabbed the top, she neatly vaulted over like a gymnast over a pommel horse. From the other side, she threw an end of the rope over to Clay's side of the wall and instructed Clay to grab hold and use it to climb. Once Clay reached the top, he also dropped to the other side and Erika continued her conversation.

"How many truly good personal relationships do you have?"

"Well, my son and I are aware of each other's powers. We have a lot in common and can talk about it...Maybe Zander Frauss. He specializes in the field of parapsychology so he understands me and seems able to accept me for who I am...I can't think of anyone else."

"So you don't trust that God gave you your powers for a purpose and you don't trust other people enough to open up to them."

"I told *you*."

"Why is that? You said you '*think*' that maybe you can trust me."

Clay shrugged his shoulders. "Maybe I was hoping you would like me again...the *real* me. Flaws and all. I decided to take a risk, I guess. Plus Zander's wife *said* I should trust you."

Since dropping from the barrier, they had been walking down an open passageway under a high ceiling and between flat, tall walls. There was nothing jutting out and no difficulties in the path. They had simply been leisurely walking along when suddenly, as if in response to Clay's answer, Erika said, "Let's stop here." Erika sat down and because she was Clay's guide, he followed suit even though he wasn't tired in the least. "You actually trust only in yourself, and that is *not* sufficient. Turn off your light." Erika flipped off her headlamp, and Clay did as he was instructed. "It's dark, isn't it?" Even as she said it, Clay knew she was smiling again.

"I can't see my hand in front of my face. Wow...it actually *feels* dark. Is that possible?"

She ignored his question. "Take off your helmet and give it to me. Your flashlight too."

"Yes, Ma'am," Clay replied in a weak attempt at humor.

"You always handle your problems in your own strength. Am I right about that?"

"I'm not sure that I understand what you're asking me."

"I said you lacked faith. When you can't see where you're going, you flounder. You press on, but you can't see the end, so you try to find the end in your own strength." Erika paused giving Clay time to think. "After we climbed over that wall, as you might remember, we walked a short distance through a wide passage. Now all you have to do is walk back to that wall in the dark."

"But I can't see *anything*."

"That's right, but you remember the passage...I'm heading to the other end. I'll wait for you there, but if you speak to me, I won't answer. When you catch up to me at the end of the passage, I'll give you back your light. Have fun," she giggled, and she left Clay alone in the dark.

Clay stood and stretched out his hand, feeling for something...anything. What exactly he was reaching for, he was unsure. There was no noise and absolutely no light, and he was unsure what to do next. He took a couple of very hesitant steps with his hands stretched out before him. He swung his right arm slowly to the side and then his left arm, making no contact with anything at all. He stood still, wondering what to do next. He took a deep breath and tried to picture the passageway, but all he could visualize was utter blackness. His heart started to race and he wanted to call out to Erika. Instead he took a deep breath and tried to compose himself. He could do this. What was it, a hundred feet? Erika said she'd be waiting at the end of the passage, but the trouble was that Clay couldn't see what was ahead of him, and he didn't know how to get there. He actually began to feel betrayed that she would leave him alone to flounder.

Clay started sidestepping in miniature steps to his right. He held his right arm out to the side and gradually worked his way toward what he believed would eventually be a wall. Minutes passed as Clay slowly shuffled no more than ten feet to the flat rock wall surface. When his hand touched rock, his legs seemed to give out and he sank to the cave floor. From there he inched his way forward, putting all his weight on his left hand and his knees, his right hand never losing contact with the wall. The only noise he could hear was the scraping of his knees and the deafening sound of his breathing. Why couldn't he seem to get any oxygen? Where was the end? Why was it taking so long? Was he lost? Was he in danger? How did Erika expect him to find his way without any guidance? But he pressed on alone, determined to find the end of the corridor.

Ten to fifteen minutes later, though it seemed much longer to Clay, he literally bumped into Erika and gasped. He'd been so focused on making his own path that he'd actually forgotten she was there all the time, waiting. "You did it," she whispered.

"Why was it so hard?" Clay whispered back as he held onto Erika like he was afraid she'd vanish once again.

"It's always hard when you don't know where you're going and you try to make the journey on your own. When you're not walking by faith, you stumble along on your hands and knees in fear of what you can't see. What kind of way is *that* to live?"

"I wasn't exactly enjoying myself," Clay admitted.

"Here. Put your helmet back on, but don't turn on the light. And here's your flashlight. Hook it to your belt." Clay did as he was told. "Now stand up and take hold of my hand." She pulled him four or five steps to his right. "Hold your free hand out in front of you, okay?"

"Okay."

"It's still pretty dark, isn't it?" There was that giggle again. "Let's walk. Trust me, Clay. I'm here with you, and I know the way. You just hold on for the ride." They began walking in silence at a casual but steady pace. After about thirty to forty steps, in about thirty seconds, Clay's hand hit a wall and they stopped. Erika turned and flipped on her headlamp. "There. That wasn't so hard was it?"

Clay also turned and looked at the passage that they had just navigated. It was wide open. No rock outcroppings, nothing in the path, smooth walls and floor—just as he now remembered seeing it after they had dropped from the wall at the other end. "I feel like such a fool," Clay confessed. "Do you mind if I keep hold of your hand and trust you the rest of the way?"

"I don't mind at all, but there are still lessons to learn, Clay. Flip your light on and help me over *this* wall too."

***

It appeared to Marshall Mortonson that Logan rolled his eyes when Marshall's car pulled up at the school to pick him up. His head dropped and he walked the twenty-five or thirty feet about a foot and a half per step. He plopped down in the front passenger seat without so much as a "hello."

"Hi, Logan," Morty said with as much enthusiasm as he could muster.

"Hey."

"You don't look too happy."

"Nope."

Morty hesitated but then asked where he'd like to eat. All he got was a shrug of his shoulders. "Well, obviously we don't have much to choose from since there's only McDonald's, Wendy's, and Subway in Durand. Let's go to McDonald's...unless you'd like someplace else." Another shrug of the shoulders. The kid sure knew how to make a person uncomfortable. His father was good at that too, he thought. Except his father did it in a much different way.

They ordered their meal and found a table in the corner away from everyone else. "Why does my mom think I need a babysitter?"

"*Hmmm...a regular conversation starter, this one,*" Morty thought, but he figured he'd better take advantage of actual words coming from Logan's mouth. "Maybe she just wants you to have some company. Since your father disappeared, you..."

"I hated him," Logan interrupted. That was all he said.

"Um, well, a lot of people felt the same way, Logan. But people love your mother, and we all want to help the two of you."

"Why did other people hate him?"

"He was *my* best friend, but he was running the business into the ground with his wild living, and in the process, he hurt a lot of people. He put people out of business, offended, cheated, embarrassed, and took advantage of people. From where I sat, he didn't treat people with respect and didn't mind hurting them if he thought it benefited himself. I'm sorry to tell you that." He paused. "Logan, why did *you* hate him?"

He simply shrugged his shoulders again. He wasn't willing to say.

***

When Clay dropped to the other side of the wall, he expected to see another passage similar to the one they had just vacated. Instead, there was a series of structures that they had to spot and assist each other to climb and descend. Occasionally formations were too steep, too high, or too treacherous to climb, and in those occasions they were forced to crawl through a freezing channel of running water *beneath* the cave walls. The way was getting more and more difficult to navigate, but Clay, wet and unsure of himself, did his best to keep up with the ball of energy that was leading the way. After descending a particularly dangerous drop, it appeared that they had reached a dead end. Clay assumed that Erika would lead the way back up the structure they had just dropped from, but she had no intention of retreating. As far as Clay could see, the only way forward was a waterway near the base and along the side of a huge stalagmite. There was only a clearance under the rock of about a foot and a half, maybe less, and when Clay tested it, there was about six inches of standing water. Erika sat down on a rock and smiled as Clay bent over and shined his light below the rock.

"What do you see?" she asked.

"Well, it appears to be a narrow passage filled with water that goes under this rock about maybe fifteen feet or so. We're heading back, right? I mean there's no other way to pass unless we crawl under." Erika just smiled while Clay began to comprehend what she was thinking. "You're planning to crawl under, right?" That would be absurd, Clay immediately deduced, but Erika simply continued to smile. She was wet and dirty, her curly blond locks damp and hanging over her eyes, which coincidentally were not making any eye-contact with Clay in case he had any ideas of telling her what to do next. "Erika, listen. I've crawled through freezing water several times to get to this point, but never while smashed between two giant rocks. I don't think I can fit through there." Clay was starting to feel desperate. "Tell me you're not gonna ask me to squeeze through that opening? Please?"

Erika just continued to smile. She had beautiful, pearly white teeth. *What a dumb thing to notice,* Clay thought, *when I'm about to die.*

"It's like this," Erika explained. "I'm your guide, and this is the way I'm leading you out of the cave. I told you that there were lessons still to be learned and you said you were gonna trust me the rest of the way. So, now's the time to trust me. You *can* fit through that opening, so except for the fact that the water's gonna be bitterly cold, you'll have no problem getting through."

"I hate cold water," Clay complained, but Erika took it as a good sign that the complaint wasn't about the size of the opening.

"Let's see. You're about six feet two inches, 195 pounds. That's about twice as big as me; I hope you don't get stuck," she giggled. "Follow me." She ducked her head, and started wiggling through the water. Clay began to panic again, but he got down on his knees, ducked his head, and plunged into the water. He gasped at the temperature. There was probably ten inches of clearance for him to breathe, but each time he tried to push himself forward using his knees, he banged his back on the rock. He began to feel claustrophobic because the farther he pushed himself the lower the rock ceiling became. It had dropped maybe three inches before he emerged from the crack that he was half swimming, half crawling through. There had barely been enough room to keep his face above the water and breathe. Erika was sitting on a rock with her helmet in hand when Clay dragged himself out of the water. He looked around and was shocked to see that they were trapped between two walls. The rock ceiling in front of them appeared to be lower yet.

"You'll need to take your batteries out of the headlamp and give them to me. I'll put 'em in this watertight bag. The last leg of the journey is too tight a fit for you to wear the helmet. You'll have to hold it in front of you while you squirm through the last fifteen to twenty feet."

"How will I see?"

"Well, that's where you're gonna have to trust me when I tell you that you can make it through. You aren't going to be able to see, and the ceiling is gonna gradually drop from about thirteen inches to approximately eight. The water'll remain at about six inches deep. The helmet won't fit through on your head, so hold it out in front of you and use your other hand to help push yourself through. Your flashlight is water tight, but I honestly don't see how you can hold it and use it. You're gonna have to make it through in the dark."

"You're kidding right? I can't fit through an eight-inch opening. And it's filled with water. I'll drown. And if I can't see, how will I know how far I have to go and when I'm through?"

"Believe me. You'll know when you're through...plus I'll have a light on when you get there. And you'll have to trust me also when I tell you that you can fit. You won't drown—not if you care to survive. Clay, this is the way out, the last leg of the journey.

This is where you're gonna have to have the most faith. There's room for you to move side-to-side. You won't be completely hemmed it. It's just that the ceiling's very low—as low as eight inches for the last eight or ten feet—and the water fills most of the opening. Keep your face turned up and keep moving. I'll have you tie this rope under your armpits and if you stop moving, I'll pull you through. The only obstacle is fear. Franklin Roosevelt once said 'Let me assert my firm belief that the only thing we have to fear is fear itself—nameless, unreasoning, unjustified terror which paralyzes the effort needed to convert retreat into advance.' At no time does that quote apply more than at this moment. Bigger men than you have made it through this opening. You'll have to trust me about that. You can't be afraid; you can't retreat."

"What are you trying to prove to me, Erika? This isn't fun. This is life and death."

"Clay, you've had the power most of your life to control things. In the living out of that life, you have developed the habit of trusting only in yourself. It's time for you to learn to let go. You're never gonna experience life like a normal person because you have a gift that isn't normal, but you can begin to experience life differently than you have in the past. You have to put some faith in something besides yourself—whether that be God or people that you care about. It's time you took a step of faith and trusted in someone else. You can make it through this, and then maybe you can move on with your life and experience it fully—experience it abundantly. I'm going through, Clay, and you need to come too."

"Okay, so I *believe* that I can make it because you say I can, but believing doesn't get me through the opening. What if I really can't do it?"

"You can either show me your faith by what you say, or you can show me by what you *do*. Faith isn't a concept....It's an action verb. Get on your chest, stick your face in the water, and make it to the other side."

Erika moved to loop her rope around Clay, but he stopped her. "I'll do it without the rope."

"That's the spirit." She smiled her awesome smile once again, stuffed the rope into her bag, and lowered herself into the water.

Terrified but determined, Clay left his flashlight on but inserted it into his belt knowing that he needed to keep his hands free but hoping that at least a bit of light would mar the blackness. He took a deep breath and crawled into the water. It was freezing. His plan was to hold his breath and scoot along on his belly as fast as he could manage, but his heart was beating so fast and the water was so cold that he was out of breath in just a few seconds. Only the top half of his frame was under the rock before he had to lift his head out of the water and take several breaths. His body was already getting numb and he felt like he was going to hyperventilate. He took as deep a breath as he could manage and scooted a couple more feet, but the movement managed to turn his flashlight off and he was plunged into absolutely complete darkness.

He felt the same disorientation that he felt while trying to walk from one end of the tunnel to the other in the dark. How was he to know if he was even going in the right direction? He needed another breath, so he lifted his head as high as he could and banged it on the rock ceiling so hard that he was certain that he had drawn blood. From the overhead rock to the floor beneath, there was approximately a ten-inch clearance. Water filled his mouth and he coughed and choked slightly. Anxiety and fear began to take over, but as he wondered if he would make it out alive, his mind began to spin. "Faith is the substance of things hoped for and the evidence of things unseen…the only thing we have to fear is fear itself…it's time for you to let go…it's time you took a step of faith and trusted in someone else…stop trusting only in yourself…show me by what you *do*." Erika's words started to flood Clay's mind, and he realized that he was moving along in a regular pattern, a couple of short pulls forward, a turn of the head for a breath, a couple more pulls forward, another breath. He was making progress even as the gap tightened to no more than eight inches. "Trust me…You can't be afraid; you can't retreat…When you're not walking by faith, you stumble along on your hands and knees in fear of what you can't see. What kind of way is *that* to live?...I don't think your problem is that you have a gift, Clay. I think you're a person who is lacking faith."

Clay slid forward another foot or so and turned his head for another breath. His head turned freely and didn't bang into rock. His head was out of the passage! A renewed energy possessed him as he slid the rest of his body out of the enclosure. He had made it! As he was standing, a light flipped on. Clay smiled and climbed completely out of the water. He put his arms around Erika and lifted her off the ground in the most genuine hug he had ever given. Erika giggled that sexy laugh she had used several times that day. "I didn't think I was going to make it," he told Erika. "But I started flashing back to *your* words. I made it because you said I could and I trusted you."

"You trusted me," Erika repeated proudly. "How do you feel about that?"

"I feel great—well, I'm *freezing* to death, and my head hurts, but otherwise I feel great!"

She grabbed his arm, and they starting walking up a steep walkway toward the cave exit. The polypro started to warm his body, but it was Clay's heart that was truly warming up. He had a lot to think about—things he'd learned and things he needed to work on, but his faith had been stirred by Erika, and now he knew he had some things to do. It was time that he used his gifts to help someone else, and according to Zander Frauss, there was a mystery to be solved, and Erika and her son were in need of some aid themselves.

CHAPTER 7

Clay had dropped off Erika and was stopped at a train crossing waiting for the longest train he'd ever seen, so he checked his cell phone and saw that he had a message from Tanner. He couldn't get his mind off the events of the day, but mostly he couldn't get his mind off Erika. The message said to call right away, so he speed dialed Tanner.

"Hi, Dad. How was your day?"

"Pretty memorable, to say the least, but I'll tell you about it later. What's up?"

"Well, Dr. Frauss told me a little more about your caving adventure, and we were discussing the mystery surrounding the train wreck in Durand. We talked about the news articles some more, and then he told me about some things he had learned about the Depot. Anyway, last night I had another one of my dreams, and there was a picture calling to me."

"A picture? How would you ever find a *picture*?"

"I think my dream located it *for* me. As it played out, it kind of closed in right on the picture. First there were railroad tracks and a train. I had to wait for the train to pass before the vision continued. Then it zoomed in on a building. It was a huge two-and-a-half story building with pointed peaks that were like turrets on a castle. It was roofed in red, claylike tiles. I looked up the Durand Depot, Dad, and it looked just like my dream, so I'm sure the picture is in that building. When the vision zoomed inside, I saw something like museum exhibits, but right at the entrance to the

Depot, the vision went to the right and eventually down a hall and up a set of winding stairs. There was a long hallway with framed displays on the walls and then some offices. In the second office on a wall to the right was a family picture of a man, woman, and boy. It was that picture that was calling to me."

"Do you have any idea from the dream why the picture was calling to you?"

"No. Nothing at all was familiar about it. But Dr. Frauss said there was a mystery there that he wanted you to check into. Maybe because I was there for the explanation and because I read the articles, I got connected somehow. You're gonna check into it, right?"

"Ya know, I think so, Tanner. Zander said he had some sort of intuition that there was a mystery to be solved, and I'm even more curious about that now than I was before. Plus, there's a family that maybe could use my help. *Our* help. I don't know how exactly, but your vision makes me think we should check things out. You wanna come with me?"

"Sure. Is tomorrow too soon? A bunch of guys on the team have been sick, so Coach gave us a day off and tomorrow I only have a lab in the morning. I could be at the house by eleven."

"That sounds like a plan. I'll make arrangements for our visit. See ya tomorrow."

***

Clay described his previous day's activities to Tanner as they drove from Flint to Durand. He finally decided as they neared the Durand exit off from I-69 to tell him that Erika was the high school girlfriend that he'd told Tanner about nearly a year ago. "Remember? She was the one that I told to like me, and then told to break up with me."

Tanner laughed. "Does she still just wanna be friends?" He thought that was funny because that is what Clay had told her to say when she broke up with him.

"Of course. She's *married*, Tanner. But her husband *is* missing." Then he decided to include with a slight smile, "And she still looks really good. She claims she liked me long before the eleventh grade. I guess my mind-control kinda screwed up a golden opportunity. I'd really like to help her if I can."

Erika had suggested that they meet at her house and go to the Depot together, so after stopping for three trains within about a tenth of a mile, they pulled into her driveway at about 11:30 in the morning. They stepped past neatly trimmed shrubbery to the porch of her cozy, cream-colored, ranch-styled home and rang the doorbell. Thinking again of her blue eyes, he noticed the house trim and front door were of the same color. Powder blue? Sky blue? The front door pulled open to the inside of the house, and Erika pushed open the front screen door. As she did so, a bird flew over Clay's head and right into the house. Erika shrieked, ducked, turned, and tumbled over the side of a living room chair, falling to the floor. Clay stepped in to help her, but she was off the floor like she had bounced off a trampoline. She grabbed a couch cushion and started chasing the bird around the house, screaming and swinging at it every chance she got. Tanner and Clay both started laughing hysterically. Tanner held the screen door open and Clay opened the front window in hopes that the bird would find its way out before it got pummeled by a couch cushion. "Go out the window, you stupid bird! Go out the window!" Erika was yelling at it like she was Dr. Doolittle and the bird could somehow understand her ravings.

As it flew down a hallway and banged into a wall, both men wiped tears from their eyes, but then Clay had an idea. The bird flew back into the living room with Erika running close behind. "Hold on, Erika! Wait just a minute!" Clay extended his hand and concentrated on the bird. The bird started fluttering in the corner of the room near the ceiling. It was like Clay had caught it in his hand. The bird continued to flutter, and then he swung his arm toward the window and the bird flew right outside. Erika and Tanner looked on in amazement, and Clay was kind of surprised himself. Then the men looked at Erika, still holding onto the couch cushion, and they began to laugh again.

She was wearing an attractive sweater, a cute, navy-blue skirt, and matching knee-high leather boots. Hair, eye shadow, mascara, blush, and lipstick were all done to perfection. Her eye shadow was a bit darker today, making her eyes appear to be a deeper blue. She sat on the couch, but continued to cling to the cushion. She smiled and said to Tanner, "Hi, I'm Erika." Then she began to laugh too. When her laughter died down a bit, she turned to Clay. "You can control the minds of birds? You could be an amazing hunter. You could join the circus." She started to laugh again.

"Telekinesis," Clay smiled kind of awkwardly. "I didn't get around to telling you about *that* talent. I never tried it on an animal before. I'm just as surprised as you. This is my son, Tanner, by the way."

"Nice to meet you," she giggled. "I hope I didn't make too bad of a first impression. I have to admit—if you hadn't noticed—that bird kind of scared me for a minute. And, Clay, since *you* just made a confession, I have to admit there *is* something I'm afraid of…There's a midget who terrifies me."

Everyone started laughing again. "What? A midget? Why is that?"

"Well, there's this midget in Durand—name starts with a *J*…Jester or something like that. Anyway, to this day, he rides around on a kid's bicycle. When we moved here that first summer, I was walking downtown on East Main near the clock tower. Out of the corner of my eye, I saw somethin' comin' at me, so I threw up my arm to protect myself. That midget ran his bike right into me, and I hit him right in the throat with my forearm." Tanner was already laughing. Erika looked at Tanner and said, "Just wait. He was cussin' and yelling as he got up off the ground, and *then* he saw that his handlebars were crooked and started swearing at *me* even worse. I don't know how he did it, but he was so mad that while he was swearing, he started kicking himself in the head."

"What? Say again?" Clay interrupted. "He was kicking his own head?"

Out of the corner of his eye, he saw Tanner do a leg kick, which only came about waist high. He grabbed the back of his leg and said, "I think I just pulled a hammy."

"Yes! He was literally kicking himself in the forehead. Then he picked up a handful of stones and started throwing them at me. My friend, Dan—he's a cop in town now—stepped in and saved me. He got the little guy to settle down and got him on his bike, and he started riding away." Tanner and Clay were cracking up. "His forehead was swelled up, and his handlebars were turned at a crazy angle, so he kept veering to the right and jerking back to the left." Now Erika was laughing. "He was steering all over the place, so when he turned back to me and threatened to 'get me' someday, he hit the curb and flipped off his bike again. That scary little man points at me and yells at me every time he's seen me since. He terrifies me. So, yeah, I'm kinda afraid of midgets. Dan's always been kinda my 'protector' ever since. He keeps an eye on the little monster for me, and he watches out for Logan too."

Everyone was still laughing as they finally left Erika's house and headed for the Depot to take a look at the picture that had called out to Tanner. Tanner liked her and found himself hoping that Zander was right about her. Maybe she really could help his dad finally move on from the loss of his wife. He was also beginning to sense that there really was a mystery to be solved and maybe his dad was the one to figure it out.

CHAPTER 8

Roberto Gomez was heading to his truck so he could drive home for lunch when Erika, Clay, and Tanner arrived at the depot. Erika introduced the employee to everyone.

"Nice to meet you, Roberto. What do you do here?"

"Grease monkey, air monkey, snipe, diesel mechanic, gandy dancer, juggler…anything besides an engineman or a white shirt."

"That didn't sound like Spanish, but I didn't understand a thing you just said," Tanner quipped.

"Si, Señor Thomas. I was just messin' with ya. I'm a train car and equipment oiler, brake repairman, track laborer, engine repairman, and unloader. Whatever they ask me to do besides drive the trains and supervise."

Tanner and Clay liked him right away. "Not to mention, he's a really good friend," Erika interjected. "Say hi to Stacy for me."

"Sure thing. Buenas tardes, amigos."

"Let's head on in, Gentlemen," Erika said.

After Roberto drove away, Tanner said to his dad, "If we go in those front doors, we should walk in and turn to the right to go to a waiting area. If we go straight through the lobby and down a hallway, there'll be a stairway on the right, heading to the second floor." He led his dad and Erika through the doors, and sure enough, it was just as he described it. They headed up the stairs. When they reached the second floor, Tanner turned to the right and walked down a hallway. When he reached the second office door, he turned right, then looked to the wall on the right and pointed at a family picture of Erika, Adrian, and Logan Payne. Logan looked to be about nine or ten years old. "There it is."

"*That* is what called you here? That picture in *my* office?"

Tanner shrugged his shoulders and smiled. Clay marveled at his attitude. Clay had lost his wife, but Tanner had lost his *mother*. She loved Tanner with all her heart, and Tanner knew it. Yet, less than a year later, he could smile, laugh, and not take himself too seriously. They had found the picture, and now it was everyone else's responsibility to figure things out. His cell phone buzzed; he took it out of his pocket, read the message, and laughed. "Big Jake came to our room to see if we had any flu medicine—he's a player on our team who's been sick," he explained to Erika—"so my roommate, Mike, let him in and they headed for the bathroom. Mike says, 'You don't look so good, Jake,' and Jake says, 'How can you live in here? It smells so bad!' and the next thing, he was puking his guts out in the toilet. Mike says he couldn't leave fast enough."

Clay and Tanner started laughing again. "Tanner hypnotized Jake 'cause he was hangin' out too much in their room. Every time he's there in the room and hears his name, he believes the smell's so bad that he leaves."

"Or he pukes and then leaves. That's priceless!" Tanner was laughing again, and so was Erika.

Clay was intrigued by the mystery, however, so he was right back to business while the other two were enjoying their laugh. He was studying the picture. It was simply a family picture of Erika, Adrian, and Logan Payne outside the Depot with an old orange-colored train caboose in the background. Nothing seemed out of the ordinary. He removed it from the wall and looked at the back of the picture, feeling it to see if possibly there was something hidden on the back. There was nothing unusual that he could see. "Erika, do you mind if I take the picture out of the frame? Maybe there's something inside."

She gave the okay, so he took a couple of minutes to remove the picture and check everything thoroughly, still discovering nothing unusual. He flipped the picture over again and studied the photo. He began to feel a coolness in the room, like the temperature had just rapidly dropped a few degrees. Clay looked up to see if someone had opened a window, but Erika and Tanner were standing and talking about some wooden carvings that were on Erika's desk.

"Yeah, Logan is really talented. I'm planning on getting him some real wood carving knives for Christmas. He did this with his *jackknife.*"

"Wow," Tanner said. "Look at this, Dad. He carved a train, some train tracks, and look at this horse. This one is *really* good."

As Clay started to look away from the picture, he heard, *"I'm looking a dead horse in the mouth."* It was a kind of whispery male voice. He looked around, expecting to see someone else in the room.

"Did you hear that?" he asked.

Erika shot him a curious look, but Tanner quickly said, "I didn't hear anything. What did you hear?"

Clay clipped the picture back into the frame and leaned it against the desk before he said, "I heard a voice say, 'I'm looking a dead horse in the mouth.'"

Immediately, Clay heard, *"I'm straight from the horses' mouths."* He turned around again, assuming there was someone else in the room. "I'm straight from the horses' mouths?" he said in wonderment. The room seemed to drop a few more degrees.

"I could be beating a dead horse…"

Clay repeated what he had just heard to the others.

"Some sort of extra-sensory perception, Dad?"

"I don't know…It seems different. And who would be talking to me? And what do horses have to do with anything? And why is the room so cold?"

It didn't seem cold to Erika and Tanner. Erika didn't understand Clay and Tanner's gifts, but she was certainly curious about what was going on. Tanner set the horse carving back on Erika's desk, so Erika reached to replace the train and tracks. As she did so, she noticed that the picture of her and Logan was lying face down on her desk. She gasped. Carefully, she set the frame back up correctly, then looked at Clay and walked straight to the wall where the family picture usually hung. There on the floor beside the wall was the picture that Clay had been studying. It was also lying face down.

When Clay saw the picture, he said, "How did that get over there? I just leaned it against the desk."

"It just *can't* be!" Erika said as she stared at the picture and the men stared at her. She looked back to her desk, and sure enough, the carvings were missing. She walked over to the wastebasket, reached in, and pulled them out. Erika said, "A ghost did it."

"A ghost?" Tanner repeated. "This is *so* cool! Dad, can you hear ghosts?"

***

Dan Duncan pulled into his garage, unlocked the back door, and headed for the kitchen for a late lunch. He looked out his back kitchen window as he was pouring himself a glass of V8 juice. What he saw was a squirrel squatting on one of his birdfeeders, eating the birdseed. He slammed his drinking hand down on the counter in anger, chipping his glass and splattering the red juice all over his police uniform. He yelled a couple of choice swear words toward the squirrel. Dan was a firm believer that the smartest, most talented and athletic squirrel on earth occupied his backyard. No matter what he did to try to discourage the squirrel, it somehow managed to continue to antagonize the police officer.

Since fall had made its way to Michigan and many species of birds had migrated South, Dan filled his feeders in hopes of attracting black-capped chickadees, blue jays, dark-eyed juncos, white-breasted nuthatches, and northern cardinals. He loved watching birds, especially in the winter mornings when Michigan's depressing gray skies and frosty temperatures threatened depths of discouragement. He'd had some luck attracting his chosen species, but he'd also attracted a squirrel that was determined to drive the bird-watcher crazy. After the six weeks of late October and the month of November, Dan was considering using his police revolver to put the pest into eternal hibernation.

Dan had mounted new feeders on six-foot poles. His super-squirrel made the leap with ease. He raised the height of the feeder. The squirrel climbed the pole just as easily. He spread the poles with black auto grease. The squirrel tracked it all over his deck as if to mock the foolish man. He tried plastic baffles, but the vermin would adjust the positioning and climb over them anyway. When he went to metal baffles, the squirrel began jumping from a nearby tree. He cut off branches and the squirrel began climbing his house, leaving scratch marks all over his woodwork prior to each flying leap. He moved the poles and the squirrel jumped from a nearby fence. He tried safflower seeds because squirrels weren't supposed to like them, but his squirrel ate them like dessert.

He had put up the feeders so he could bird watch and relieve stress. Instead he was feeling more stressed than ever. Before he went to change his uniform, he slid open the window and yelled, "Get out of my feeder, you stupid squirrel!"

"Tchrring...tchrring," it seemed to call back while flicking its tail as if to say, "Get away."

Dan Duncan unholstered his Glock 22 police issued handgun and leveled it at his intruder. With 15 rounds in the magazine, he was sure he could end its irritating life, but he'd also blow several holes in his neighbor's vinyl siding. So he slid it back in the holster, put on a new uniform, and made himself a sandwich for lunch. He needed to pump some iron—maybe spend a little time at the soup kitchen. He found that it was getting harder and harder to live with himself.

***

Each new power that Clay possessed seemed to surprise him less. He wondered, "Is hearing a ghost a parapsychological power?"

"Maybe you're a ghost whisperer, Dad. Jennifer Love Hewitt's a ghost whisperer." Tanner was smiling again.

"She's an *actress* and that's a TV show. Get serious for a minute. Erika, you're telling me that there's a ghost in your office?"

"People have believed for as long as I've been in Durand that the Depot is haunted. Roberto's wife, Stacy, has claimed for years that she saw a ghost more than once while she was working here. It was a woman in a wedding dress. She saw her running from the women's restroom on the first floor, and she saw her sprinting into the attic down the hall when she was pulling out Christmas decorations. There're other stories of circus performers who roam the halls at night performing various circus activities, but no one around here has ever seen or heard anything to verify those stories."

"Are any of the circus performers supposed to be midgets?" Tanner quipped.

"You're not serious too often, are you?" Erika replied with a smile.

"I am when I play sports, but other than that, usually only when my stuffy dad's around."

Clay rolled his eyes and smiled. "So why would circus performers be roaming the halls?"

"Well, in 1903, the Wallace Brothers Circus was traveling by two trains through Durand and while stopped at the Depot, the first train was rear-ended by the second train. More than twenty circus performers were killed and twice that many were injured. Ten of the bodies were laid to rest in Lovejoy Cemetery, just a couple of miles south of town. Two or three of the bodies were never even identified. Believe it or not, Comedian Red Skelton's father was a clown in that circus and is buried in the cemetery. An elephant, some camels, and a dog were buried along the tracks…People in Durand occasionally claim to hear the trumpeting of that elephant."

"That would be a horse of a different color," Clay heard in his head, but he ignored the voice temporarily.

There was a pause as the two men took in Erika's tale. "Clay, exactly one hundred years later—to the day—the train my husband was on crashed into a semi-trailer carrying horses. Only the conductor was killed, but Adrian has been missing ever since. The horses were also buried along the tracks as a kind of symbolic gesture in remembrance of the circus disaster."

"Since the wreck, there have been supposed sightings of the ghosts of harness-racing horses pulling their carts," Erika added.

"So you think a ghost is playing with your office decorations?" Clay asked sincerely.

"Actually, before today, there have been over a dozen break-ins here in the Depot over the last six years or so. Each time there is no evidence of a burglary. Things are simply moved. Marshall's office furniture is always rearranged like Adrian used to keep it, drawers are opened and papers scattered, and a shovel is always found on his desk. My office always has pictures turned over and any personal items I have of Logan's are thrown away—just like you witnessed just now...but I don't think it's one of the circus performers..."

"It's your *husband*!" Tanner interjected.

"*Good horse sense, that one,*" Clay heard.

"I don't know, but *maybe*," Erika replied. "Most of the time since the accident, I figured he was alive and had chosen to disappear. But as we've had more and more break-ins, I'm starting to think more and more that it could be him. Everyone but Marshall has entertained the idea that it's a ghost. Even Chief Hopper thinks it's a ghost. If we're all willing to believe it's a ghost, it has to be *someone's* spirit...and the break-ins kind of have *his* signature."

"Well, if your husband is dead, why has his body never turned up? And if he's the ghost, why does he keep talking about horses? He said 'that would be a horse of a different color' when you mentioned the elephant, and he said that Tanner has 'good horse sense' when he brought up your husband. And why does he put a *shovel* on your boss's desk?"

"*Don't put the cart before the horses.*"

Clay's brain was whirring. "He said, 'don't put the cart before the horses.' Most of the sayings he's been using aren't accurate. They're close, but not accurate. Do you think it's some sort of message? If it *is* your husband, what does his disappearance or death have to do with horses?"

Tanner was texting again when he said, "The train killed four horses in the wreck, Dad. Remember the horses were buried near the tracks?"

"The shovel!" Clay and Erika said simultaneously. "Could he be buried with the horses?" Clay asked. He picked up the picture and literally asked it a question. "Well? Is your body buried with the horses?"

"*I'm looking a dead horse in the mouth.*"

Clay gave a frustrated look at Erika and repeated the ghost's answer. "Why can't he just answer the question?"

"*Because that would be too easy.*"

Erika shrugged. "Obviously, even as a *dead* person he's not very likable."

"*Not a very nice thing to say to the only person who has any answers.*"

Then she said, "We need to talk to Luke Hopper, our police chief, about this."

CHAPTER 9

Robbie Gomez walked into the house and was attacked by his three little girls.

"Daddy!"

"Daddy's here!"

"Hi, Daddy!"

"Hola, Girls!" He got down on his knees and hugged his precious daughters. Stacey was in the kitchen. She was preparing the Thursday meal for the Paynes, an apricot chicken casserole. Stacy loved to cook and her entire family looked forward to delivering the new meal each week.

After wrestling and tickling his girls for several minutes, Roberto finally escaped the grasp of the little ones and entered the kitchen with Anna, the seven-year-old, holding him around the waist and standing on his feet as he walked. He kissed Stacy as he remarked, "That looks great! I hope you made a double batch for us, or else the Paynes are gonna be missing a couple scoops. What's for lunch? I'm *starving*."

"You'll have to get the leftover pasta from the fridge. The girls had tacos, but since you don't eat them, you can have leftovers."

"Tacos?" Robbie scrunched up his face in disgust.

"For a Mexican, you sure aren't big on Spanish food."

"How many times did Adrian Payne call me 'Taco' or 'Roburrito'? I swear I'm never gonna eat Mexican food again as long as I live simply 'cause it makes me think of him."

"Why did he call you Roburrito, Daddy?" asked Anna.

"He was simply a horrible man, Sweetheart. He liked to be mean." He peeled his daughter's arms from around his waist and told her to go play with her sisters while he ate his lunch. To his wife he said, "She's such a beautiful girl. I'm so glad she looks like you. And she has your heart too. She loves Logan Payne like a brother."

"She wants to play basketball with him today, so we need to go a little early so they have some time. Do you want me to heat something up for you?"

"No, I can do it. Thanks." He kissed her on the cheek and opened the refrigerator.

***

Clay and Tanner left Erika at the Depot so she could get some work done. She had invited them over for dinner. She explained that the Gomezes always brought plenty of food. Logan had basketball practice after school, but she wanted her son to meet her two new friends. Erika had put in a call to Chief Hopper and set up an appointment for her and the Thomases to meet with him, but the meeting wasn't until about an hour and a half later. The two guys headed out to get something to eat and to talk. It was exactly one mile from the Depot to the restaurant, but they crossed two railroad tracks, *both* of which had slow moving trains. It took close to fifteen minutes to get there.

"It must be nice knowing you have to give yourself an extra fifteen minutes to get wherever you're going in this town," Tanner remarked as he opened his menu in the restaurant.

Clay shook his head in frustrated agreement, but he decided to take the high road and change the subject. No sense dwelling on things he couldn't control. They were eating at Nick's Hometown Bar and Grill. Tanner ordered a Southwest Burger and Clay ordered a Quesadilla Burger.

"So tell me about basketball, Tanner."

"It's goin' pretty well," Tanner said while taking a sip from his Coke. "DeMarco's kind of a head case for a senior, though. I don't know. He doesn't take it too well when Beilein yells at him—and he yells at him a lot. Know what he yells at him most for? DeMarco's *always* steppin' on the three-point line when he shoots a three. Coach calls it the worst shot in basketball, and he claims DeMarco must have clown feet. 'Are you a clown, DeMarco?' he says. 'You must be 'cause you definitely have clown feet.' It's hard not to laugh when he says stuff like that."

"What *I* notice about DeMarco," Clay interjected, "is that he's always passing the ball on the break when he should be shooting and shooting when he should be passing. His decision making isn't so good, and in that close game against Western Michigan, it almost cost you the game."

"Yeah, he gets yelled at for that too...and for one-handed passes...and for not talking on defense. But he's a baller if ever there was a baller. It's tough workin' against him every day in practice, that's for sure."

"Well, keep workin' hard and make the most of the chances you get. You've played pretty well in the chances you've had so far."

When the food arrived, Clay became serious. "In order for this police chief to help us, he's gonna have to believe I can hear a ghost, and I'm gonna have to tell him what I can do. I was thinking that maybe we shouldn't tell him about *you*. Hiding your powers may come in handy somewhere down the road."

"What're you gonna do if he doesn't believe you or he won't help you?"

"Um, I'd just have to *make* him, I guess. But I don't wanna do that, so let's just pray that he'll be on our side."

After a little more small talk, Tanner excused himself to go to the restroom. He was washing his hands when a strange feeling came over him. He leaned forward toward the restroom mirror and looked into his own eyes. He began to feel dizzy, and then for a brief time, he lost track of his current circumstances and began to see into the future. First, he was sitting in an office with Erika, his dad, and a tall, thin, red-haired man he'd never seen before who was wearing a tie and sitting behind a desk that had a nameplate that said Chief Hopper. He was talking on the phone. "Yeah, I know, Morty, but what we'd really like is your permission to dig into the horse graveyard, so we can find out for sure." When he hung up, he said, "Morty says no."

There was a spinning sensation and Tanner saw two men with shovels and one with a large pick standing near a granite memorial. He could see "Amtrak Train Wreck Memorial" and "August 7, 2003." Though it was dark, Tanner could still clearly see that the men were wearing brown denim, suspendered overalls, navy blue denim jackets, small-billed railway caps with the Durand Depot logo, and black work boots. Time seemed to spin forward, and then he could see that two of them were down in the hole they had dug while the other knelt on the edge and shined two flashlights into the gravesite. The men were digging very carefully when one proclaimed, "This one is the head of a horse, but these bones beside it are *definitely* human. Someone buried a human body in this grave!"

The spinning sensation began again and Tanner saw flashing police lights and again saw the police chief from his office vision. The human skeleton had been removed from the grave, and a man in a white lab coat was examining the remains. To the side was a short, stocky officer nervously working to set up crime-scene tape. A pot-bellied, balding man wearing a blue dress coat over a white dress shirt and loosened necktie was standing next to Clay, Tanner, Erika, and a teen-aged boy. The man was strangely sweating though it was cold enough that condensation was coming from everyone's nose and mouth. They were standing behind the crime tape. Erika was holding the teenager around the shoulders while he was crying.

The vision swirled again and Tanner was looking into his own eyes in the restroom mirror. He felt a little disoriented but the details from the vision were cemented into his mind. He shook his head, opened the restroom door, and stepped out, accidentally turning the opposite way of his table. There to his right were the three men he had seen digging at the gravesite. They were at the bar, each drinking a beer and watching Sports Center highlights. Because the vision made it very clear that Erika's boss wasn't going to cooperate with the digging up of the gravesite, Tanner decided to use mind-control to tell the three railroad workers to dig up the horse gravesite along the tracks as soon as it became dark outside. He then headed back to his seat, deciding not to tell his dad about the vision just yet. He assumed he still had circumstances to manipulate, and he didn't want his dad to stop him.

***

As Erika was leaving for her meeting at the police department, she ran into Marshall Mortonson, who was returning from the bank. "Hi, Morty. I'm heading out to a meeting with Copper at the police station. I may not be back to work before tomorrow."

"Is there something wrong?" Marshall asked.

"No, not really. I think we have some information about Adrian's disappearance. We're talking with Copper to see what we can do about it."

"*We?*" Marshall seemed a bit concerned.

"A friend of mine is kind of helping me. He has a theory, sort of." Erika was trying to say as little as possible.

"*Who*, Erika? What is this about? It's been years since you've had any interest in finding out what happened to Adrian. Shouldn't you just let it go? I mean, it's been more than seven years. We can start the process to have him declared legally dead."

"He's just a friend. I was hoping to maybe find some closure for Logan, to be honest. He needs to know what happened. He needs to know that his father didn't just abandon him. Maybe knowing the truth will help him."

"Well, I'm all for helping him, you know that, but I don't see how bringing up the past can do that."

"I'm not sure it can, Morty, but I need to try. I've got to get going. Have a good day."

Marshall went into his office, put his elbows on his desk, and put his face in his hands. He had a bad feeling about Erika's meeting.

***

Clay and Tanner were waiting in the parking lot when Erika pulled in and parked in the space beside the Thomases. They walked into the police department together. A gusty, chilly wind was blowing. Winter was making its way quickly into the Michigan town. Before they were directed into Chief Hopper's office, Clay told Erika their plan to keep Tanner's powers secret for the time being.

"Come on in," the chief said. "Hello, Erika."

"Hi. I'd like you to meet my friends, Clay Thomas and his son, Tanner." Clay stepped forward first to shake his hand. "Clay, this is Luke Hopper." Erika smiled. "I usually just call him Copper," she teased.

"Nice to meet you, Lou," Clay said. "I appreciate you meeting with us."

"The name's *Luke*, Clay."

"Oh, I'm sorry," Clay apologized. "*Luke* Copper. I misunderstood."

Erika giggled. She knew he hated to be called Copper.

"That would be Luke *Hopper*, Clay—spelled kinda like the name on my nameplate. Me being a cop and all, people kind of have a hard time grasping the name." He glared somewhat playfully at Erika. She was too cute to get mad at.

Tanner started laughing. "So much for a good first impression, Dad. I'm Tanner, Mr. Hopper. It's nice to meet you." He gave the police chief a firm handshake. Without question, Luke Hopper was the man that was in Tanner's vision.

"*Finally*, a person who knows how to treat an officer of the law. Nice to meet you, Tanner. I believe I saw you playing ball on TV the other day against Western Michigan on the Big Ten Network. You had a good game. The buzzer beater you hit at the end of the first half must've been from about thirty. *That* had to feel good."

"Yeah, it did. Thanks. Sir, we appreciate your time. We have something important to talk to you about."

"All right. Pull up a chair everyone. No offense, Clay—meant or taken. Any friend of Erika's is a friend of mine. I hope I can be of help."

Erika took a deep breath and started right in. "We think we know where Adrian's body is, Luke. And we need your help to uncover it."

"Whoa! Hold on a minute. This is pretty much from out of left field. Slow down and explain."

"You know those break-ins at the Depot? Well, we're pretty sure it's Adrian's ghost. And we're pretty sure he's buried with the horses that were killed during the train wreck."

Luke looked at Clay. "Didn't I just ask her to slow down and explain? Tanner? You want to help me out here? You seemed pretty reasonable a minute ago."

"Mr. Hopper, we know this is going to sound unbelievable, but a ghost in the Depot spoke, and my dad heard him. We think it was Adrian Payne, and we think he was telling my dad to look where the horses are buried to find his body."

He looked at Clay again. "You can hear ghosts?"

"Not before today," Clay confessed. "But before today I could control minds, read minds, receive extra-sensory messages, and use telekinesis."

"And telekinesis *is*?

"I can move objects with my mind."

Now he turned to Erika. "Where'd you find this guy?"

"We went caving together. And we went to high school together before I moved here. Listen, Luke, it's true, and as soon as you accept the truth that Clay has mind powers, we can get back to the purpose of our visit. We believe that Adrian's buried alongside the railroad tracks with the horses from the train wreck."

"I don't know what to say," Luke said in disbelief.

"Luke," Erika continued, "you and I both know that you've said many times that you believe the break-ins were done by a ghost. Well, now we know for sure."

"Yeah, I said it, but I didn't really *believe* it. I mean, when there's no explanation for something, why not make up an explanation? But to really believe it is a different thing."

"Listen," Clay interjected. "Make a call to Dr. Zander Frauss. Maybe he can convince you that I can do what I claim."

Clay gave Zander's phone number to Luke, and the police chief finally agreed to make the call against his "better judgment."

"Excuse me," Luke said. "I'll make the call from another office."

As soon as he left the room, Clay voiced a concern. "We weren't going to tell him about your powers, Tanner. How can we keep Zander from saying something?"

"I'll take care of it," Tanner said as he followed the police chief out of the office.

"What's he doing?" Erika asked.

"I'm not exactly sure, but there's something going on. I sensed it at the restaurant. I trust him, Erika, so all we can do is wait and see."

***

Tanner followed Luke Hopper to a conference room where he stood outside an open door and listened. As soon as he heard Hopper introduce himself to Dr. Frauss, Tanner stepped into the room, and he sent a message to Zander through the phone. He told Zander to tell about his father only, and to leave Tanner's talents out of the explanation. Then Tanner asked Chief Hopper where the restroom was and, for good measure, used mind-control to tell Hopper to believe Dr. Frauss. Tanner's mind-control powers were at a completely different level than his father's. Tanner was able to control groups if necessary, and he didn't need eye contact like his father. He was going to have to wait to hear from Hopper to confirm his belief that he controlled Zander's mind through the airwaves from the Durand end of the phone, but he was confident that he'd been successful. When Tanner returned to the office, he plopped down into a chair and started texting, as if nothing at all had happened.

No one spoke for several minutes, but everyone sat up when Hopper returned to the room. "Okay, Thomas. Just for fun, let's say that I believe you. What do you suggest I do?"

"Zander explained things?"

"I don't know what the heck a medulla oblongata is, but I guess yours is completely open and you get sensory messages that the rest of us don't get. And you're able to control the messages. Does that sum everything up?"

"Pretty much."

"And what do you think I can do?"

"You could start by taking us to the horse graveyard, and then we can dig up the body."

"Well, the first problem is that it's private property, so Marshall Mortonson will have to give his permission. If he doesn't, we'll have to get a warrant, and the trouble with *that* is that we don't have any proof there's a body there. It's my guess that a judge is going to be hesitant to issue a warrant based on a stranger's story that Adrian's ghost told him to look there. Oh, but if I tell him you have 'mind powers,' that ought to convince him, don't you think?" he asked sarcastically. "Maybe you can *make* him believe, Clay. Let's start with Morty. I'll give him a call and see if he's willing to help us out."

Hopper asked Erika for the number to Marshall's office and made the call.

"Hi, Morty. This is Luke Hopper...I'm fine, thanks. Any new break-ins to report?...Well, that's good to hear...Listen, Morty. We've been given some information here at the office that suggests that maybe Adrian Payne might be buried with the horses along your railroad tracks...Yeah, I know, Morty, but what we'd really like is your permission to dig into the horse burial ground, so we can find out for sure...No, there isn't a warrant, and no we don't have any physical evidence. Just a tip...Well, Morty, I understand your concern, but Adrian Payne's been missing a long time, and this is the first time we think we know something about his disappearance...Yeah, of course, Morty, we could be wrong, but if we're right, we could finally give Erika and Logan some closure…I *know* it's a historical landmark. I don't know what to tell you, Morty. Can we dig or not?…Okay, if that's what we need to do, we'll try to get a warrant. I sure wish you'd be more reasonable…I understand. Have a good day, Morty."

Luke Hopper got off the phone, and with more than a little disappointment in his voice, he said, "Morty says no."

The hair on Tanner's arms stood up. Those exact words were the second confirmation that his vision was legitimate. Clay looked Tanner in the eyes and sent him a message. *"Are you going to do something?"*

Tanner nodded back at his father, and then with as much concentration as he could gather, he sent a message to Chief Hopper. *"At 7:30 tonight, go check on the horse gravesite along the tracks."*

CHAPTER 10

Clay, Tanner, and Erika left the police department with only a promise from the police chief that he would definitely call the local judge the next day and attempt to get a warrant to dig up the horse graves. As they walked to their cars, they were discussing taking a visit to the burial site. Clay suggested that they take a look before they headed to Erika's house to meet Logan Payne and to eat dinner.

"What I've heard while working at the railroad," Erika explained, "is that the circus animals from the Wallace train wreck were buried about fifteen hundred feet west of the South Oak Street crossing, but there's no way to confirm that anymore. There was no memorial placed at the site. The current memorial for the circus wreck is at Lovejoy Cemetery, about a half mile west of Durand Road on Prior Road. There's like a five-foot tall granite monument explaining that the elephant, camels, and dog from the circus were killed and buried after the wreck. When the horses were killed seven years ago, they were legitimately buried approximately fifteen hundred feet west of the South Oak Street crossing. A similar monument to the one at Lovejoy was erected. If Adrian is buried with the horses, we can know right where to look."

Without a seeming care in the world, Tanner said, "We can't go there, Dad. We should just go back to Erika's and make sure some people see us. I'm thinking that we're gonna need an alibi later today." When Clay and Erika gave him questioning looks, he said, "Trust me on this one, okay?"

***

Once they reached Erika's house, Tanner and Clay spent some time raking leaves. For an early December day, the weather was fairly mild, but the cool temperatures were dropping as they worked. In case they needed an alibi, they intentionally waved at several neighbors and many passing cars. Tanner explained to his dad what happened in the restroom at the restaurant and then explained how he had manipulated Chief Hopper and the railroad workers. "I expect that sometime after 7:30, all hell's gonna break loose, and Erika will get a call."

"You're right about the alibi, Tanner. I think it's best that we stay visible until that family comes with dinner. I don't want to be accused of digging up that grave. By the way, seeing into the future is called precognition."

Tanner smiled as a train roared from a nearby railroad track. "I could make a fortune betting on games," he nearly yelled.

"Great idea, Tanner," Clay yelled back sarcastically. "That way you'll never have to get a job and be responsible. You'll make me so proud."

At about 4:45, Logan arrived home from school and basketball practice. He was thin and about five feet ten inches tall. His dark hair hung over his eyes and he barely looked up when his mother introduced him to her new friends. When Tanner asked Logan about how practice was, he said, "Okay." But he didn't elaborate.

"Tanner's a freshman on U of M's basketball team," Erika said.

"Cool" was all that Logan said in response. Then, because Tanner manipulated his mind, Logan said something he wouldn't have said of his own free will. "Do ya wanna shoot some hoops?"

For the next fifteen to twenty minutes, Clay and Erika watched from the front window while Tanner and Logan shot baskets in the driveway. They seemed to actually be carrying on a conversation, and Clay remarked that Logan had a pretty nice shot. When he noticed that Erika looked a little sad, he asked what was wrong.

"You know when I told you I was afraid of midgets?"

"Yeah," Clay laughed.

"Well, I *am* kind of afraid of them, but that's not what I'm *really* afraid of. I'm afraid that I'm failing him as a mom," she said as she glanced Logan's way. "He's going to be eighteen on his next birthday, and I'm afraid I'm not doing my job. He's so depressed and unhappy, and I can't fix it. I take people like you out into a cave and teach them what it means to have faith, but in my *own* life, I have a hard time believing that I'm not failing *him. A*nd why can't I get *him* to have faith in something? Why can't *he* be happy? Why can't I fix whatever it is that's eating away at him? It scares me more than anything to think I might not be an adequate mother."

"I don't have the answers," Clay gently responded, "but I have a hunch that we may be able to help him if we can solve this mystery."

"I'll be praying with all my heart that you're right about that," she said. Then she changed the subject and said, "Good. The Gomezes are here. The one thing that always seems to bring a smile to Logan's face is their oldest girl, Anna. I've learned to treasure these moments. Come on." She grabbed Clay's hand and led him to the door.

***

When the Gomez pickup truck parked in the driveway, a side door flew open and little Anna jumped out, smiled a big dimpled smile, and yelled, "Logan!"

Logan brushed the hair from his eyes and smiled his own terrific dimpled smile. Erika elbowed Clay, and with tears in her eyes, said, "See what I'm talkin' about? That girl brings joy to our lives."

Tanner strolled over to the couple as Logan began lowering his basketball hoop so Anna could easily make some shots. "Hi, Anna. I'm Tanner. How old are you?"

"Seven and a half," she said. But she was more interested in playing with Logan than talking to Tanner, so as soon as the basket was low enough, she squealed and grabbed the basketball, not minding the cold whatsoever.

Logan spent a few minutes reviewing how to dribble with her fingertips. Then he made her dribble with her left hand too because "if you only dribble with one hand, you're only a half a basketball player." It sounded like something a coach probably said to him over the years.

The Thomases were introduced to Stacy Gomez, and Roberto said hello to them again. They all stepped into the house and Erika put the food in the oven to keep warm. She returned the dish from the previous week and spent a few minutes playing with the younger Gomez girls. When it finally got too dark for Logan and Anna to play anymore, they came inside. "Mom and Dad, Logan says I'm a good basketball player! And I'm gonna be a superstar!"

"You're already a superstar to me, Sweetheart," said Roberto. "But if Logan says you'll be a star, then I'm certain he's right."

"A *super*star, Daddy!"

Everyone laughed and then Stacy suggested it was time to leave so everyone could eat dinner. During dinner, Erika broke an uncomfortable silence by telling Logan that the police were investigating information that might soon lead to the discovery of his father. "*Sooner than you think*," thought Tanner. Logan shrugged his shoulders like he didn't really care, but Clay caught a glimpse of one of his eyes and he heard the boy think, "…*hate him.*" Logan claimed he had homework, and he excused himself and went to his room.

Clay somewhat anxiously explained to Erika that he and Tanner would leave at 8:00 or so if they didn't hear from Chief Hopper. But he also explained that Tanner was *very* sure they would hear from him. The next hour or so dragged as the friends waited, but time wasn't dragging elsewhere.

CHAPTER 11

The three railroad workers started digging as soon as it was dark. They were a bit drunk and quite confused as to why they were there, but everyone agreed it was something that they needed to do. Once they had dug close to six feet deep, they seemed to sense that they needed to be careful. The worker with the large pick went to his truck and returned with two flashlights. He kneeled at the hole and lowered the flashlights below the ground surface in an attempt to hide the beams. One of the men used his hands to clear dirt from one skeleton while the other man cleared dirt from a second skeleton. Eventually the bones became recognizable. "This one is the head of a horse, but these bones beside it are *definitely* human. Someone buried a human body in this grave!"

After very little discussion and a unanimous decision, the man with the flashlights helped pull the other two men out of the grave, and they practically ran to their truck and drove away vowing to never tell anyone what they had just done and seen.

At 7:30, Luke Hopper drove a police cruiser near the burial location and then walked to the horse gravesite, shining his flashlight to lead his way. First, he saw the mound of dirt. He quickened his pace and approached the hole. What he saw next he found quite disturbing. His powerful flashlight beam shone directly on the skull of a horse. To his left of the horse was the skull and upper body of a human. "*Clay Thomas, what have you done?*" he thought. He headed back to his car and made the call announcing he'd found a dead body. He requested a call be placed to the Genesee County Medical Examiner and he ordered a couple of backup units to be sent to the scene.

Dan Duncan received a call from Chief Hopper personally. "You need to get over here, Dan. I think I've discovered Adrian Payne's body at the monument along the tracks. I'm gonna have to call Morty and Erika too. It's probably best if her friends are here when she shows up." Dan felt sick. He rushed around and left his house almost immediately.

Hopper called Marshall Mortonson next. "Yeah, I know you said no, Morty. I had a bad feeling and took a look, and someone dug up the grave. I think we've found Adrian's body. I'm calling Erika next, but I think you should be here when she arrives." Anxiously, a disturbed Mortonson threw on a coat. He too left almost immediately.

When Hopper called Erika, it was a little before 8:00. "I think your friend dug up the grave, Erika. But there's a body. I think you need to get over here. I'm sorry, Erika; I really am."

"It looks like he was right about the grave, Luke, but he didn't dig it up. He and Tanner have been with me ever since we left your office. There's no way it was Clay. We'll be there in a minute." Erika called to Logan and then told Clay that his theory was right. A body had been discovered.

"I'll drive," Clay said.

When they arrived at the gravesite, Tanner saw a man in a white lab coat kneeling over what he was sure was the skeleton of Adrian Payne. A short, stocky police officer was setting up crime scene tape. The policeman, Dan Duncan, looked anxiously at Erika as she arrived. Erika walked right up to a pot-bellied, balding man wearing a blue dress coat over a white dress shirt and loose necktie. The man, Marshall Mortonson, gave Erika a hug. It was so strange to Tanner to see his final vision coming true before his eyes. Condensation was coming from the noses and mouths of everyone present, but Adrian Payne's partner was sweating. Luke Hopper walked up and glared at Clay with obvious distrust. "We don't know for sure yet, but if Clay here was right, we've found

Adrian's body." As the words escaped his mouth and entered Logan's ears, the teenager began crying. Erika put her arms around him and held him tightly as he wept. It was going to have to be confirmed, but Tanner, Clay, and Erika were certain that Adrian Payne's body had been discovered after seven years. And since it had been secretly buried, Adrian might have been murdered.

CHAPTER 12

The next morning, as Clay was eating a late breakfast, his phone rang. It was a call from Chief Hopper, asking Clay to come back to Durand for a meeting. The previous evening Tanner had driven back with his father to the house in Flint and then had continued on to his apartment in Ann Arbor, so during a mostly sleepless night and restless morning, Clay had been alone, thinking about the events of the past day. He found that he was very attracted to Erika, and realized that for the first time since Jessie's death, he was interested in another woman. Yet, he knew that his purpose in Durand was going to have to be to solve the mystery. It worried him that discovering the unknown might not have the desired romantic outcome, but he felt confident that he needed to do whatever he could to help Erika and Logan. He would worry about the rest later.

As Clay's mind wandered, he began to realize that he needed to find answers to a lot of questions. He needed to know what actually happened on the night of the train wreck. How did Adrian's body disappear? Was he actually murdered? Who would have the motive to kill him, and how could it have been done? If the coroner's report confirmed the identity of Adrian Payne, would the coroner be able to discover the cause of death after seven years? And who could have buried the body? And why? Those questions and more flooded Clay's mind. Why did Logan hate his father? And if he hated him, why was he so upset when the body was found? He also wondered, now that the body was discovered, if the ghost at the Depot had found some sort of peace and would stop communicating with him. Is a ghost some sort of entity trapped in a type of spiritual state until his or her purpose is achieved? After Clay cleaned up the kitchen, he brushed his teeth, grabbed his keys, phone, and jacket, and headed out the door, feeling a wave of anxiety. Was he getting into something that was over his head?

***

During breakfast at the Payne household, there was nearly complete silence, except for the continuous opening and snapping shut of Logan's jackknife. Logan looked like a wreck. He was slouched in a seat at the kitchen table, a plate of uneaten waffles before him. His unwashed hair was hanging over his puffy eyes, and a look of misery clouded his face. Erika wanted to cry. She had no idea what to say. She was personally hopeful that the coroner would be able to identify the body and that she might be able to know for certain that Adrian would not someday surprisingly show up in their lives again. She knew she was happier without him, and she found that she was already looking forward to seeing Clay again. Once the investigation was concluded, maybe Adrian's funeral would mark a new beginning. Her thoughts then switched to her parents in Florida. She wondered if they would remember the crush she had had on Clay. Additional questions began to swirl in her mind. How could she help Logan? He was going to have to get some additional counseling if he continued to feel so upset over the loss of his father. What if she and Clay dug into the mystery and found out things that she didn't really want to know? Would it be better to let things go as they are, or could finding answers finally help Logan to move on with his life?

There was a knock at the back door. It was 10:30 in the morning. Erika had no desire to fight Logan about going to school, so she hadn't even tried. When she opened the door, it was Stacy with little Anna. Stacy had brought a vegetable pizza that "you can eat anytime." She explained that she kept Anna from school and brought her in hopes that she would cheer up Logan. Logan smiled, grabbed Anna's hand and led her to the living room where they started hitting a soft volleyball back and forth to each other. Erika gave Stacy a hug and thanked her for her kindness.

"Robbie seemed really upset when he heard the news from last night. He said he was worried about you and Logan, so I volunteered to come to see you. So, how're you doing?"

"I'm okay. At the beginning, I figured he'd disappeared on purpose. It didn't make sense that there was no body after the wreck, but as time passed, I believed he was gone for good and maybe he *was* actually dead. Stacy, life has been hard, but it's been better without him. I worry so much about Logan, though. He was sad and withdrawn *before* the wreck, but he's been getting worse since his father disappeared. He doesn't talk about it—even to a counselor—so I don't know how I can help him."

"Well, kids love and need their dads. I'm sure it's been tough on him to not have one."

"If you ask me, Logan didn't love *or* need his dad. I don't believe Adrian loved *him*. Logan had to see that. And Adrian never took an interest in him either. He was mostly only interested in himself. Logan could see that too. So I'm just simply confused about his reaction to losing him *and* his emotional reaction to finding him last night."

"Well, we'll do whatever we can to help you, Erika. It's obvious to us that he has a good heart. He treats our girls like princesses…especially Anna. We love him."

***

Clay showed up at the Durand Police Station by 11:00. He was told to head into Chief Hopper's office. Dan Duncan stuffed a fist full of sunflowers seeds in his mouth as he glared at Clay. Clay walked past and heard, *"Who do you think you are?"* as he glanced at the police officer. Clay saw "Duncan" on the cop's desk. He remembered the policeman stretching out crime scene tape at the gravesite the night before and remembered his name as the cop who was Erika and Logan's "protector." Clay figured he was probably a good guy who was just a bit jealous. As he made his way through the station, Dan grabbed his jacket and headed home to do some yard work and relax.

Clay entered Hopper's office. "Mornin', Clay. Can I get you some coffee?"

"Mornin', Chief. No thanks. I don't drink it."

"Call me Luke...and have a seat, Clay. We have some things to talk about."

"Okay."

"All right, listen. We checked out your alibi. Obviously Erika and her son vouched for you, but we also talked with neighbors who confirmed it was you and Tanner that had raked up those piles of leaves in the Payne's yard, and Roberto Gomez and his wife confirmed you were at the house during the time we figure the grave was dug up, so you're not a suspect. But I'm still trying to figure out if you had something to do with it anyway. So, did you?"

"No."

"Don't you think it's kind of a coincidence that we've never had a clue about the location of Adrian's body and then you show up and claim it was in the horses' grave, and that very day the body is dug up and discovered?"

"Yeah, it's quite a coincidence, but I didn't have anything to do with it." No sense telling about Tanner. "You mentioned that it was Adrian's body."

Hopper ignored Clay's comment. "I don't understand your interest, Clay. We all know that Erika's about as hot as a woman can be, but there has to be more to it than that."

"I'm just trying to help her, Luke. And maybe help her son. My friends, Zander and Lydia Frauss, asked me to help her."

"He's the doctor I spoke to yesterday?"

"Yes."

"He told me that he set you up with Erika so she could help *you. W*hat's that about?"

"I went caving with Erika. Zander is my friend. He felt that I wasn't doing myself any good sitting around mourning my wife's murder. I suppose you've checked me out and know about that by now? I feel quite a bit responsible for her death, Luke. It was my powers that caused the whole chain of events to transpire. Erika helped me to see that I might be able to use my gifts for something good. I can't help but feel that I can help Erika discover some peace and maybe help that troubled son of hers."

"I know about the murder. I'm sorry, Clay. I have to admit, you seem like a straight up guy, and I admit to taking a liking to Tanner too. So I'm going to include you in this investigation. I'm hoping it's the wisest course of action. This being my first homicide investigation, I don't exactly have a plan of action. Durand's not exactly a hotbed of violent crime. There hasn't been a murder since I've lived here."

"You mentioned it was Adrian's body." Clay's question still hadn't been answered.

"Okay. Here goes. Fortunately we didn't need to do any DNA tests. After seven years the body was completely skeletonized and all cloth remains or other evidence was completely decomposed. However, we were able to match up dental records and X-rays from his past. We're certain that the body is Adrian Payne's. The forensic pathologist from Genesee County, however, has determined that the cause of death is almost certainly trauma caused by the train wreck. Many, many bones were broken, including his skull. His best guess as to why so many bones were broken would be that he jumped from the train and one of the overturned train cars landed on top of him."

"So if he died in the train wreck," Clay asked, "how did the body end up in the horse grave?"

"That's a question we need to attempt to answer because the graves weren't dug until the second day after the wreck, and certainly Adrian's body wasn't buried along with the horses until later. Someone would have had to hide the body for at least two days and then dig up the grave after the fact."

"Any suspects?"

"Let me tell you something about Adrian Payne, Clay. I don't think anyone really liked him. And I can tell you that there wasn't much mourning over his disappearance. People's lives simply moved on—except many people have gone out of their way to help Erika. Logan is the only one who seemed affected by the loss of Adrian. It could have been anyone."

"Did *you* like him?"

"Nope. And you wouldn't have either. I never met another person who cared less about others and more about himself. We all pretty much felt a shortened life was pretty much what he deserved. So, you have any ideas of what to do next?"

"I have two. Number one, let's find out what happened on that train. You're a detective...detect," Clay said with a smile. "Number two, let's go back to the train station and see if Adrian's ghost is still alive and kickin'...so to speak."

"I can see this is gonna be *fun* for you," Hopper rolled his eyes. "Let's head over to the Depot."

"Do you mind if I call you Copper?" Clay laughed.

"Unless you want to be kickin' alongside Adrian, I'd suggest not," replied Luke Hopper. Clay smiled again. The chief was definitely a good guy.

CHAPTER 13

Luke and Clay waited at the Ann Arbor Street railroad crossing for a good ten minutes, while a cargo train zoomed by at about two miles per hour. "Wouldn't it be better for the transportation business if the trains went, like, thirty or forty times faster than this one is going?" Clay asked in complete sincerity.

Luke laughed. "Yeah, I think I could push a train with my own strength faster than this one is going. But you get kind of used to it around here. I've taken to listening to books on CD while my life wastes away at railroad tracks."

"I'd think you wouldn't have too many high speed chases around town here in Durand. Every road is pretty much permanently barricaded from what I've seen in my short time here."

Luke laughed again. "I'll bet you didn't know that there're all sorts of stories about homeless people and teenaged runaways hopping on cargo trains as they inched through this town. Especially during the Great Depression. They go too fast, you can't jump on 'em, Clay."

Finally the train cleared and Chief Hopper drove the rest of the way down Ann Arbor Street and onto South Railroad Street before pulling into the Depot parking lot. The track superintendent, Wilson Goodrich, was organizing a group of three men, Roberto Gomez and two of the workers that Tanner had manipulated in the restaurant, to fill the dirt back into the grave and reestablish the memorial site. Chief Hopper nodded at the men and led the way inside.

Their first stop was Marshall Mortonson's office. He was looking a bit ill, but was busy making entries in an account ledger on his desk. "Morning, Chief," he said as he finished an entry and flipped the book shut. "I figured I'd see you today. Any idea who it was that trespassed on my property and dug up the memorial?"

"Sorry, Morty. Nothing yet. Hopefully we'll hear something that will give us a lead. This here is Clay Thomas, by the way." Clay reached over and shook Marshall's hand. "Clay's an advisor on the Adrian Payne case. He's the one who brought me the evidence about Adrian's location."

"You trust him?" Marshall obviously didn't.

"The jury's still out on that, Morty. I don't trust easily. But, yeah, I think I can trust him. What we'd like to ask you is to think back to the train wreck. What do you remember about that night?"

Marshall took a deep breath. Clay looked into his eyes. "*This can't possibly go well,*" Marshall thought. Clay was immediately *very* interested.

"We were coming from East Lansing. There was a convention honoring Amtrak employees and such. Adrian liked to go to those and be seen and heard. I usually didn't attend. But Erika was going on a caving training, I think it was, and Logan needed someone to watch him. Adrian flat out refused. He had plans in Lansing. I went along simply to keep an eye on Logan."

"What kind of 'plans' did he have?"

"Same as usual, I suspect. Some babe on the side. How could he have the nicest looking wife on the planet and fool around on her?"

"Did Erika know that Adrian was cheating on her?" Clay asked.

"What'd you say your name was again?" Marshall responded.

"It's Clay Thomas."

"Well, Clay, pretty much *everyone* knew he was fooling around, so I'd suspect that Erika knew it too. I*'ve* never said anything to her, though. Listen, Adrian was my best friend. I knew him before we purchased the Depot. He wasn't such a bad guy in those days. Couldn't have been so bad if he got Erika to marry him. But he changed—almost completely for the worse. When he had a chance—and he found lots of chances—he fooled around, and he spent a lot of our money doing it. That trip to Lansing, I suspect, was no different than any other. I tried to occupy Logan while Adrian went off to do his own thing."

"So what was Logan, ten, eleven years old?" asked Hopper.

"Something like that. He was a timid kid. Seemed afraid of his dad, if you ask me."

"So, again, what do you remember about that night?" Hopper asked.

"Well, the Lansing station is pretty much just a storage facility turned into a train station. But it's right on the west side of the MSU campus. It's really convenient for students, and the storage facility was sold at a minimal cost by the college just to get rid of it. But we've worked out a sort of partnership, so we have lots of our meetings, parties, conventions, and such right on campus. Adrian was an MSU grad and he donated money to the college, so they pretty much let him do as he pleased there. Off from the service road near the train station, there's a huge service building that we meet in. Lots of rooms. Adrian was known to take advantage of some of those rooms by paying for the services of a lady of two."

"Hookers?" Clay asked in amazement. "And he was with someone like that on the night of the accident?"

"I don't know that for sure, but it was pretty common. I never saw him with anyone on that particular night, at least not that I recall. Besides, I spent half my time trying to keep up with Logan. Lost him a coupla times."

"How 'bout the train ride back? What do you remember?" Hopper asked.

"The train left on time, so it would have been 8:20. There weren't many passengers. Fifteen to twenty, I'd guess. There were two passenger cars near the back of the Amtrak that the passengers were in. Logan and I were in the front of the two. I don't recall any problems until Logan got up to look for his dad. It's not a long ride. Forty-five minutes give or take. We'd been on the train maybe thirty minutes when Logan left to find his dad. We had seen him get on, but hadn't seen him since. I was pretty confident he'd be in the engine, piloting the train. Adrian knew the engineer—Joe something-or-other. He's the guy who died in the wreck. But Adrian would always deliver the train into the station when Joe was the engineer. He'd buy him a bottle of somethin' Joe liked to drink and then act like he was important by driving the train into the Depot by himself."

"He'd do that often?" Clay asked.

"*Everyone* who knew Adrian or was associated with the Depot knew he piloted the train into our station. Adrian was a deadhead—he rode the trains on company pass and company business all the time. I generally stayed and worked in the offices. But he fancied himself as an engineer. He could be like a spoiled rotten little kid."

"So what happened with Logan?" Hopper seemed to be constantly trying to keep Marshall on topic.

"Well, he came back after about five minutes. Wouldn't look at me. Curled up with his face against one of the seat cushions and was sniffling. He was cryin' about something, but wouldn't talk to me. Finally, just before we got to the Depot, I left my seat to look for Adrian myself."

Clay was looking in his eyes when Marshall paused. Clay heard, "*He was lying on the floor, looking like he'd passed out.*" Finally, Marshall spoke out loud. "I assume that Adrian was in the engine car, but I never saw him. I looked through the engine windows and saw something large was on the tracks. Before I could even think, Joe jumped from the train, and I just reacted and jumped myself. The train wasn't going very fast. I guess we came around the curve after the Monroe crossing, and there was the horse trailer. Word was that Joe was drinking. He must not've reacted quick enough. The 'black box' recorded an attempt to brake, but obviously Joe knew there was gonna be a crash, so he bailed, and I did too."

"What about Adrian?" Hopper asked.

"*More'n likely I killed him*" is what he thought, but what he said was, "He was on the train when it left Lansing, but I never saw him before, during, or after the wreck. I always believed that somewhere along the way, he jumped off, and went off to live a new life. Figured he'd done something so stupid he was running for his life. I always figured he was alive somewhere, living the same selfish, despicable life he always led."

"So tell me about the wreck," Hopper continued to push.

"Well, I scraped myself up pretty good. Hit the ground just before the crash. It was a horrible sound, and then the truck caught on fire and a couple of train cars tipped over. The back one just missed me. I guess the front one landed on Joe. It was a while before passengers started unloading. After that, I rounded up Logan. He had a pretty good bruise on the side of his face and was a bit shook up, but he seemed okay. The other passengers weren't hurt badly either. All the emergency services started showing up, and eventually reporters, police, and such. Then Erika came for Logan. I answered a few questions, made sure the medical teams had access to the Depot. I prob'ly got home somewhere between eleven or twelve."

"Any idea who might've buried him?" Hopper asked.

"*Yes*," Marshall thought. "No," Marshall said. "Maybe he was runnin' from someone who wanted to kill him. Maybe they caught up with him and he ended up dead."

Clay was finding detective business to be intriguing. He had a few things to share with Hopper. Marshall clearly had something to do with Adrian's death. Maybe the ghost had the answer.

Marshall looked at his watch and squirmed uncomfortably. "I got some business to do at the bank and then an appointment with my attorney. If you don't mind, I need to get goin'."

"No, that's fine, Morty. We've got some other business to accomplish ourselves. If we need to, we'll talk to you again later. Thanks for your help."

"No problem. Gentlemen," he nodded, "have a nice day."

***

Dan Duncan worked out, tried to watch his cholesterol, and tried to limit salt in his diet, but his stress level was raising his blood pressure more than his efforts were lowering it. He was thinking of taking up yoga, but vainly hated the idea of being seen in the classes at his health club, so instead, he was reading a book *about* yoga while he ate oatmeal and drank a cup of hot chocolate. He was listening to classical music, thinking it had to be better for his nerves than the country music he actually *liked* to listen to. Out of the corner of his eye, he spotted his irritating squirrel squatting on one of the feeders that he'd just refilled. How it got there was a mystery. He had just cut down several additional tree branches to keep the animal from leaping to the feeder.

So much for peaceful bird watching—as soon as Dan noticed the pest, he could feel his anxiety rising. He opened his kitchen window and yelled at the squirrel, but it ignored him completely. Dan ran to his bedroom and grabbed a BB gun that he'd recently purchased and pumped the thing about thirty times. He slid open his sliding glass door which led to a wooden deck and stepped out in his stockinged feet for a clear shot, but he stepped on the pruning-stick tree-trimmer that he'd just left on the deck. He heard a snap of the trimmer handle from the weight on his right foot, and then he yelped and cursed as he stumbled and the weight of his left foot stepped onto the pruning blade, almost completely severing his big toe.

In his pain and anger, he started yelling at the squirrel. As he raised the BB gun to shoot, the squirrel simply repositioned itself so that it was directly behind the feeder and there was no clear shot. Dan's bloodied sock was leaving bloodstains on the deck as he limped with great difficulty from one end to the other, trying to get a good view of his hated enemy. The first time the squirrel's head poked out from behind the feeder, Dan took a shot, which hit the plastic feeder dead on, cracking it. A trickle of birdseed began streaming from the feeder onto the ground and Dan swore and yelled some more. He pumped the gun about forty more times and ran into the yard like a crazy person, ignoring completely that his toe was dangling from his foot and blood was pumping out at a furious rate. Running awkwardly with only one working big toe, he saw the squirrel prepare to take a flying leap, so Dan shot the rifle from his hip like a cowboy in the movies and then, after his final left-footed, unbalanced step, he fell on his face in a heap. The BB hit the feeder a fraction of an inch from the first crack and the plastic nearly exploded as the entire collection of seeds poured onto the ground. The squirrel landed safely on the grass and scurried up the stupid-looking tree that Dan had nearly voided of branches. The policeman howled, and in a fit of anger, threw the gun at the tree, breaking the rifle and rendering it forever useless.

"Tchrring...tchrring," the squirrel called down from the top of the tree. From Dan's perspective, it sounded like it was laughing at him. Dan rolled over and for the first time noticed his blood-soaked sock. He reached down to touch his toe, which was dangling, just barely attached. He hurled his chocolaty oatmeal onto the grass and fought the urge to pass out just long enough to pull his cell phone from his belt and punch in 9-1-1. He had barely managed to give his address before he passed out on the lawn.

CHAPTER 14

As soon as Mortonson had left his office and headed down the stairs, Clay and Luke turned down the hall into Erika's office. Luke closed the door. "Any observations you'd like to share?" he asked Clay.

"Well, I don't know if you could tell, but he's lying."

"I'm a trained officer of the law, Clay. Course I could tell he was lying. But his story sounded legit, so you tell me. What was he lying about?"

"First of all, he was concerned that the interview was going to be trouble for him. But that wasn't what he lied about. When Marshall went to look for Adrian, he found his body lying on the floor of the train, looking like he was passed out. When you asked him about what happened to Adrian when he and the engineer bailed from the train, he said—well, he *thought*— that he 'more than likely killed him.' And when you asked him if he had any idea who might have buried Adrian, he *said* no, but he *thought* yes. Something happened on that train the night of the wreck, Luke."

"It looks that way. But every great detective knows that if there's a crime, there's a means, a motive, and opportunity. We need to keep digging if we want to find any of those things out. Maybe your ghost will be of help."

"*If* he's still around and feeling helpful." Clay walked over to the picture that was hanging on Erika's wall. He studied it for a minute. He could see the sadness in Logan's eyes, even in the picture. Erika was smiling her same infectious smile, while

Adrian's smile was clearly forced—the dimple on his right cheek only barely discernible. The orange-colored caboose was in the background. It was odd seeing the caboose sitting all alone because each time Clay had seen it in person, it was sitting next to the wrecked Amtrak train engine. The picture seemed sort of spooky. Maybe Clay just thought it was spooky because he was trying to communicate with the ghost of the man in the picture.

"Well, Adrian, is there any message you'd like to communicate to me?" Clay didn't really know how to talk to a ghost. He figured asking it a straight-on question might work, but there was no response. He paused and waited several seconds before speaking to Luke. "Nothing. He didn't say a thing."

"Have you ever watched that show, *Ghost Whisperer*, Clay?"

"Actually, no, I haven't. What's it about?"

"Jennifer Love Hewitt's this girl from a town in New York, I think. She can see and communicate with the dead. I was wondering if you ever saw Adrian when he supposedly talked to you?"

"No, but I'm *certain* he talked to me. It wasn't something that 'supposedly' happened."

"I'm being as open-minded as I can be, Clay. Anyway, the ghosts reach out to her for help relaying messages or completing tasks that are meant to put their spirits to rest. It's like they died with unfinished business and they aren't allowed to find peace or cross over into the afterlife until their tasks are completed. Maybe Adrian has some unfinished business or needs to find peace somehow before he's allowed to move on. Or maybe he's found it now that his body has been uncovered."

"Can't move on until my one good deed is accomplished."

The hair on Clay's arms stood on end. Adrian wasn't gone yet. He refocused his attention to the picture and said, "Adrian, you just said you have one good deed to accomplish. Maybe that deed is to find out what happened to you. Could you possibly help us figure that out?"

"Skeleton key," is what Clay heard.

"Did you say, 'skeleton key'?" Clay asked.

"*Yes. Skeleton key.*"

Clay could feel the room getting a little chilly, once again. He could see that Adrian was *not* going to be completely cooperative. He had no idea what 'skeleton key' meant, but it was a start. Luke, who was observing patiently, asked, "How did you die, Adrian?"

"*A heart attack*," he replied.

"He said, 'a heart attack,' Luke, but that doesn't sound like any funny business to me. I don't understand." Clay continued to gaze at the picture. "Why are you talking to me? What do you want?"

"*Ease the pain*," Clay heard.

"So a skeleton key will help us figure out who buried you, you died of a heart attack, and you're hoping we can ease your pain." He continued to look at the picture on the wall. "Is that what you're telling me?"

In an eerie whisper, the voice responded, "*Ease the pain.*"

The ghost didn't say another word. Clay and Luke both asked questions, but Adrian had said all he was going to say. None of his words made much sense, but they were clues. Hopefully, somewhere along the way, the words would help them figure out what happened.

***

Marshall Mortonson stepped out of Sagelink Credit Union with his legitimate account books in hand. The credit union was a consistent supporter of the Durand Depot and an active sponsor of the Durand Railroad Days. Marshall had met with the bank manager. He had been informed that they were unwilling to finance him to buy out Erika Payne if she decided to sell her fifty percent ownership of the business now that she was officially the beneficiary of Adrian's estate. An appraisal nearly a year earlier had established that the business in its entirety was worth nearly five million dollars. Marshall then collected a check as a donation toward the upcoming "Christmas in the Diamond District: Festival of Trees" holiday event that had begun the last week of November. Then he made his weekly Friday deposits and returned to his car to secret away the accurate books and to pick up the doctored ones.

The cold of early December was upon them, so Marshall buttoned up his coat and departed down the street toward Nickel and Sons Attorneys.

He stepped into the offices, a few minutes early for his appointment, and found his attorney, Toni Nickel, refilling a cup of coffee in her mug. "Hey, Morty. Come on right in. How're you doing?"

"When're you gonna change that sign outside?" Marshall asked. "Don't you think that when clients come calling that they'll notice that Oscar Nickel's 'sons' are female? Just 'cause your names are Toni and Andi Nickel doesn't mean that people aren't gonna notice you have breasts."

"Have you ever seen an attorney's office called 'Blank and *Daughters*,' Morty? How 'bout you, Andi," she called into her sister's office. "You ever hear of an attorney's office with the word *daughter* in it?"

"Nope," Andi called back to her sister.

"We were thinking of changing the name, though, Morty." She raised her voice so her sister could hear. "How about 'Daddy/Daughters, Attorneys at Law'? Or 'Nickel and Double Nickels'?"

"I like 'Nickel and Dames,'" Andi called from her office.

"Okay, okay. Forget I asked. Mind if I have a seat, or do you want to bust my chops some more? Have you looked over my contracts?"

Toni laughed. "Yeah, I've looked them over. What do you want to know?"

"I just want to know what's about to happen to my business now that Adrian's body has been found. How's it gonna affect me?"

"Well, the coroner has issued a death certificate, so he's officially deceased. That means that fifty-percent of the business legally belongs to his heir, Erika Payne. Morty, you still hold all decision-making power in the company. You brought your books, right?" Marshall nodded assent, knowing he had only brought the "cooked" books that provided the falsified numbers. "I may want to look them over. From what you've told me, Erika's been a paid employee of the company for the last six plus years and a recipient of capital gains revenue in lieu of her husband's absence. But since her husband has been dead the past seven years, she will probably be entitled to fifty percent of all earnings for those years, minus what she's already received. Plus, the contract wording indicates that if she wants to sell her half of the business, you have to buy her out, or you'll have to agree to sell."

"That's true. I just left the credit union where we talked about that. I'd need to get a current appraisal, but I can tell you that buying her out will be troublesome. Actually, it's probably impossible."

"So you'd have to sell. What are you hoping for, Morty?"

"I don't want to sell and give up my business, that's for sure. I just want you to look through my books, and figure out what a payout for the last seven years would entail. What I'm saying is that I'd like to figure out an agreement with Erika that's as quick and painless as possible. I'm sure I can manage to obtain that size of a personal loan, but—let me say this delicately—I'd be uncomfortable with other people looking through my books. And, Toni, if she wants to sell, I'm gonna have to get that appraisal, and, again, she'll probably want a look at the financial records. I don't think I can afford her looking into these books. And I mean that *literally* as well as figuratively."

***

Clay and Luke decided to stop by Erika's house to see how she was doing and to ask her some questions as well. Stacy had already left so the house was nearly silent. Erika smiled a big smile at Clay but resisted the urge to give him a hug. She did make eye contact and thought, "*Can you hear me?*" Clay nodded his head yes. "*I wish I could hug you.*" Clay smiled back at her and mouthed the words "*Me too.*"

Hopper spoke first. "Hi, Erika. How're you doin'?"

"Didn't get much rest, but I'm okay. Logan's been upset though. Would you like to come in? It's awfully quiet around here."

"Thank you." The men entered the house, took off their shoes to be polite, and each sat in a chair. Everything in the cozy home was brightly colored and neatly decorated. "We've started an investigation, but we haven't got far," Luke said. "We *do* have the coroner's conclusion that the body was Adrian's. I'm sorry, Erika."

"I was sure it would be. What else did you find out?"

"Well, the coroner determined that the cause of death was most likely from the train wreck. There were lots of broken bones. But there is no way to know that for certain. After seven years, the body is completely skeletonized and there isn't other forensic evidence to look at."

"But *Adrian* claims that he died from a heart attack," Clay interjected. "He also said that a skeleton key would help us determine who buried him. Plus he wants to ease his pain."

"Does any of that make any sense to you?" Both men shook their heads no. "Can a ghost be in pain?" Erika asked.

Hopper spoke up. "We assume he was talking about finding peace in his life or finding a way to put his spirit to rest, but we don't know that for certain either. We talked with Morty, Erika, about what he remembered from the day of the train wreck. Do you mind if we ask you what *you* remember." Clay deduced immediately that the chief didn't want to tell what Marshall had said—at least not right away.

"There's not much for me to tell. Adrian went to a conference or convention or some such thing. I remember we fought because I wanted to go to spelunker training in Indiana. I suggested he take Logan with him, but he didn't want anything to do with that. Logan wanted to go, though, because he wanted to ride on the train. Finally, somehow we convinced Morty to go too, so he could help keep an eye on Logan."

"Do you know why he didn't want Logan there?" asked Clay.

"Could have been lots of reasons. He was a very self-centered man. He didn't want to be bothered by Logan, I suppose. It could have been that he had plans that he felt Logan would interfere with. It could have been simply that he didn't like having him around. Maybe he was going to be legitimately busy and couldn't keep an eye on him well enough."

"Maybe it was because he had plans with another woman," Chief Hopper said.

Erika was immediately embarrassed and Clay was a little angry by the insensitivity of the remark.

"That was uncalled for, Luke," Clay said.

"It's okay, Clay. It's humiliating, but most likely true. I'd noticed things—evidence, comments, looks from other people. I figured he was cheating on me. I have to admit, that was one of *my* reasons why I wanted Logan to go with him—to keep him from cheating."

"I'm so sorry, Erika," said Clay.

"Please…don't be. He was what he was. I just feel stupid that I didn't do anything about it."

"So what else do you remember?" Hopper continued.

"I went to a cave in Northern Indiana. It wasn't too long of a drive. I was back home at about five thirty or six. The train doesn't leave East Lansing until 8:20 and wasn't scheduled to arrive until after nine, so I got some work done here at home."

"Can anyone verify that you were here?"

"What are you getting at, Luke?" Clay asked, obviously offended.

"I'm just asking questions, Clay. Remember you told me to detect. Well, I'm detecting to the best of my ability." He turned back to Erika. "Someone buried your husband, Erika, and I think there's more to the story than just a train wreck. I want to get to the bottom of it, so I'm just asking lots of questions, hoping things'll sort themselves out. Is that okay with you, Clay?" he asked somewhat sarcastically.

"It's okay, Clay, but the answer is no, Luke. Unless I got a phone call or something, I don't think there's any way I can prove that I was home. But I *was*. At least until around nine o'clock when the emergency sirens went off and I heard the ambulances and fire trucks. I could see smoke over toward the Depot. I got in my car and drove to the train station and saw the wreck.

Everything else is kind of a blur. I found Logan. His face was red and bruised. Morty was bloody all over, and Adrian was missing."

"Do you remember anything else that might have seemed unusual or important in some way?" Hopper asked.

"I just remember Morty saying that he thought that Adrian was in the engine car, but because they couldn't locate him, maybe he had jumped. He even suggested that Adrian had exited the train before the wreck."

"What did Logan say? Morty said that Logan went to talk to Adrian just a few minutes before the wreck. Did Logan see him?"

"Logan has never said *anything* about what happened that night."

"Could we talk to him right now?"

"I think he's asleep. This has been hard on him. Maybe today's not a good time, Luke. Can you give him a little time?"

"Sure, Erika. Thanks for the information. I've got some things to look into, but I'm sure I'll eventually want to talk to Logan. Let's go, Clay."

***

As soon as they were in Hopper's car, Clay jumped all over him. "You're treating her like a suspect! How could you seriously think that?"

"Listen, Clay. Obviously you like her. Who doesn't? But she *is* a suspect. S*omebody* buried that body. You claim Morty has an idea who buried Adrian. If it was Erika, Morty'd keep his mouth shut about that for sure. Maybe they were working together. Listen, I don't think she did anything, Clay, but I'd be making a mistake if I didn't at least keep an open mind about the possibility. That's why I didn't tell her what Morty was thinking yet. She had a good motive for him to disappear. He was cheating on her. She claimed he didn't love Logan. She had the opportunity to bury him—at least she hasn't been ruled out yet. Let me do some investigating, and something will turn up. It always does—at least on the TV shows it does." He smiled.

"Okay. You do your job, and I'll do whatever I can to help you. What's next?"

"I guess I'll look into the records of the train wreck and see if I can find anything unusual. I'll check Erika's phone records. Maybe someone *did* call her. I'm gonna have to find out for sure if she really *was* out of town that day. Maybe the reason she needed Logan to go with Adrian is because she had some diabolical plan." Clay gave him an unhappy stare. "I *know*...I'm reaching for possibilities. We also need to figure out what Adrian meant by the skeleton key helping us discover who buried him. We need to talk to Logan eventually too. If Morty saw him lying on the floor, maybe Logan saw him too. Maybe *you* can get him to open up with your mind tricks."

"I wouldn't do that unless Erika gave me permission. These powers I have are not toys to be played with. When I influence people, there are often consequences. I've learned that the hard way."

As they pulled back into the police station, Hopper said, "I'll speak to the medical examiner again too. Maybe he can tell us something about the heart attack that Adrian claims he had...and I'm especially interested that Morty thinks he might have killed him. Could there have been a murder or attempted murder? Nothing much makes sense yet, does it?"

"Nope, not yet. By the way, Tanner has a game tomorrow at Crisler Arena. I'll be out of town most of the day."

"Give him my best wishes. I'll call you when I have information. Thanks for your help, Clay."

CHAPTER 15

Michigan's men's basketball team was playing a Saturday afternoon game against Clay's alma mater, Eastern Michigan University, at Crisler Arena in Ann Arbor. Clay was seated in the stands with Zander Frauss and his wife, Lydia. Though Clay was actually grateful, he pretended to be a little put out and said, "By the way, you two, thanks for setting me up. Here I was thinking I was doing Erika Payne and her son a favor and I find that you sent me so she could help *me*. Seems a little sneaky to me."

"That was completely Zander's idea, Clay. I actually made first contact in the real hope that *you* could help *them*. That Logan Payne is troubled, and I can't seem to find a way to help him. Maybe *you* can."

"I plead the fifth," Zander said with a grin. "Anything I say can and will incriminate me. But now that you've met her, it's my guess that you're actually not too upset with me. How do you like her?"

"I'd like to tell you that you're wasting your time messin' with my personal life, Doc, but actually, as hard as it is to admit it to you, I like her." Then Clay proceeded to catch Zander and his wife up on the case. "Tanner made a bit of a connection with Logan, Lydia, but it's going to be hard to get them together because of college and basketball. The police chief and I are hoping to find out what Logan saw on that train, but getting him to open up sounds like a difficult proposition."

"You can always *make* him talk if you decide to," Zander reminded Clay.

"Hopefully I don't have to resort to mind manipulation, but if that's what I have to do to solve the mystery, I just might do it."

The Star Spangled Banner played and the lineups were introduced, so Clay's attention was diverted. He was hoping that Tanner would get some quality playing time and do well.

***

Darius Williams, Michigan's starting point guard was having a great first half. He played the first eight minutes, scoring eleven points and dishing out four assists. Tanner subbed and played three uninspired minutes—his entire stat line consisted of one foul and one turnover—before Williams reentered the game. Clay was a bit disappointed, but he rationalized that freshman often had to go through some growing pains. A guard from Eastern dribbled the ball across half court and tapped his head to indicate a play. He faked a pass to his right and then fired a pass across the court to a teammate, but Williams anticipated the pass perfectly and intercepted it. Williams dribbled quickly down the court, intent on taking the ball to the basket for two more points. The guard from Eastern Michigan who had made the bad pass sprinted down the court and set himself in the lane, hoping to draw an offensive foul. Williams took the ball right at him, jumped, and then did an amazing three hundred and sixty degree spin in mid-air to avoid the charge, but the defender leaned into him anyway. Williams flipped the shot up and into the basket just before taking the hit, which caused him to turn awkwardly before returning to the floor. The crowd erupted in a tremendous cheer in appreciation of the amazing shot, but the crowd noise turned into nearly a complete hush as they heard both the loud snapping of his right ankle in a complete fracture and the near scream of painful agony as Williams crashed to the floor.

The sight was awful. Williams's foot was twisted in a grotesque angle causing the snapped anklebone to poke nearly through the skin. The foot was twisted sideways and down while the bone poked in the opposite direction. A cheerleader who saw the damage fainted right on top of the referee who was bending down to aid Williams. Other shocked cheerleaders and players alike turned away to avoid the horrific sight. Clay felt sick, the injury was so gruesome. The EMU player who committed the foul literally ran down the players' tunnel where he threw up. Tears came to his eyes as Tanner watched his friend continue to yell out in pain. He fell to his knees in front of the bench and began praying for his teammate. Coach Beilein ran to Williams's aid and held his hand while his starting senior point guard writhed around on the floor in anguish. Medical trainers rushed to his aid and the aid of the unconscious cheerleader. Once the referee pulled himself from under the girl, he helped his partners herd the players away from the scene.

The next ten to fifteen minutes dragged by in near silence as a medical team padded, iced, and wrapped Darius Williams's foot and eventually lifted him onto a stretcher to wheel him away to an ambulance. The entire Michigan team was noticeably as upset as Coach Beilein. They gathered around their coach and he suggested that the players say a prayer for Darius. Tanner volunteered to lead his team, but as he was praying, he decided to make use of his mental powers. He had sensed accurately that his team was in no mental state to effectively continue the game. "As we finish out this game," Tanner 'prayed,' "we will be able to block out our worries and concerns for Darius, and we will maintain one hundred percent focus and intensity. We will do everything in our power to win this game for Darius. Amen."

As the Wolverines broke their huddle, their focus was undeniable. Tanner had to shoot the free throw that resulted from the foul on the Williams basket. He made it, and for the next twenty-eight minutes of playing time, the Michigan team put on an unbelievable performance. They turned a seven-point lead into a fifty-four-point victory. Tanner, as the only player whose mind was not manipulated, was the only player to miss a free throw the rest of the game. The defensive intensity was ferocious, drawing nine offensive charging fouls, diving recklessly all over the floor, and setting a team record for defensive deflections. And as their scoring onslaught indicated, their offensive execution was excellent as well.

In the locker room after the game, Tanner reminded his teammates about Darius, and the players simply congratulated each other without celebrating. Coach Beilein complimented his team on their focus and intensity and praised them for having a common goal and carrying out its execution as a team. Players looked into each other's eyes in a seeming realization of how much they could accomplish when they were mentally focused. Tanner couldn't help but wonder if it would be a turning point in the team's season. He knew he'd influenced their mental toughness, but he knew that each player had simply played to the best of his God-given ability and gave the most that he could give. Maybe in the future, they'd be able to do it again on their own.

***

Tanner greeted his dad with a bear hug after the game. Clay looked in his eyes and saw sorrow. Maybe regret. Clay knew the feeling that regret brought when he felt he had abused his powers, so he was hoping the look was one of sorrow for the horrible injury to his son's teammate. He led his son to an arena seat and they sat down next to each other to talk. "What's on your mind, Son?"

"As a coach, you never manipulated any of your players, did you?"

"Getting my players to always play their best would be a nice advantage, wouldn't it?" Clay responded. "But, no, Tanner. I assumed when I was young that manipulating others was wrong. As I got older, I figured it was *my* secret and as long as I didn't use the power I possessed, and never told anyone about it, I could be happy and content. I wasn't either of those things, but I kind of decided that my power was my own personal cross to bear, and I needed to simply accept the burden. When your mother was killed, I blamed myself. I told myself that it was because I had used my powers that all of the chain of events occurred that led to her murder. I've been grieving her loss ever since. But lately I've started to have a change of heart. The powers I possess are a gift that God has given me to use for His glory. Now it's my job, or my goal, or my desire, to figure out how and when to use my gifts in a way that I'm proud."

"Do you think you would have been proud of a decision to make all your team—or all your teammates, like in my case—be able to play with one hundred percent focus?"

"I have to admit, you're a little more reckless in the use of your powers than I tend to be, but that doesn't mean you're any more selfish or any more inappropriate. The way I saw it—and Zander and his wife agreed—you helped your teammates deal with a very difficult situation, and they came out of it as a better team. Maybe it *was* the wrong thing to do, but we as individuals are forced to make tough decisions and moral decisions over and over again. We learn from the wrong ones and try to do better the next time. I don't know if what you did was wrong or not, and I'm not sure if I would have done what you just did, but I'm proud of you for caring about whether you were right or not."

Tanner had listened intently and seemed to be thinking deeply about what his father had said. He leaned over and gave his dad another hug. "Thanks, Dad...Let's go get something to eat. I'm starving."

Clay simply laughed. Tanner bounced back from everything in what seemed to be a blink of the eye. "Sounds good."

"I'm gonna have a hard time gettin' that broken ankle out of my head. You wanna get in my head and make me forget it?"

"Nope. It'll help you remember what happened tonight."

Tanner laughed too. "By the way. I have another picture in my head that I can't seem to shake. It's a gray, metal cabinet, about the size of a two-drawer file cabinet. It looks like it has a drawer and a door. There's a metal handle that you'd probably turn down and then pull out to open the door. It looks like there's a keypad, but it's kind of semi-dangling loose from the door. The vision's been in my head all day. I was hoping you'd know what it was."

"I don't have any idea, but I wouldn't be surprised if it has something to do with the mystery we're working on. I'll keep my eyes open for something that looks like that. Maybe it'll be important."

CHAPTER 16

Logan Payne didn't go to school again on Monday. His woodshop teacher, Mr. Jorgenson, called to see if everything was all right, and his basketball coach called to give his condolences. Logan had spent the entire morning working on a wood project that he planned to give to Anna Gomez. He took a one-inch by one-inch by four-inch piece of soft balsa wood. He drew a circle at the center of each of the four sides and then drew two rectangles on each side of the block—one to the right and one to the left of each circle. He took a chisel and chipped away each of the eight rectangles until the piece of wood looked like a cage for the remaining portion of wood in the center. He then took out his jackknife and began to whittle away at the piece of wood remaining in the center, rounding it into the shape of a ball that was too big to slide through its cage. When he was done, he had created a toy for Anna. She would be amazed at how he got the ball inside the cage since it was obviously too big to be taken out.

Erika marveled at his talent and was grateful that he was using it to be kind to someone else. Her phone rang for the third time that morning. It was Clay and Luke Hopper, wondering if they could stop by again to talk to Logan. Erika told them that he wasn't in school, so they could visit any time.

The men left right away. Clay was excited to see Erika again, so when Hopper's car pulled to a stop at a railroad crossing, he was more than a little disturbed. Lights were flashing and the crossing arm was lowered, but there was no train. Clay leaned forward in his seat and looked to his left and right to locate the train, but he didn't see anything. "You're a cop. How 'bout you drive around that arm so we can get going?"

"I'm an officer of the law, Clay. That would be illegal."

"But there's no train, Luke."

"It does appear that way. Maybe some tests are being done. Happens all the time around here."

"And you don't just drive around? You sit here until the arm goes back up?"

"I usually just listen to one of my books or listen to sports talk. Sometimes I finish my coffee and read the paper. Today I'm blessed to have *you* and your stimulating conversation to keep me entertained. There's usually not much reason to hurry around here. Relax, Clay. Enjoy the sights."

"What sights? I see some overgrown bushes, a dilapidated storage shed, and some telephone poles. Is that the best you have to offer?"

"Sometimes, if you're patient, you might see some wildlife cross the road," Hopper joked. "By the way, we checked out Erika the best we could so far. She made a phone call to Mortonson's home on the morning of the train crash, and he made a call from East Lansing back to Erika's house before the train left the station. There are no records of any purchases through her credit card, which would be strange if she drove to Indiana and back."

"The calls make sense, you know," Clay responded. "He was watching her son. And maybe she didn't drive. She was with other people. Have you checked with any of them? Maybe she paid cash. I can't believe you think she's a suspect."

"I wouldn't be doing my job if I ruled her out before I was sure. It's called police work." The lights stopped flashing and the crossing arm raised. "See there? Patience is a virtue, you know. You could use some patience as we muddle our way through this *case* too."

Clay just rolled his eyes and started thinking about Erika again.

***

Erika had to get Logan back out of bed when Clay and Chief Hopper arrived. One side of his hair was flattened to his head; the other side was sticking straight out. His bangs were still covering his eyes. Erika explained to him that the men were there to ask questions about the day his dad disappeared.

After Logan plopped down on the couch and grabbed a pillow to hug, Chief Hopper asked his first question. "What do you remember about that day, Logan?"

"Nothin' really."

"You were in a train wreck and your dad disappeared, and you don't remember *anything*?"

"Logan, be cooperative," his mother ordered.

There was a long pause, and finally Logan said, "I remember my loser dad being a jerk."

Hopper was practicing amazing interview skills. He continued to remain silent. There was another long pause. "He didn't want me to go. I remember that. So Mom had to send Morty to baby sit. I wanted to ride on the train. I wanted to be in the engine with my dad and have him pay attention to me. Maybe let me drive the train. But like *always*, he didn't want to be with me."

That was a lot of words for Logan. Erika was amazed. She looked at Clay and pointed at her eyes, then his, hoping that he'd understand what she was suggesting, but Clay shook his head. He hadn't controlled Logan at all.

"Tell me what you remember about the train ride home," Hopper suggested.

"I was waiting with Morty to get on the train, but I was looking for my dad. I didn't see him anywhere—didn't see *anyone* I knew, except Morty, who was with me, and I think I saw Robbie. He was carrying a chain and a toolbox away from the train. Finally, my dad showed up and stepped up into the engine car. When we got on, we went to the back of the train and sat."

"Mr. Mortonson said you got up after about a half hour and went to look for your dad."

Clay had been struggling to get a look at Logan's eyes, but they were mostly covered by his bangs, and he rarely looked up. It appeared that he wasn't going to learn anything by reading the boy's mind. But miraculously, he actually looked up and they made eye contact. "*Don't look away*," Clay ordered him.

"I wanted to ride in the engine with him."

"Did you see him?" asked Hopper.

"*Yes*," thought Logan. There was a pause. He didn't answer.

Clay had eye contact, so he asked, "Was he lying on the floor of the train?"

"No," Logan answered quietly.

"What happened, Logan?" Clay responded just as softly.

"*We argued and he hit me in the face*," Logan thought. "Nothing" is what he said.

When Clay heard what Logan was thinking, he lost eye contact in order to look at Erika. When he looked back, Logan was looking down again.

Hopper rejoined the interview. "Nothing happened? You didn't see him?"

"No." Logan was back to his usual one-word answers.

Hopper paused again and seemed to sense that he was fortunate to get Logan to say as much as he did, so he thanked Logan and allowed him to go back to his room.

As soon as Clay heard the boy's door close, he looked at Erika and quietly said, "He saw your husband on the train."

"Are you just saying that because it's what you believe or do you know something that I don't?"

"I read his mind. He saw Adrian, and Adrian hit him in the face."

"What?" Erika was clearly shocked.

"Had Adrian ever hit him before?" Luke asked.

"No. Not that I ever knew of...How can you be sure that's what he was thinking?"

"I'm sure, Erika. But the only things that I read from him were that he saw your husband, and that your husband struck him in the face."

"Ex-husband. And if he was alive now, I think I'd kill him."

***

Luke Hopper was being very contemplative in the car on the way back to the station. When the first of two trains zoomed by—actually at a reasonable speed—Luke turned his CD player on and listened to Harlan Coben's *Tell No One*. "You ever read this book, Clay?"

"No, actually, I haven't. Isn't Coben the guy with the Myron Bolitar character?"

"Yeah, but not in this book." He stopped the CD. "This one is about a guy whose wife was taken and killed. Eight years later, he gets a message that he's convinced only his wife could have sent, but he gets warned to 'tell no one.' Well, the guy isn't about to sit still. He needs answers—closure. He wants to know what happened to his wife. Erika, in my opinion, doesn't seem quite as concerned about finding out what happened to her husband. I don't want to believe that she's somehow involved in this, but she had two pretty good motives to kill the guy. And she also quite likely had the opportunity. She as much as admitted that she could kill him."

"Well, you keep following your little rabbit trail if you want to, Luke, but she's innocent of any wrongdoing, and I intend to prove it. In the meantime, maybe we'll find what really happened that day."

"What's especially troubling," said Luke, "is that the medical examiner said that Adrian died from the accident, and Adrian's ghost said he died of a heart attack. But the body was definitely buried after the fact, and people are lying about it. And we just started asking around. And one more thing. Logan said he thought he saw Robbie at the train in East Lansing. I have the passenger lists. Robbie wasn't a passenger. What was he doing there?"

CHAPTER 17

Clay got in his car and considered driving back home. He was feeling a bit helpless, not knowing what to do next, so he did what he *wanted* to do. He called Erika. She asked him to meet her at Durand High School, where she was dropping her son off at basketball practice. He'd agreed to go even though he'd missed school and wouldn't be able to participate. His first game was only one day away.

At the high school, Erika got out of her car and got in Clay's. She affectionately squeezed his hand. "If you don't mind, I'd like to go give my friend, Dan Duncan, a visit. He's at home after emergency surgery on his big toe. We can ask him what *he* remembers about that night."

On the way, Clay was driving behind the one lone car on the road, a car that was slowing down as they were approaching a railroad crossing. The crossing was in a wide-open space where both directions of track could be easily seen and where there was no crossing arm. As they cautiously—for no apparent reason that Clay could perceive— approached the tracks, the crossing lights began to flash and the driver slammed on his brakes and came to a screeching halt. Clay slammed on his brakes too and managed to skid to about an inch of the car in front of him. After breathing a sigh of relief, he craned his neck in both directions, looking for the train. Ten to fifteen seconds later, he caught sight of the engine about a quarter-mile away. There was still plenty of time to cross the tracks, but the car in front of Clay never budged. As Clay impatiently started to back up, another car came to a stop behind him, blocking any hope of maneuvering around the waiting car. He was stuck. There was no end to the adventures of train crossings in Durand. When the train *finally* arrived, it was at least a mile long and took a good five minutes to pass.

"So what do you think of Durand?" Erika laughed.

"It's a nice place to visit, but I wouldn't want to live here," Clay responded with his own laugh. "So far, you're the nicest thing about this place."

"Aww, that's sweet. You're pretty okay yourself, Clay Thomas." Erika wrapped his arm warmly with both of hers and actually placed her head on his shoulder.

When they reached the front door of Dan Duncan's house, he could be heard yelling and swearing. Erika rang the doorbell. When Dan finally opened the front door, he was on a pair of crutches and his police revolver was tucked into the waistband of a pair of sweatpants.

Dan smiled a friendly smile at Erika and then lost the smile immediately when he saw Clay. "Hey, Danny. I'd like you to meet my friend, Clay Thomas…Clay, this is Dan Duncan."

Dan's left foot was in a cast, but while balancing on his right, he gave Clay a handshake that was intentionally a bit too hard. "Clay," he said.

Clay squeezed back just as hard but gave no indication to Erika what he was doing. "Dan," he responded. "*What a jerk*," Clay thought.

"What's the gun for, Dan?" asked Erika. "Expecting trouble?"

"It's for a squirrel in my backyard. Because of that stupid pest, I ended up in the hospital, and now he's back again. I'm gonna shoot it, Erika, I swear."

"Do you mind if we come in? How's the toe doing?"

Dan directed them to seats in his living room, which was a jumbled mess. "I'll be fine. What's up, Erika? Why the visit?"

"I wanted to see how you were doing, and I towed Clay along—no pun intended—because he's trying to help me figure out what happened the night of the train wreck. Now that Adrian's no longer missing, I'm hoping that figuring out what happened will bring some closure for Logan."

"And Clay here is what? A private investigator? A cop?"

"No, Dan, I'm just a friend, but Chief Hopper asked me to stay on and help him with this case. I'm volunteering my services as a favor to Erika, so Hopper doesn't have to foot the bill—no pun intended, of course."

"I see," he said. *"You're after my Erika,"* Clay read from his mind. "So what do you want to know?"

"We're just hoping that maybe you can remember something about what happened that night that will help us figure out how the body ended up in the grave with the horses," explained Clay. "Would you mind telling me exactly how you were involved in the incident that night?"

"I ain't tellin' you nothin'," he thought. "Anything to help Erika and the boy, but I don't have much to tell."

"When were you at the accident scene?"

"Before and *after I killed two people."* Those words got Clay's attention, but he did his best to not show any reaction to Dan's thoughts. "I arrived after the wreck. I was at the Shell gas station by the expressway when I heard the emergency call on my radio. The truck driver saw me and explained that his rig had been stolen. He gave me a description, and I called it in. Dispatch claimed that the train had smashed into a semi-truck carrying a load of horses. So I drove the truck driver to the accident scene, and he identified his rig. It was on fire, and the horses were all dead."

"Why were you at the Shell station?"

Dan was looking at Erika, so Clay had no chance of reading his mind. "I don't remember. I was on my shift, in my police cruiser, cruising around Durand. I just happened to be there when a truck driver needed my assistance. There was no particular reason for my being there that I recall." He turned back to Clay. *"Sooner or later this was all bound to come back to haunt me."* Dan decided to try to change the subject. "Would either of you like something to drink?"

"Sure, Dan. Get us a couple of tall glasses of ice water and we'd love to watch you carry them back." Erika giggled. She liked to laugh, and Clay liked that about her. Obviously, Dan liked a few things about her too. "Really, that's not necessary," she added. "But thanks for offering."

Clay was a little concerned about his interviewing skills. He didn't know where to go with his next question. "So you just happened to pull into the gas station, and the truck driver saw you and told you about his stolen truck?"

"Yeah, that's pretty much how I remember it. I may have been heading into the store to get some gum or seeds." As if the thought compelled him to do something, he opened a bag of David BBQ flavored sunflower seeds and stuffed a few in his mouth.

"Do you recall where you were before you ended up at the Shell station?"

"Drivin' around town, I assume. Donut shop maybe." Dan gave a weak laugh at his poor attempt at humor.

"Were you anywhere near the Depot where you might have seen something suspicious?"

"*I ain't tellin' you squat, Dude.*" Dan replied, "First time I was near the Depot was after the accident. There were firemen startin' to put the truck fire out, a smashed train engine, a couple of grounded train cars, and lots of people millin' around. Other emergency vehicles were there."

"Did you happen to see Adrian?"

"I don't believe anyone saw Adrian, 'cause he'd disappeared."

"Did you look for him?"

"*I checked to see if he was dead,*" Duncan thought. "Of course not. Why would I care about *him* in particular?"

"Excuse me for saying, Dan, but you don't seem all too sympathetic about Adrian passing away. Did you have something against him?"

"Look, I don't know who you are, but since you're supposed to be Erika's friend, I invited you into my house. Dredging up my problems with Adrian isn't somethin' that I wanna talk about right now, if you don't mind."

"*Yes, you do*," Clay told Dan as he looked into his eyes and manipulated his mind. "*Tell me what you had against Adrian Payne.*"

"He treated Erika and Logan like crap, and he put my dad out of business!" Dan nearly shouted before looking embarrassed and unsure of why he just spit that information out."

"Did you know he was going to be on that train?"

"*Everyone* knew he was gonna be on that train. Anytime there was a convention, banquet, ceremony, *anything*, Adrian was there front and center, seeking attention. E*veryone* knew he engineered the trains back into Durand. He was an ego-maniac; so *sure*, I knew he'd be on that train."

"Do you know anything about how the body ended up in the horse cemetery?"

"If I knew somethin', he would've been dug up a long time before now."

There was a long pause while Clay tried to sort out his thoughts. Finally, Erika wisely suggested that they should get going. She could see that Dan was getting angry. She already knew about his father, so she hadn't heard anything new or interesting in the interview. She told Dan again that she was concerned about his toe, and she added that she hoped he'd be better soon. She hugged him, and the men did another handshake squeeze, and then they left.

As Clay was opening Erika's door, they heard Dan screaming obscenities at the squirrel from the backyard, and then they heard a gunshot. Clay decided to drive away before Dan shot at *him*. What they didn't know was that the squirrel was somehow eating from the other feeder—the one that hadn't been shot apart—and when Dan shot at it, he demolished the second feeder too. The squirrel simply ran to safety. Dan's blood pressure rose once again.

***

As they pulled away, Clay spoke first. "Dan's a little on edge, don't you think? I hope he didn't shoot someone."

"Always has been a bit uptight, but it *does* seem a little overboard to be shooting his gun at a squirrel. Regardless, I'm sorry you didn't really learn anything new."

"Sure I did."

"Oh, that comment about Adrian treating Logan and me bad and how he put Mr. Duncan out of business? I could have told you that. By the way, he *said* he didn't want to talk about it, and then he shouted it right out. What do you make of that?"

"Um, actually I *made* him tell me."

Erika giggled. "Did you make him shoot at that squirrel?"

Clay laughed too. "No, I'm not as crazy as he is."

"So, what did you learn?"

"First of all, he thinks you're his girl."

Erika laughed harder. "We could get married and I could open my own donut shop. I could call it Duncan Donuts. Wait, that name's taken."

"Don't get your hopes too high. The dude says he killed two people that night. Also, he was at the scene of the wreck both before *and* after the crash, and when he returned with the truck driver, he checked to see if Adrian was dead."

"That doesn't make sense."

"You're telling me. The coroner says Adrian died as a result of the train crash. Adrian says he died of a heart attack. Mortonson says he probably killed him, and now Duncan says he killed two people, one of which is obviously Adrian. Logan says he argued with his dad on the train and Adrian struck him in the face, but Mortonson said Adrian was passed out on the floor. How did he get off the train, I wonder? Then Marshall suggested he knew how the body was buried, but Dan had no idea. Yet he was checking to see if Adrian was dead after the wreck. None of this makes any sense to me."

"Why would Dan want to kill my husband?"

"The nut had a crush on you and resented Adrian for how he treated you, and he hated Adrian for putting his father out of business. It appears he had a motive or two." Clay paused. "Tell me what happened with the trucking business." They were approaching town and there was a long line-up of cars stopped at a train crossing. Clay slowed down, sighed, and shook his head in frustration.

"When Adrian and Morty bought the business, Morty settled right in as the business manager. He was in charge of the books and the daily running of the business. Adrian was more front and center. He was very aggressive in his attempts to improve the company, and one of his primary goals was to get shipping contracts for the freight trains. Dan's father had a trucking company in town that was a family-owned business. Dan probably would be a trucker instead of a cop if Adrian hadn't convinced people to ship by train rather than truck. When Adrian took over the Duncan's business contracts, Dan's father lost everything."

The train finally passed and cars were beginning to move forward, but because of stoplights in town, the entire line-up of cars came to a halt again. Clay impatiently observed the lack of forward movement as a few cars made it through the stoplight and then the light turned red again.

"I assume that happened a long time before the train wreck. Why would Duncan all of a sudden feel the urge to get revenge?"

"The takeover was probably at least ten years before the wreck, but as I recall now, it seems like Dan's father passed away shortly before the train accident. Mr. Duncan's health deteriorated after he lost his company. Maybe his death motivated Dan to get revenge."

"All this is well and good, but *how* could Dan have killed Adrian? He wasn't on the train, and clearly he was on a work shift when everything happened. It doesn't make sense."

Cars had made it through a couple of lights, so Clay's car was finally nearly at the railroad tracks when the crossing lights started flashing and the arm lowered once again. Clay looked at Erika in absolute frustration, and she began to laugh.

All of a sudden, Erika's passenger side window exploded. She screamed and ducked her head. When she looked up and out of the window, she screamed again. There was her little midget friend standing beside his bike with another rock in his hand. He was screaming incoherently and pointing at Erika threateningly. He hurled another rock that ricocheted off the side of the car.

Clay's frustration with the train was already apparent, so the midget's act of vandalism put him over the edge. He jumped out of the car, ran to the edge of the train tracks, and picked up two nice-sized rocks of his own. He hurled the first one with tremendous velocity at the midget's bike, breaking the left-side pedal. The midget recognized the strength of Clay's arm and dropped his next rock. Clay accurately fired the second rock and bent several spokes of the midget's back tire. The little guy jumped on his bike in an attempt to escape. He started pedaling furiously but his left foot kept slipping of the broken pedal and his back tire was wobbling crazily. The little man was swearing furiously. He looked back over his shoulder and flipped Clay off with his middle finger, but his foot slipped off the pedal again and he lost control of his bike, which smashed into a cement commercial parking block, throwing him over the handlebars and onto the downtown sidewalk.

The midget slowly climbed up off the cement and picked his bike off the ground. The handlebars were bent at a crazy angle and the front tire was completely flat. He hurled his bike back on the ground and started flailing his arms in a crazy temper tantrum. Then he did an amazing thing. He started kicking himself in the head, just like Erika explained. Cars were honking as Clay realized that the train had passed and he was holding up traffic. He had thoughts of helping the lunatic little man, but the honking cars made him realize he had no choice but to return to his car and drive away.

"That little dude is *definitely* terrifying, Erika. Did you see him kicking his own head? I totally thought you were kidding."

Erika's eyes were as big as saucers. Finally she smiled. "I have a new protector."

Clay couldn't help but laugh, even though he knew there was damage to his car. "There's no doubt about that," he said.

"You have quite an arm there, Rocket. Your baseball players must be very impressed."

"Makes you kind of proud that you know me, doesn't it?" Clay joked.

"I was kind of feeling that way even *before* I was rescued."

CHAPTER 18

"Here's my report, Chief," said Officer Verne Gilbert as he handed Chief Hopper a file folder. Hopper had assigned the officer the responsibility of checking into Roberto Gomez's movements on the night of the train wreck seven years earlier. It was gnawing at Hopper that Logan Payne believed he had seen Gomez at the train station in East Lansing. Was he really there? If he was, what was he doing?

Hopper was disappointed as he flipped through the file folder. There were no credit card purchases, though he did fill up his gas tank at the Durand Shell station at about 6:30 p.m. There were no phone calls to his house or from his cell phone that were suspicious at all. Roberto was not working that evening, so he was available to leave town, but there was no evidence that he had gone anywhere except for Logan's belief that he saw Gomez at the train station.

He decided to call Clay. They needed to give Roberto Gomez a visit, and Clay's mind-reading ability could come in handy. Clay and Erika were eating at Uncle Tony's Pizza Company, while Logan finished up his basketball practice. Hopper invited himself to crash their date.

***

When Hopper arrived, Clay and Erika had already started on their pizzas. They had ordered two-for-one specialty pizzas, a BLT pizza and a Chicken, Bacon, Ranch pizza that Erika claimed Logan liked best. Clay was impressed with the variety of food choices on the menu, including pasta dishes, Mexican food, stromboli, salads, and wings.

Hopper had a seat next to Erika. "You didn't order The Uncle Toninator? I think I'm hungry enough to eat one myself."

"A 28-inch pizza all by yourself? You have a couple of hollow legs? You got here pretty quick. Must not've hit a train."

"Nope. I think you're bad luck, Clay. The train gods are picking on you. Did I see that your car window is smashed out there?"

Clay retold the story about the midget, and Hopper got a good laugh out of it. "You wanna file a complaint against the little pest? It won't be the first, and I'm afraid it won't be the last. Bet you didn't know he holds a law degree. In front of a judge, he's an expert at making himself look like the victim. A regular wordsmith. Another interesting fact is that he claims he's an heir of one of the circus performers that died in the Wallace train wreck. He says one of the unmarked graves is the burial site of his great grandfather."

"Well," Clay said, "I don't think I'll file a complaint—especially if he'd have some sort of advantage in front of a judge—but I have to say the tiny man is hugely unstable. You should have seen him kicking himself in the head."

Hopper laughed again. "I've heard reports of his flexibility, but I've never seen it myself. I have to tell you, one of the funniest things I ever witnessed was an incident during the Railroad Days several years ago. He was riding his little bike while holding onto a helium balloon. The balloon was weighted, but apparently not enough that, when he lost hold of it, it started to slowly rise out of his reach. Somehow he stopped that bike, jumped onto the bike seat with his feet, and leaped for the balloon—the little dude's as nimble as a gymnast. The bike crashed, and he missed the balloon. He landed off balance, but he fell forward onto his hands and did a somersault back onto his feet. The balloon kept slowly rising, so Jasper—that's his name, by the way—climbed the no parking sign on the side of the street. He got all the way to the top and just as he was reaching for the balloon string, the sign started to bend backward. Jasper was hanging there by one hand and flailing for the balloon with his other one, and the sign was slowly bending until he landed right on his feet on the ground. But that's not the end of it. Jasper's pretty handy with a rock, as you've seen, so he picked up a small rock from the street and while swearing a stream of cuss words that would've made a sailor blush, he hit that balloon with his first throw, and it popped immediately. The weight fell straight down and hit him on the head. You couldn't make up something like that."

Erika was giggling, which made Clay smile and laugh himself. "Have some pizza, Luke. We ordered plenty."

The chief helped himself and then got down to business. "We can't find anything linking Roberto Gomez to the Lansing train station, but since Logan believes that he saw him there, I think we should go and have a talk, Clay. The longer this case goes, the more questions that pop up."

"Just wait 'til you hear what we have to share. We went to visit Dan Duncan. Dan didn't want to talk, but I read his mind. Luke, what I learned was that Duncan was at the accident scene both before and after the crash. When he was there after the wreck, he specifically tried to find out if Adrian was dead because he claims to have killed two people."

"What?" Hopper asked in disbelief.

"I asked him when he was at the accident scene and what I read from his mind was 'both before and after I killed two people.' Without question, he was hiding things and didn't want to cooperate."

"That just doesn't make sense, Clay."

"That's what we've been saying, but he has a motive and opportunity. How he could've killed somebody is the troubling question, especially since Adrian seems to think he died from a heart attack."

In frustration, Hopper was rubbing his hands over his face and, eventually, with his elbows on the table, hid his face completely in his hands. In Hopper's mind, Erika was still a suspect of some sorts, so he didn't want to say too much, but what he was hearing was difficult to digest.

Their meal together continued without much conversation. Eventually Erika announced it was time for her to get back to the high school to pick up Logan. Chief Hopper suggested that Clay return the next day, Tuesday, and come with him to visit Roberto Gomez. "I'm gonna need to get my window fixed, but I'll come as soon as I can tomorrow."

Clay paid the bill and everyone said his and her farewells. Clay walked Erika to the car, and once he was also seated and buckled in, he grabbed her hand and held it. Erika smiled that beautiful smile of hers and squeezed his hand. "I'm sorry we've reunited in such trying circumstances, but I'm glad anyway," Clay said.

"I'm glad too, Clay. Thank you for being here for me."

When they made it back to the school parking lot, Clay leaned over and gave Erika a light kiss on the lips. It felt good. He wasn't sure if it was the right thing to do, but he was glad he did it anyway.

Erika looked to actually be blushing, but with tears misting her eyes just a little, she said, "Thank you." Then she exited Clay's car and entered her own to wait for Logan. Clay drove away feeling like a school kid with a crush, but it felt good, so it made him happy for the first time in a long, long time.

CHAPTER 19

When Clay got up the next morning, he had his window replaced, made a stop at a store, and then made his way back to Durand to meet with Chief Hopper. Hopper was all business when Clay arrived, and he wasted no time in leaving for the Depot to have a chat with Roberto Gomez. Clay drove separately because he was planning on stopping to see Erika at the Depot offices when they were done with the interview. He slammed his hand on his steering wheel as he watched Hopper drive across the railroad tracks just before the lights flashed on and the arm lowered. Hopper couldn't help but laugh as he saw Clay waiting for the train, but he waited for him patiently in the Depot parking lot.

They found Roberto in a maintenance shed hanging a long-handled track wrench onto a stout metal peg. Roberto gave a questioning look when he saw Hopper, but still gave a friendly greeting. "Hola, Chief. Hola, Clay. Can I help you with something?"

"We're here to talk to you, Robbie. Do you have a minute?"

"Sure, Chief. I just got done tightening some bolts on the tracks. Next, Morty's rushin' me to do some brake work on that engine on the wye, but I can talk for a few. Is there a problem?"

"No, Robbie. We've just been doing some investigating, trying to figure out how Adrian Payne's body ended up buried in that horse cemetery. The medical examiner is looking into the possibility of foul play, but the original conclusion is that Adrian died as a result of the crash. As you know, the body was never found after the train wreck, yet someone buried him sometime later." Hopper turned to Clay. "Clay here gave us some information suggesting the body was buried near the tracks, and then someone dug up the grave. Since you work here full time, we were wondering if you knew anything about the disappearance, the burial, or the discovery of the body. Clay has a few questions for you."

"Okay." Robbie looked nervously at Clay.

"Robbie, could you tell us where you were on the night of the train wreck?"

"*Dios, no…No, por favor.*" Roberto's thoughts were begging as well as his eyes. "I was home with Stacy and Anna."

"You didn't go anywhere that evening?"

"*They can't know I was in Lansing, can they?*" Roberto's hands were shaking and his voice was cracking, but he tried to stay composed. "Not that I recall. It was a long time ago. I know that I was home when the accident happened. We heard the sirens and watched reports on the news. I never left the house."

"You seem a little nervous, Robbie. Do you know something that could help us?"

"*I'm gonna go to jail for killing two men. They know. What am I gonna do?*" Then he had an idea. "Why are you asking me these questions? Is it because I'm Mexican? You figure because of my race, I must be guilty of something. Is that it? You're no better than Adrian Payne if that's what you think."

"Did you have some problem with Adrian?" Clay asked.

"*Like that he raped my wife?*" Roberto thought. "Yeah, he was always calling me 'Taco' and 'Roburrito' and making racist comments. He hired me, and then treated me like dirt while he sexually harassed my wife. Yeah, I had a problem with him, but so did everyone else who knew him. He was scum."

Hopper joined the conversation. "Relax, Robbie, we're just asking questions. You've proven to be a good man. This isn't about race; it's about finding answers to some troubling questions. Let's just back up a bit. You've established that you weren't anywhere near the Depot during the accident. But did you know that Adrian Payne was on that train?"

"Everyone at the Depot—practically everyone in general—knew about the convention in East Lansing. Of course Payne would be there, and everyone knew he would be on the train coming back."

"Did you know that Logan or Morty would be on the train?"

"No," he replied. "After the accident, I heard they were passengers."

"Did you hear any talk, or see anything that would lead you to believe that Adrian's body had been confiscated and set aside to be buried later?"

"Chief, I was just like everyone else. I didn't know what happened to Payne. I figured he must not've been on the train, or maybe he got off somehow."

Clay interjected again. "Robbie, I have one more question for you. Were you in Lansing on the day of the accident?"

Robbie had his head down, avoiding eye contact with Clay when he lied. "No, I wasn't."

"Logan Payne seems to think that he saw you at the Lansing Depot."

"He must be mistaken, Señor. I was at work and then home with my family."

"Robbie, we're still looking to find out what happened that day," Hopper said. "If you think of anything, please let us know."

The men all shook hands and then Hopper led Clay back to his car and told Clay to get in for a minute. "Did you learn anything?"

"You're not gonna believe this. He wasn't being honest with us."

"Really?" Hopper said sarcastically. "How many times do I have to tell you that I'm a trained police officer? Course he was hiding something. You have any idea what it is?"

"Adrian raped Robbie's wife, Luke. That's the problem he had with Adrian. And he *was* in East Lansing. Now he's worried that he's going to go to jail for killing two men."

"Do you make this stuff up, Clay? Payne raped Stacy Gomez, which would be a good reason to want to kill the guy, and then Robbie admits to killing two men that night? How could all these people have all killed Adrian, yet the coroner and Adrian don't seem to agree?"

"I don't have any idea; I'm just as confused as you are."

"Have you asked Erika if *she* killed her husband? Maybe *she* did it too! Maybe they all did it together and tricked Adrian into believing they were all innocent."

"Erika *is* innocent, Luke. But as for the others, we're gonna have to keep digging."

***

Clay made his way into the Depot, his heart pounding with excitement to see Erika. He entered the building, made his way up the stairs, and turned down the hallway toward her office, but it was empty. When he looked back at Morty's door to ask where Erika was, he saw there was a meeting going on with Morty, Erika, and an attractive dark-haired woman. He returned to Erika's office to leave a note asking that she call him when she got a chance. Though it was unnecessary, he jotted down his cell number and wrote that he had an errand to run but to please call him. Before he could leave, he heard, "*Skeleton key, Clay. Skeleton key.*"

Clay turned to the picture hanging on the wall. The ghost was talking to him, yet he was thinking, "*Wow, you are beautiful, Erika. I never get tired of looking at you.*" Eventually he checked himself and decided to talk to Adrian. "Why do you keep talking in riddles and clues? Why can't you just tell me what happened? *Everyone*, it seems, wanted you dead, and everyone seems to think he killed you. How about Erika? Or Logan?" he added sarcastically. "Did they kill you too? Do you think maybe you could help me out?"

"*What fun would that be?*" he whispered. "*I give clues; you solve the mystery...if you can. By the way...ease the pain. Ease the pain.*"

"Why would I want to ease your pain? You cheated on your wife, spent your partner's money on prostitutes, didn't care about your son who you physically abused, raped Stacy Gomez, ran people out of business, and gave alcohol to the train engineer, endangering lives just so you could play engineer. You're stuck in some state between Heaven and Hell, haunting your friends and family, and instead of helping us figure out what happened, you leave indecipherable clues and ask me to ease *your* pain. You're priceless, Adrian. No wonder no one cared about you. People were actually happy you were gone. How does that make you feel?"

"*Solve the mystery, and I'll be on my way to Hell.*"

Clay exited the room in frustration.

***

Marshall Mortonson had asked Erika into his office. His attorney, Toni Nickel, was present when Erika entered and sat down. Toni was an attractive woman in her mid-to-late thirties with long, dark hair and a polished smile. She seemed friendly enough, but Erika was a little leery of the surprise meeting. She felt like she was being ganged up on even before the conversation began. She found herself wishing that Clay was there with her.

"We have some important issues to deal with now that Adrian's legally deceased. I asked my attorney to come in to answer questions you might have. Toni Nickel, this is Erika Payne."

They shook hands and then Erika smiled and said, "I think we get our hair done at the same place. Your hair is beautiful, by the way. I've seen you at the salon and around town a few other times."

Erika's genuine kindness was apparent to Toni, and she decided immediately that she liked her. Within seconds, the attorney had determined that she liked Erika more than the cheating, conniving client she was representing, and certainly more than Erika's ex-husband, who she had known in a Biblical sense of the word, and had found to be a disgusting human being. She had no idea he was married at the time. "I've been looking over the contract that Morty and Adrian put together when they purchased the entire business. As you probably know, you've inherited fifty-percent of the business. Morty contractually does not have to share decision-making power with you, but he *does* have to share profits and losses, including the profits over the last seven years.

"After perusing the company books, it appears that the business has been somewhat profitable since the time your husband went missing, so Morty is bound contractually to be fair and pay you your share. We'll have to sort out an accurate number, but Morty is hoping that you will be satisfied with the amount and agree to not sell the business."

"I can't afford to buy you out, Erika, but I want to keep the business. The bank is not willing to loan me what I would need. I'm hoping we can agree to the partnership as it is currently working. I can keep doing what I am doing, and you can continue to work in the office just as before—if you choose to. But we'll split all financial interests fifty-fifty."

Toni suspected that Mortonson wasn't being honest. She wasn't an accountant, but from what she had seen of the books thus far, she couldn't see why Marshall would be so adamant about not wanting Erika to look at the numbers. It made her think that maybe what was written in the books wasn't exactly the truth. It didn't appear from the ledgers she had seen that the business was making large amounts of money, yet when she looked into the worth of the business, she learned from the bank that they'd done an appraisal for Marshall less than a year before, and it was determined to be worth about five million dollars. She didn't know that Marshall was using two different sets of books for her and the bank. She could see how Marshall couldn't afford to give Erika two and a half million dollars, but she couldn't comprehend how the business, according to the books in her hands, was making so little profit.

"Erika," Marshall continued, "we'll talk about this again. You can have as much time as you need to think about it, but I wanted you to know that I'd really like to keep the business as it is." He reached over and grabbed the books from Toni Nickel and then reached into his jacket pocket and unconsciously pulled out his skeleton keys to prepare to lock everything back up.

Erika noticed the keys and remembered Adrian's words. "*Was he talking about Morty's keys?*" she wondered. "Morty," she said, "how much is the business currently worth?"

Marshall nervously stuffed the keys back in his pocket. "Um, I really don't know, Erika. That's so hard to say."

Toni raised her eyebrows as she glanced at her client. She didn't say anything, but she already knew that Marshall was lying. The bank had told Morty the same thing they had told his attorney.

CHAPTER 20

Because Erika was in her meeting, Clay headed back to his car, checked the purchase he had stored in the trunk, and started out toward town. He had an errand that he wanted to accomplish. He called the police station and was connected right away with Chief Hopper. He asked Luke a question, waited briefly while the police chief found the answer, and then he wrote down the information. He programmed an address into his Garmin GPS, and headed away from the Depot to an address on South Oak Street.

When he found the house he was looking for, Clay pulled into the driveway and nervously exited his car, climbed the porch steps, and knocked on the door. There was no answer after the first knock, so he tried again, only harder.

"All right already!" screamed a voice from inside. "Don't get your panties in a bunch; I'm coming!"

Clay's heart started beating faster. He was beginning to understand how Erika could be afraid of midgets because that's exactly how he was feeling. *"There's nothing to fear but fear itself"* were words that came to his mind—words that Erika herself had spoken to him in the cave. He took a deep breath and waited a few seconds more before the door swung slightly open, but when it did, there was no one there. He began to survey the area inside the doorway, but there didn't appear to be anyone there.

"I'm down here, you moron!"

Sure enough, there he was. He was probably a few inches short of four feet tall. He had curly reddish hair, several crooked teeth that Clay could see as the little guy seemed to be growling at him, and a big purplish bruise on his forehead. "Um, excuse me," Clay said nervously, "I assume you're Jasper?"

"No, I'm Barney the Dinosaur. Go away before I bust your knees with a baseball bat!"

"I'd like a minute of your time, if you don't mind."

"You have somethin' stuck in your ears, you meathead, or do you just enjoy pain?" he growled angrily. "You want me to hurt you? Stick your head inside the door and I'll kick you in the teeth."

"You're an angry little midget aren't you?"

The door flew open and the crazy little guy jumped right on Clay, knocking him backward off the porch. Clay managed to keep his footing, and then he threw the maniac off his body. Jasper landed on his back on the lawn. Clay pressed his foot on the lunatic's chest and held him down with his foot.

"You call me a midget one more time," the psycho yelled, spit flying from his mouth, "and I'll be all over you like white on rice! I'm a little person, and I have a name like any other man!"

Clay looked him in his wild red eyes and said, "Jasper, stop being angry right now, you hear? You will settle down right now and listen to me!"

Mind control did have its occasional benefits and there before him was a prime example. Jasper settled right down, and Clay removed his foot from the little person's chest. "How about we have a talk, Jasper? I'm actually here to do you a favor."

"You're the guy who broke my bike, aren't you?"

"I'm ashamed to admit it, Jasper, but yes."

"You have a good arm."

Clay smiled. "My name's Clay. Nice to meet you. And you, by the way, you're the guy who broke my car window and dented my door and tried to hurt someone who's very important to me. Why are you always trying to scare her like that?" They both sat down on the porch steps.

Jasper hesitated a minute then said, "The first time I ran into her—I literally ran into her—I was a teenager. She knocked me off my bike and bent my handle bars. She looked down at me and screamed and said something like, 'Oh, no, I've killed a midget.' Do you know how offensive that word is?" He waited a second for a response. "*Obviously* not—anyway I lost my temper. I know; it's hard to believe, but true. I don't recall any other confrontations for years, but I could tell she was afraid of me. Then one day while doing some legal documents for Adrian, he gave me some extra money and asked for a favor. Said he'd keep me as his attorney as long as I kept terrifying his wife. He thought it'd be a hilarious practical joke. I've been doin' it ever since."

"Adrian Payne was a bigger creep than you—no offense, Jasper."

"None taken, Clay."

"You know that Adrian's dead, don't you? You certainly don't have to worry about losing his business now. I can tell in just a minute of conversation you're an intelligent guy. Why are you still scaring Erika?"

"Didn't know he was dead until just recently. He's my last real client. Last time we met was a couple months before he disappeared. I've been holding his documents ever since. I've learned to be a little bitter about life, and I know I can be a real nasty creep at times, but I'm actually still his attorney, and I made him a promise. I went overboard with that rock, though, didn't I? Sorry, Clay."

Clay got up from the porch steps. He walked to his car and popped open the trunk. As Jasper walked to the car in curiosity, Clay pulled a small, new mountain bike out and set it on the ground. "This is for you. When you jumped me like a wild animal, I had second thoughts, but I've changed my mind again."

"Why would you do this for me?" Jasper actually had tears in his eyes. From Clay's perspective, a look of shame seemed to cross his face. "I'm not a nice person, and I threw the first rock."

"You know, Jasper, I'm still learning how to live my life effectively, but one thing I've learned recently is that if I'm not helping other people, I'm not only being disobedient to God who loves me, but I'm missing out on some tremendous blessings in life. I'm trying to help Erika and her son find out what happened to

Adrian Payne. Erika helped me to renew my faith, and I'm trying to renew her peace. She's lived long enough without answers. And her son's a troubled kid who really needs a break in life. In the meantime, I saw an opportunity to do something nice for you too…I didn't realize I'd be risking life and limb, but here I am."

A train whistle sounded in the distance just as Jasper reached out in a sincere gesture to shake hands with Clay. Clay grabbed and shook his tiny hand while at the same time realizing where he was standing.

"Clay, how 'bout I make another promise to *you*? How 'bout I promise to stop scaring your girlfriend."

"I'd like that, Jasper, but I just thought of another way you might be able to help me too. You're just a stone's throw from the South Oak Street crossing, aren't you? What can you tell me about the accident seven years ago?"

***

Erika walked back into her office and closed the door. She saw the note that Clay had left on her desk and called him immediately. When Clay answered, she didn't even wait to say hello. "Morty's got two skeleton keys that he carries around all the time. I saw them again today, and I think maybe that's what Adrian was talking about. One of them is for the attic door. Maybe Adrian wants you to look for something in the attic."

Clay explained that he would be a while before he could make it back to the Depot, so Erika impatiently hung up and stepped back into the hallway. Marshall and Toni Nickel were still in the office, but just as she looked in, Toni got out of her seat and shook Marshall's hand. Erika quickly scampered toward the stairs and headed down to the first floor. She stepped back into a doorway until Toni exited the building and then she carefully proceeded back up the steps. She actually giggled as she considered how she was sneaking around, trying not to be seen, but as she reached the top of the stairs and looked down the hallway, she cut her quiet laughter short. She saw Mortonson with his ledger books, taking a peek into Erika's office. When he saw that she wasn't there, he did his own sneaking down the hallway, stopping at the attic door. The decorative wooden door was never locked, so he pulled it open and then took out a skeleton key to open the second, vault door.

While Erika watched, he slipped inside, where he disappeared for barely more than a minute before peaking his head back outside the door. Erika ducked back and made a second trip down the stairs. She waited a minute or two and then walked as casually as she could back up the steps. When she reached the hallway, she saw that the wooden door was closed again, and as she passed Marshall's office, she saw he was busy at his computer on his desk. Then she went into her own office and closed the door to wait anxiously for Clay.

**

The train was chugging by no more than sixty yards from Jasper's house. The noise was a bit too loud, so Jasper suggested that Clay step inside. On the wall on the left was his legal degree from Kaplan University. Jasper was an estate attorney, and based on Clay's prior knowledge, it appeared that Jasper had earned his law degree on-line. Jasper saw him looking at the degree. "Estate attorney. I studied to do wills, living trusts, estate planning, etc. Passed the bar and everything. I also have a real estate license. But people don't take dwarves too seriously, and I've never made a decent living from either thing. Turns one a little bitter—I'm sorry to admit—because living a life of selfishness and bitterness is not an enjoyable way to live." Again, Clay saw shame and guilt written on the man's face.

On the wall to the right was a blown-up, poster-sized picture of the Wallace Train Wreck of 1903. There were pictures of circus performers and circus animals, and there was a picture of Jasper with Red Skelton. "Erika told me that Red Skelton's father died in that wreck."

"He did. Red was known to ride the train into Durand occasionally and visit his father's gravesite in Vernon. His father and my great-grandfather were close friends, and they both died during that wreck."

"I'm sorry to hear that," said Clay. He paused, and then asked again. "Jasper, what do you remember about the train wreck seven years ago?"

"I remember it like it was yesterday. It was a Thursday, just a little after 9:00. You never really *hear* the train coming. You get used to it and block it out. But the crash is a sound I'll never forget. I was taking a shower. It took some time to finish up before I got a chance to step out on my porch and look. By then everything was in chaos. Both sides of the street were lined with emergency vehicles and other cars from gawkers. The semi-truck that was hit by the train was on fire and firemen were just starting to put out the blaze. It was pretty clear that two of the train cars were lying on their sides beside the tracks on the right side of Oak Street. I headed to the left because I don't like being around people that much."

"Really? I would've never guessed."

"You're so funny, Clay. Do you want me to finish the story?" he said sarcastically. "The two images that I'll always remember most are seeing the charred remains of the horses when they were pulled from the trailer, and seeing Marshall Mortonson step out of the storage shed near the tracks, covered with blood."

"You saw Morty do *what*?" Clay asked in total surprise.

"They had just finished putting out the fire. A few people were watching from the street, but most were paying attention to all the people near the overturned train cars. I happened to look the opposite direction and saw Mortonson step out of the storage shed just down the tracks a bit. He looked scared, and he looked hurt. There was blood all over his shirt, arms, face, everything. He walked right past me and went to the other side of the street where all the people were. When I looked back at the truck, they were pulling the burned-up horses from the trailer. I'll never forget that."

"What were you thinking?"

"I was thinking that it was horrible what happened to the horses. I like horses."

"What were you thinking about Marshall Mortonson?"

"Well, I heard later that he had to jump from the train. I figured when I saw him that night, he was in some sort of shock, wandering around hurt and confused."

"Jasper, I'm thinking it was a little more than that."

CHAPTER 21

As Clay was nearing the Depot, he phoned Luke Hopper. "Luke, I just spent some time with Jasper."

"I was worried about that. You didn't hurt him did you? I shouldn't have given you that address. I had a bad feeling."

"No, no, it was nothing like that."

"He hurt *you*, didn't he?"

"No, Luke. Stop! We had a nice chat. You need to get right over to his house and take an official statement. And then I have a feeling you're gonna want a search warrant to search one of Mortonson's storage buildings. Jasper saw Morty exiting the building after the train wreck. He was bloody and looking awfully suspicious. I think we may have discovered who hid and buried the body."

"I'll get right on it, Clay. What are you doing next?"

"Erika has a lead on the 'skeleton key.' I'm going to check it out."

"I know you think she's innocent, Clay, but use good judgment. She may be involved in all of this."

"You're dead wrong, but I'll watch myself anyway. I think we may be on the verge of breaking this open."

Clay pulled into the parking lot of the Depot as Marshall Mortonson was driving away. They nodded at each other. Clay tried not to glare in disapproval. He headed right up to Erika's office. She jumped up in relief when he showed up. "Is there something wrong?" he asked as she gave him a hug.

"No. Well, yes *and* no. I'm so glad you're here. I'm just nervous about finding something that could help Logan and maybe end all of this."

"So tell me what's going on."

"I had a meeting with Morty and his attorney. Now that I own half the company, he wants to continue running the business as it is with me as his new partner. He wants me to take a payment for the earnings of the company the last seven years. He says he can't buy me out if I want to sell, so he'd have to sell too, and he doesn't want to do that. I had a gut feeling that he was hiding something, though, so I watched him when his attorney left, and he snuck to the attic with his account ledgers and used the skeleton keys to lock them away. Only Morty has keys to the attic, but we need to get in there somehow and look around for his books."

"I saw him leave just as I got here. Do you have a way to get in there?"

"Actually, no. But maybe we can break in. You know? Pick the lock."

"You think you can just stick a Bobbie pin in the keyhole and wiggle it around until it unlocks?"

"Or maybe you can use a credit card."

Clay laughed. Erika laughed. She grabbed his hand and squeezed. "Come on. Let's take a look," said Clay. "You own the building…at least fifty percent of it. And those books are as much yours as they are Morty's. We have every right to enter that room."

Erika pulled open the wooden door, exposing the vault door. She tugged on it, but it was definitely locked. Clay began looking at the hinges, then at the door edge, wondering if he actually *could* use a credit card to unlock it. He looked through the keyhole, but it was dark on the other side of the door, so all he could see was shadows. "Too bad it's not a person. I could tell it to open and it wouldn't have a choice." Both people laughed more out of nervousness than anything else, but Clay's comment made him think of something. "What if I used telekinesis? Maybe I can manipulate the lock mechanism."

He didn't have any idea what he was doing, but he began to use his mind to twist, turn, and manipulate whatever would move, hoping that there was something in the locking mechanism or some sort of switch inside the lock. What he didn't know was that there was a toggle that resembled a light switch inside the mechanism. All he had to do was to flip the toggle up and the door would unlock, and eventually he did just that. He heard the toggle sort of click, so he tried the door and it popped right open—they were inside the attic.

Erika flipped on a light switch, and she and Clay began to wander around the attic looking for Marshall's financial records. It was basically just a storage facility. There were a couple of windows that were mostly blocked by storage supplies. There were shelves and boxes haphazardly stocked and stacked all around the room, but they didn't know what they were looking for—at least not until, tucked in a corner just steps from the attic door, Clay saw a gray, metal cabinet, about the size of a two-drawer file cabinet. It was exactly what Tanner had described in his vision. It had a drawer and a door with a metal handle. There was a keypad, dangling loose from the door. Upon closer scrutiny, Clay was sure that it was a safe, and the keypad was no longer in working order. Behind the hanging keypad was a slot for a skeleton key. That would explain the second of Morty's two keys.

"Erika, I'm pretty sure I've found what we're looking for. Tanner saw this safe in a vision. It has a slot for another skeleton key, which is probably a backup system to open the safe now that the keypad is inoperable. I'm gonna see if I can get this open too." Once again his used his mind to manipulate and flip up the toggle that unlocked the lock. He turned the metal handle. The safe popped open and there was a pile of books that were the financial records for the company. Clay and Erika emptied the safe, shut the door again, and exited the attic, relocking and shutting the doors.

They carried the books back to Erika's office. It took about three minutes to grasp the obvious fact that Marshall Mortonson had two completely separate sets of ledgers, each detailing records for the same time periods, but in two distinctly different ways. Mortonson was doctoring the books.

Erika walked straight to Marshall's office, searched his things for his attorney's phone number, and called Toni Nickel.

"Nickel and Sons. May I help you?"

"Toni Nickel, please."

"May I ask who is calling?"

"Erika Payne."

"One moment, please."

There was a pause, and then Toni spoke. "Hello, Erika. What can I do for you?"

"Hi, Toni. Thanks for taking my call. Toni, I've discovered Morty's books. He has two completely different sets. I assume one is accurate and one is completely made up. I'm pretty certain that the made-up ones are the ones he had in our meeting. I think I'd like to hire you to go over the books. I think he's trying to cheat me."

"Erika, I understand your concern, and, off the record, I had my own suspicions, but I cannot be your attorney. It would be a conflict of interest. But if you don't mind, I'd like to recommend someone else."

"Okay. Let me get a pen and paper to write down the name and number."

"Oh, that won't be necessary. It's my sister. I can transfer you to Andi right now."

Erika could sense the smile on Toni's face, and it made her smile as well. "How about I just come right to your offices?"

"I think that would be a super idea, Erika. I'll tell her you're coming."

***

Erika hung up the phone and looked at Clay. She said, "Okay, Clay, I can tell you know something that you're not telling me."

"I'm that transparent?"

"No, I can read minds too," she said sarcastically, but she said it with another amazing smile, and Clay was helpless when she smiled that way.

"Hopper thinks I need to be careful about what I say, but I'm going to tell you what I think. I had a talk with Jasper, your little friend…"

"The midget?"

"*Little* person."

"So you're telling me you're friends now with the scariest person alive."

Clay laughed. "There's no need to be afraid of him. You're never going to believe that Adrian was paying him to scare you. Adrian thought it was funny. He was a peach of a guy, Erika."

Erika did a three-hundred-sixty-degree turn around the room. "If you can hear me, Adrian, I'd like to say you're the biggest jerk I've ever known."

"I'd have to agree. Anyway, Jasper saw Morty coming out of one of his storage sheds, all bloodied. I think he hid Adrian there and buried him after the horses were buried. That would better explain the shovel clue that Adrian kept leaving on Morty's desk. Hopper's talking with Jasper right now."

Just then Clay's cell phone rang. It was Hopper. "Hey, Luke."

"Clay, I just finished talking with Jasper. He seems to like you. I'm afraid to ask what you did to him. Regardless, you're right about the warrant. I'm working on that right now. I think we'll have it within the hour. Do you want to be there when we check out the building?"

"I'd love to. I'll be at your office as soon as I can."

"See if Erika can supply some DNA evidence. Hairs from a comb or brush or an electric razor, or maybe an old toothbrush. If Adrian's body was stored in that shed, there may be blood evidence and we can match it up to the hairs or toothbrush."

CHAPTER 22

While Erika was visiting Andi Nickel's office, Clay met with Chief Hopper. Clay presented Hopper with three different Ziploc bags, each with separate "evidence" from Adrian Payne's bathroom drawer. Luke had his search warrant and a crew of two forensics experts in tow, and they departed for the storage shed as soon as Clay arrived. They parked back in the Depot parking lot. Once they ascertained that Mortonson wasn't in his office, Hopper headed for the maintenance building and found Roberto Gomez.

"Robbie, I need you to open up the storage shed closest to South Oak Street. I have a warrant to search the building."

"What's up, Copper?"

That wasn't a wise thing to say. Hopper glared at Roberto in a way that made Gomez backtrack with amazing speed. "I mean Hopper. *Chief* Hopper. I'm sorry, Chief."

"Grab your keys, and let's go, Robbie. Police business."

It took a few minutes to make the walk, which was done mostly in uncomfortable silence. Once there, Roberto unlocked the shed and stepped aside. There was a light inside, but the crew had ultraviolet lights as well, and a quiet but thorough search was made. Finally, in a back corner under a workbench, a discovery was made. The ultraviolet lights picked up some stains on the wooden floor and, when the bench was moved aside, the wooden walls were stained as well. Wood samples were carefully removed and then bagged and tagged as evidence.

"We'll have all the evidence sent for DNA analysis," Hopper explained to Clay.

"How soon will you know something?" Clay wondered out loud.

"Forty-eight hours, max".

"Isn't that awfully quick?" Clay asked. "I was under the impression something like that could take a month or two."

"It could unless you know the right person, and he owes you a favor, and he's family, and you bribe him with a steak dinner."

"I assume that moves you right up to the front of the line," Clay joked. He was starting to like Luke Hopper quite a bit.

"It's not what ya know; it's who ya know." Hopper turned and marched away. He was all business.

He was followed closely by the forensics "crew." Roberto and Clay lagged behind as Roberto shut the door and relocked it. Then he turned to Clay and asked, "What's going on?"

"We're just gathering evidence of foul play, Robbie. We may have figured out how the body was buried."

"Does that mean the investigation is over?" Robbie asked with concern in his eyes.

"Possibly," Clay responded honestly.

"*Dios, gracias*," Roberto thought. "No more search warrants?" he asked.

"You don't have any reason to worry, do you?" Clay asked.

"*Just about the train engine*," he thought. "No. I was just wondering if I could get back to work, or if I would be needed for something else."

"This is the only thing I'm aware of. I'm sure you're free to get back to work, Robbie. Thanks for the help."

When they all got back to the parking lot, Clay caught Luke up to speed about the discovery of Marshall Mortonson's two sets of books and Erika's appointment with an attorney. Then he told about Roberto's unspoken concerns, especially his worry that another search warrant would be issued to search the train engine. Clay and Luke both agreed that Roberto was probably talking about the engine from the wreck, the very engine that was on display in front of the train depot. It was just one more thing to think about in an already confusing case, but Hopper said that he'd find someone to look over the train engine.

***

Because Erika was busy, and there was nothing else for Clay to do, he shook hands with Chief Hopper and headed home. Hopper promised to call with the DNA results. He would want Clay present for any arrest and interview. Clay's mind was wandering, and he was driving too fast when he hit a railroad crossing with a terrible bump. He heard what sounded like a gunshot. He ducked and actually wondered if Dan Duncan was shooting at him. None of his windows exploded but a warning light lit up on his dashboard, and based on how the car was driving, he realized that he had a flat tire from the railroad track. There was no end to his railroad track adventures.

Clay got out of the car, popped open his trunk, unscrewed everything related to his spare tire, and pulled the mini-spare, tire iron, and jack from their storage compartments. A few snowflakes were swirling in the air. Clay put on a pair of gloves, quickly read the tire-replacement directions to be sure he didn't do something stupid, and then he proceeded to loosen the lug nuts from the tire. Next, he used the lug wrench to raise the jack to a height nearly equal to the car frame level. He positioned the jack and continued to raise the wheel. After the wheel was suspended a couple of inches off the ground, he stopped and grabbed the tire to pull it off, but all he managed to do was disturb the perfect balance he had fortuitously established and the car fell off the jack, bending the metal at a ridiculous angle. It was ruined, and there was no way for him to continue. He was stranded on the side of the road with no way to change his own tire. Clay had managed to do something stupid anyway.

If he was the swearing type, he'd have been tempted to let out a stream of curses that would have certainly made himself feel better, but he resisted the urge and pulled out his AAA card to make a call from his cell phone. He couldn't help but wonder what kind of damage Jasper would have inflicted upon the car, or his own forehead for that matter, had *he* been the unfortunate victim of the flat tire. He laughed out loud at his vision of the little man, his seat squished as far forward as possible. He pictured his head tilted back and his neck craned to just barely peer over the steering wheel while his toes stretched for the gas pedal.

The AAA service representative gathered Clay's information and let him know that someone from the Shell gas station in Durand would be there to help him shortly. It was only a matter of minutes before a truck rolled up to his car and a man jumped out and retrieved his own jack to help Clay change his tire. He laughed at Clay's story, but he was gracious enough to not make Clay feel any more stupid than he already felt.

As they talked and the man worked, Clay had an idea. The man's name was Roger. "Roger, do you remember the night of the train wreck about seven years ago?"

"Sure do. Was actually workin' the cash register at the station that night. Missed all the action at the railroad, but I sure remember the truck driver comin' in there claimin' his truck'd been ripped off."

"What happened?"

"He came in, paid for his gas, I got him his receipt, and then he asked for the key to the restroom outside. Quite a few minutes later, he was back inside claimin' the truck had been stolen."

"What else do you remember?"

"Well, he disappeared outside to look again, like maybe he missed the truck the first time he looked." Roger laughed at the absurdity of the thought. "Saw him walk from one side of the building to the other. Finally, he saw the cop car that was parked in the lot. He went to the car, then came back in and asked me if I seen the cop that belonged to the car. I hadn't seen nobody, and I told him so. Asked if he wanted to use the phone to call the police station. He took a coupla minutes to tell me about the horses he was deliverin' and how he was worried about 'em. Then he made a call to the horse owners or his boss or someone. I asked him if he wanted me to call 9-1-1, but he shook his head and finished his call. Then he went back outside like he was hopin' it might be there if he only looked one more time. Lo and behold, that time the cop was there."

"Do you know the cop?"

"Naw, I'm a law-abidin' citizen. Never had a run-in with no cops before."

"Ever find out where the cop was?"

"Nope. No one ever came back inside, and I couldn't leave the register. The truck driver got in the cop car and they drove away with lights flashin' and siren blarin'. I heard about the train wreck from another customer awhile later. Heard the train blasted the dude's truck and killed his horses."

"Yeah, that's exactly what happened."

Roger finished, Clay signed paperwork, and the conversation was over. Even though the flat was inconvenient, Clay actually thanked God for the good fortune of running into Roger. Clearly, his story and the story told by Dan Duncan were different. What was Duncan hiding? Where was Duncan when the truck driver discovered that his truck was stolen? As always, after another day of "investigating," Clay still had more questions than answers.

CHAPTER 23

After two days of sitting around going crazy waiting for a call from Hopper, Clay decided to get on his treadmill to run off some pent-up energy. Tanner had a game against Bowling Green that evening, and it appeared he would be getting his first start. Clay put some headphones in his ears and started to run. He had called Erika five times in two days. In their last conversation, it was confirmed that Marshall Mortonson was a crook. First he embezzled, then he stole to cover the embezzlement. Then he manipulated numbers to cover financial losses that Adrian was more than likely racking up. He had evaded paying taxes. Most importantly to Erika, he had made one set of books appear that the business hadn't made much money over the past seven years. He owed Erika a lot of money, but Andi Nickel was confident they could easily prove his dishonesty. Marshall would clearly be in financial straits with Erika and in legal trouble with the Department of Treasury.

Clay had run more than a mile and was getting a little fatigued when he looked down at his iPod to determine the artist of the song he was listening to. His right foot stepped off the treadmill onto the side of the machine. The misstep spun his body sideways and Clay started to lose his balance. He was practically running sideways, but it was clear in a fraction of a second that there was no way he was going to survive the misstep. He fell straight to the course black belt that was rotating through the rollers and it shot him right off the back of the machine. His knee and palm were scraped raw and his body was shot headfirst right into the weight machine set up on the floor behind the treadmill. He hit his face on the metal stanchion, and lay on the floor with a welt below his eye. His pride was hurt as much as his body, but eventually he started laughing, imagining that his fall was captured on video. Spending time with Erika sure had given him a more optimistic outlook on life. He found himself laughing more easily and worrying less. When he dragged his body off the floor, he headed to the kitchen for some ice for his eye. Once he looked into a mirror, he could see that he would have a black eye and a lot of embarrassing explaining to do.

***

"What happened to your eye?" Zander Frauss asked as Clay took his normal seat next to his friend at Crisler Arena.

"Um, I fell," said Clay as he attempted to avoid the truth.

"On your eye?"

"Okay, I fell off the treadmill and hit my eye on my weight machine."

"Likely story. Who hit you?"

"Let's just watch the game, okay?" The anthem played and starters were announced. Then Clay quickly caught Zander up on the news of the investigation in Durand. Tanner made a turnover on his first possession as a starter, just like his first possession in his first game off the bench, but he settled into a very solid performance—three turnovers, six assists, four rebounds, and nine points in a fifteen-point victory. Clay waited patiently for Tanner to emerge from the locker room after the game, and gave him a smile and a hug. They talked briefly about the game, Clay giving a few pointers like a dad tends to do and words of encouragement and confidence as dads also tend to do.

"What happened to your eye?"

"I fell."

"On your *eye?*"

Zander laughed.

"Is déjà vu a parapsychological gift?" Clay said.

"You've had this conversation before?" Tanner asked.

Clay changed the subject. "Wanna head back to Durand with me tomorrow? There may be some excitement. I was thinking we could watch Logan play in his basketball game too."

"Coach has a clinic he's speaking at Friday night and Saturday morning, but we still have a shortened practice tomorrow morning from 11:00 to 12:30. If you can wait, I can make it after that."

* * *

Dan Duncan was itching to go back to work after being off for seven consecutive days. There were rumors at the police department that something big was going down concerning the discovery of Adrian Payne's body. Developments in the case since he had severed his toe were mostly a mystery. Dan had convinced doctors to remove his cast, so he was limping around in a walking boot when he wasn't using his crutches. He'd made it out to Walmart the day before, on Thursday, and he'd made several purchases that had left him in a very good mood. He was thinking: "*Two new birdfeeders—$44.98. One 3-9x power rimfire rifle scope—$84.99. One Mosseberg .22 semi-automatic hunting rifle—$99.99. One dead backyard varmint squirrel—priceless.*"

Dan kicked back with his police scanner turned on and classical music quietly playing on his Bose radio when he heard some scraping on the roof of his house. Soon, he heard what sounded like little clawed feet running on his roof, and then everything was quiet. Dan cautiously eased himself from his chair and spied out of his kitchen window, and sure enough, the squirrel had leaped from his roof and was perched on the bird feeder, stealing seeds. He began sneaking his way to his bedroom closet, giving the distinct impression that he didn't want the squirrel to know he was planning its murder.

Dan had already installed the scope but he had to take a minute to load the rifle with ammunition. Then he sneaked the best he could while hopping on one foot back to his kitchen window. He peeked out of the window, imagining that the squirrel was worriedly looking for him. He quietly slid the glass open a crack and poked the barrel out. Dan's heart was beating wildly and sweat was forming on his brow and upper lip. If he had known anything about hunting rifles and scopes, he would have known that he needed to zero in his scope before he used it, but what Dan was naively thinking was that an assembled scope would simply insure accurate aiming. Dan gazed through it with deadly focus. Within seconds, he believed, his squirrel would deservedly be executed and eliminated from his life completely.

Once the crosshairs of the reticle were perfectly aimed and focused on the squirrel's little head, Dan took a couple of deep, slow breaths and gently began squeezing the trigger. One shot was all that he'd need and all of his problems would be over. Finally, the bullet was ejected from the barrel. Dan watched carefully through the scope in anticipation of the squirrel's demise, but nothing happened except for a noise that sounded remarkably like glass breaking. The squirrel itself looked up in curiosity. Dan stood up, looking in the direct line of his shot, when reality sank in. His scope had not been properly sighted, and Dan had just shot out his neighbor's bathroom window.

***

Clay received a call from Chief Hopper at 10:00 a.m. on Friday morning. The DNA results were conclusive. The bloodstains were from the body of Adrian Payne. Luke agreed to allow Tanner to come and witness the arrest and interview. He found he wasn't doing many things "by the book" since he let Clay be part of the investigation. Clay also informed Luke about the conversation with Roger from the Shell gas station. He suggested that Hopper track down the truck driver so they could have a chat with him. Maybe he would remember something.

Tanner arrived at his dad's house by 12:45 and they were at the police station by 1:15. "I thought you said that Jasper didn't hurt you, Clay," said Hopper. "What happened? That's a nice shiner you have."

"It wasn't Jasper. I fell."

"On your eye?"

Clay rolled his eyes.

"More déjà vu?" Tanner laughed.

According to Erika, Mortonson had left for an appointment with Toni Nickel, but he was expected back for a phone conference at 1:45. Hopper drove his own vehicle and Officer Verne Gilbert brought a back-up squad car to the Depot to wait for Mortonson's arrival. DNA results confirmed that the body had been hidden in the storage shed, and Jasper's eyewitness testimony was compelling evidence that Marshall Mortonson was the person responsible for hiding the body after the train wreck. Hopper was planning on arresting Mortonson and charging him with a felony for concealing the corpse of Adrian Payne.

Mortonson's hands were shaking as he headed back to his office at about 1:35. While at the attorney's office, Marshall had poured himself a cup of coffee in the lobby and happened to see a stack of books on the desk of Andi Nickel. He could tell immediately that they were his account ledgers—both sets. Erika either knew or was soon to know that he was not being honest with her. He was sure to lose her trust along with probably hundreds of thousands of dollars. After passing the last set of railroad tracks, he entered the Depot parking lot and saw Chief Hopper, Clay Thomas, and an additional uniformed police officer waiting alongside a police car. Marshall panicked. He hit his brakes, paused to think—though he wasn't thinking sensibly—and then did a U-turn in preparation to drive away. Where to? Canada?

Everyone immediately recognized that Mortonson was attempting a getaway, and they all leaped into either the police chief's car or the patrol car in preparation for an exciting car chase. As Marshall started to accelerate away from the Depot, a train roared by, blocking the tracks and forcing him to stop abruptly. The cop and his chief of police skidded to a stop after about a fifty-yard drive. Ironically, a train had trapped Mortonson.

"That was exciting," Tanner quipped.

"I always get my man," Hopper wisecracked.

"What you got under the hood of this thing?" Clay asked. "It's a wonder you were able to keep up."

"I'm like a bloodhound. Never lost sight of him the whole time." Hopper got out of the car while Tanner and Clay laughed.

They took a minute to gain their composure before exiting the car themselves.

"Marshall Mortonson," Hopper began, "you are under arrest for conspiracy to conceal a dead human body. Morty, it is a Class 5 felony to move or hide a dead body. You are further charged with preventing a lawful and decent burial."

"I don't know what you're talking about," Mortonson lied.

"Morty, we have ample evidence to charge you with the crimes. You *must* know that it is unlawful to move a dead human body with the intent to abandon or conceal the corpse. Verne," Chief Hopper ordered the officer, "cuff him and read him his rights."

"Please, no handcuffs. That's so humiliating," Mortonson begged. "Take me up to my office and we can talk. There must be a misunderstanding."

Hopper looked at Clay who was smiling a big smile. The chief shook his head. "Why not. This whole investigation has been unorthodox. Let's go upstairs and talk, Morty, but, Verne, read him his rights first. And Clay, make yourself useful, and get his car out of the way."

CHAPTER 24

After Marshall was read his rights and led inside the Depot, he was allowed to call his attorney. Erika, who was at work in her office, heard that Toni Nickel had been summoned, so she called Andi Nickel and asked her to attend as well. Consensus was that potential charges of tax fraud and tax evasion and a suggested civil suit by Erika might motivate Marshall to break down and cooperate. Furniture was organized in the banquet room for everyone that would be present for the interrogation.

Erika gave Clay another tender hug when she finally got a chance. Then she pulled back and gently touched his black eye. "That looks painful. What happened? Did you fall?"

"On my *eye*?" Clay said without thinking. Then he laughed. "Actually, yes. I fell off the treadmill and hit my eye on a weight bench."

She raised her eyebrows and looked at Tanner as if to say, "Really?"

"That's the story he seems to be sticking to. I prefer the one where he got slugged by the midget."

"*Little* person, Tanner," Clay corrected.

At approximately 2:25, all of the key players were present: Chief Hopper, Officer Verne Gilbert, Marshall Mortonson, Clay and Tanner Thomas, Toni and Andi Nickel, and Erika Payne.

After a few introductions, Chief Hopper explained to Toni Nickel why her client had been arrested. She turned to Mortonson. "Have they read you your rights?"

"Yes."

"And you understand them?"

"Yes…This is just some sort of mistake."

"I would advise that you don't talk, Morty. I don't even know what evidence they have."

"*You want to talk,*" Tanner calmly told him inside his head.

"I want to talk," Marshall announced.

"I need a few moments with my client," Toni said. Officer Gilbert followed them to Erika's office and then let them have their private meeting, a meeting in which Toni told Marshall not to talk. When they returned, Toni announced, "My client would rather not talk right now."

Just then, Logan Payne appeared in the banquet room doorway, arriving at the Depot after school had ended.

"*Tell her you want to talk,*" Tanner spoke inside Marshall's head.

"I want to talk, Toni."

"What? We just decided *not* to!"

"I feel like I want to talk."

"Good," Hopper quickly said. "Here's the situation, Ms. Nickel. Your client is being charged with a felony for moving and hiding the body of the late Adrian Payne on the night of Friday, August 8, 2003. Later, he moved the body a second time, at which time he concealed the corpse at the gravesite along the railroad tracks about a quarter of a mile west of the South Oak Street crossing where the body was eventually discovered. We have DNA evidence that confirms that the body was stored in his railway storage shed just east of Oak Street before it was buried, and we have a witness that will testify that Mr. Mortonson's bloodied body exited said storage shed just minutes after the train wreck. Additionally, we have our forensic experts working diligently to determine the possibility that Adrian Payne may have been murdered by Mr. Mortonson."

"I didn't murder him!" Marshall nearly yelled.

"What happened, Morty?" Erika asked.

"We were on our way back from Lansing. Logan went to see Adrian and came back upset."

"That's because Adrian had struck him in the face," Clay said.

Logan noticeably flinched from the doorway of the banquet room. He had never told a soul that he had been hit. It appeared to Clay and Erika both that he was very embarrassed that people knew what his father had done.

"Well, I can believe it, but I didn't know it at the time. I just went to talk to Adrian about the boy, you know? He wanted a ride in the engine with his dad. When I approached the engine, Adrian appeared to be passed out on the floor. I looked up and saw we were approaching something on the tracks much too fast. I hit the emergency door release switch and picked up Adrian. The train was going to crash and the engineer jumped, so I jumped with Adrian. I tried to *save* his life. We hit the ground and I tumbled away, but Adrian landed and barely moved. The train crashed and two cars tipped. I guess the front one landed on the engineer, but the second one I know for sure landed right on Adrian and then slid off. He was crushed. I tried to save his life," Marshall ranted. "Instead, I may have caused his death. He could be a horrible person, but he was my best friend."

"So why did you hide and then bury the body?" Hopper asked.

"Don't answer that question," Toni advised.

"*Answer the question*," Tanner commanded with his mind.

"As soon as I saw him, I knew he was dead. That meant that Erika would be my partner. Fifty-fifty. She didn't know a thing about the railroad business. And she must have hated the man. She had every reason to. She would have wanted to sell her half, and I would have had to buy her out or sell. I couldn't do the one and didn't want to do the other. Our contract stipulated that Erika would inherit Adrian's portion of the business upon his death, but only I would have decision-making powers. I figured if Adrian disappeared instead of dying, I could build the business back up. I knew without Adrian wasting the company's money, I could make it a respectable business."

"Are you suggesting," Andi Nickel interrupted, "that stealing from Erika and committing tax fraud is a respectable way to run your business?"

Before Marshall could respond, Hopper interjected and looked at Toni Nickel. "That brings us to another issue, Ms. Nickel. Based on the books currently in the possession of your sister, I believe we have enough information to take to the Criminal Investigation Division, who will most certainly file charges of criminal tax fraud, tax evasion, and possibly money laundering."

"Listen to me, Morty. Do not say another thing."

Tanner's thoughts invaded Marshall's mind. "*You have more to tell us.*"

"But I have more to tell. I took money from the business and lost it all. I was doctoring the books so Adrian wouldn't find out, but he did, and he blackmailed me. He started acting and spending irresponsibly. Whenever I approached him, he threatened to press charges. He told me however I could cover his spending, I'd better do it, or I'd lose my share of the business. He forced me to lie, steal, and file false tax reports. I did everything I could legally *and* illegally to fix the books so I could show Adrian I no longer owed the company, but he was killed in the wreck before I could get out from under my debt. I was still in such a hole that there was no way to buy out Erika. I realized that as long as Adrian was missing, Erika wouldn't inherit the business from him. I did my best to provide for her. He was a sleaze, Erika, but I'm not. I didn't leave you out in the cold."

"You think by giving me a low-paying office job, you were *providing* for me. I have your books that show that just this week you were plotting to offer me a payment for the last seven years *far* below my rightful share. Is that what you call '*providing*' for me? Jeez, Morty, if he'd been declared dead, I'd have had a two million dollar insurance policy to cash in. Maybe I wouldn't have felt the need to sell if I had the insurance money."

When she said "two million dollar insurance policy," Hopper made eye contact with Clay. "*A good motive to kill the man, don't you think? I told you that you might be wrong about her.*"

Clay could read Hopper's mind, and he didn't like what Hopper was thinking, but as much as it pained him, he had to admit for the first time there was doubt in his mind about the woman he was falling in love with. The last person he truly loved was unfaithful and was murdered. Could his relationship with Erika end just as tragically, with him proving that Erika somehow pulled off a murder?

"I'm sorry, Erika. I'm truly sorry. Chief Hopper, I've done some bad things, but I didn't murder my partner. I tried to save his life."

"Is there anything else you'd like to share, Morty, before we take you off to jail?"

"I knew this day was inevitable. I worried about it for seven years. No, there's nothing else to share."

"Okay, Verne, take him away. Book him, print him, and lock him up. It looks like we've solved our mystery."

As Officer Gilbert led him away, Marshall pulled his skeleton keys from his pocket and placed them into the hand of Erika Payne.

***

Eventually, Clay, Tanner, Erika, Logan, and Luke Hopper made it into Erika's office. Logan looked embarrassed, but when Erika hugged him, he hugged back.

"Logan, why didn't you ever tell me that your father hit you?"

"I don't want to talk about it, Mom. Not here; not now."

Erika nodded in understanding. "We'll talk about it later when you're ready. But Logan…now that we know what happened to your father, and we know he won't be back, maybe you can be happy again."

Clay felt a coolness in the room, a temperature drop that he alone could sense. He was sure that Adrian Payne was present. Logan stood still for a few seconds then reached into his pocket and pulled out the jackknife that his father had given him so many years ago. He looked at it as if he was thinking some deep thought. "I don't want this anymore," he said. Then he slowly walked to the wastebasket and tossed it in.

As the knife hit the bottom of the basket, Clay heard, "*Waste not; want not.*" Logan then walked out of the room, followed by Erika.

Clay took a confused look at the picture on the wall, but then he heard again, "*Waste not; want not.*"

Clay turned to Tanner and Luke. "It's Adrian." Then he said to his ghost. "You want me to get Logan's jackknife, right?"

"*Yes. Can you figure out what's the point of it?*" Adrian replied.

"Now you're asking *me* questions? I hardly understand anything you say, so how can I have answers to your riddles?"

"*Do you think I care about you?*"

Clay got out of his seat, walked to the wastebasket, and pulled out Logan's knife. He turned back to the picture. Tanner looked on, wondering what was going on while Luke seemed more than a bit distracted. "You have anything meaningful to say to me, Adrian?"

"*Skeleton key.*"

"What? Is there something else back there in the attic? I don't understand anything you're saying to me!" Clay said in frustration.

There was no answer.

Clay walked back to the family picture that was hanging on Erika's office wall. He wanted to wipe that stupid, dimpled grin from his face. There he was in all his selfishness, sitting next to his beautiful wife and his son who wanted nothing more than his love and attention. "Tell me, Adrian. Did Erika have anything to do with your death?"

"*It was a heart attack. Ease the pain,*" was the response he was given.

Clay turned to his son and the chief in frustration. "He wanted me to get the knife, and then he asked me if I could figure out the point of it. He's still saying 'skeleton key' and 'heart attack,' and he still wants me to ease his pain. I don't care about his pain, and I don't know what I should be looking for." He remembered that Hopper didn't know about Tanner's gifts, so he looked Tanner in the eyes and spoke telepathically to him. *"Have you had any other visions?"*

Tanner shook his head no.

Finally Hopper blurted out what was bothering him. "I need to know if you made Morty talk in that banquet room."

"No, I didn't."

"I was hoping that was the case. So, what do you think? Since Adrian hasn't made his way to the light, or whatever he needs to do, I assume there's more to this than just Marshall Mortonson. If we figure it out, maybe he can make his way to the next life."

"I want to get away from here. One good deed and I can move on."

"Maybe Morty killed him," Hopper continued, "but maybe Erika did, or maybe Robbie Gomez or Dan Duncan. Or maybe he was passed out and just died unfortunately by getting squashed by a train. Or maybe he had a heart attack and died. If there's more to this, how do we figure it out?"

"Well," replied Clay, "Robbie doesn't want us to check out the train engine, so we should start there."

"Done. I have an expert coming in today."

"And maybe we can learn something from the truck driver. Did you figure out how to contact him?"

"Way ahead of you, Clay. Contacted his work, and he's still a valued employee. Guess they overlooked that he managed to get his rig stolen while he was takin' a leak. Considering his entire precious cargo was killed as a result, they seem to be pretty forgiving. He's been making Michigan deliveries regularly over the past seven years. You're the luckiest investigator I've ever known, my friend, so it's par for the course that he just happens to be on his way to Michigan today and will be at Sports Creek Raceway tomorrow a little after noon. Name's Lawrence Maloney. Company's Equine En Route, Inc. from Louisville, Kentucky. I'll bet if you show up there around noon, you'll get a chance to talk to him. Forgive me, but I'll be doing some more digging into Erika. Believe me, I hope I'm wrong, but I wouldn't be doin' my duty if I didn't investigate. That insurance policy is a mighty good motive for foul play."

Clay said, "Morty, Dan, and Robbie all said they killed him, but there's no real evidence. The medical examiner assumes he died in the crash, and Adrian himself thinks he died of a heart attack. Erika was out of town, so why is she a murder suspect?"

"You're right. I don't even know if Adrian was murdered, and if he was, there are better suspects than Erika. But what I *do* know is that there is a lot more to that night than an accidental crash. We'll just keep trying to figure out what happened as we go along."

***

The Thomases had an early dinner with the Paynes. Tanner and Logan were both very quiet during the meal. Afterward, they headed out to the driveway to shoot baskets. Clay and Erika were sitting on the couch, snuggling closely and holding hands, both temporarily caught up in their own thoughts. Finally Clay said, "Two million dollars?"

"Yes. I guess I need to call the insurance company, don't I?"

"You haven't called them?"

"Unlike a lot of other people, I wouldn't have been surprised if Adrian was alive. I figured he'd gotten himself into trouble, and was on the run. I figured he didn't really care about us enough to call, but someday, he'd come strolling back into our lives. I knew about the insurance policy because I signed it, but I never checked into it or his will or trust. The break-ins made me think of ghosts, and Morty's office especially made me think of Adrian, but there was no other reason to assume he was dead."

"You didn't even call your insurance company now that you know for sure?"

"I hadn't even thought of it. Besides, they're still holding the body. Isn't there supposed to be a funeral and such before I would look into my inheritance?"

That made sense to Clay, so he asked something else that was on his mind. "What do you make of Logan?"

"Clay, I've become really a simple woman. I care about him more than I care about myself, and I'd die for him if I had to. It hurts me more than I can say to see him unhappy. Now that I know that Adrian hit him, I assume he did it other times too. Maybe that's why Logan was withdrawn before the accident. Losing a father has to be traumatic, so maybe that's why he was unhappy *after* the accident. Maybe he's lived under fear that his dad would return, or maybe his last encounter with his dad was so traumatic that he can't get over it. Whatever it is, it has caused me just as much pain as it's caused him."

"But you were hoping once the body was found, he'd change for the better, weren't you?"

"Yes, but it didn't seem to happen. I was hoping that learning his father didn't abandon him would help too. Then I was hoping that finding out Morty was involved would make some sort of impact, but he still doesn't want to talk about it."

"What can I do?" Clay asked sincerely.

"Pray for him. Be a friend. Keep bringing Tanner around. Find out what happened. All of those things, I guess."

"What do you want me to do with his knife?" Clay told her that Adrian wanted him to take it from the wastebasket.

"Adrian gave that to him. It always seemed important to Logan. I figured it symbolized something, or there was some sort of sentimental value to it because it was something he got from his dad. I was surprised to see him throw it away. Why don't *you* keep it? Maybe someday, he'll want it back, and it would be nice if he got it from you."

Erika hugged Clay and gave him a soft kiss on his cheek that made the hairs on his arms stand up. She felt so good to him. He wanted to help her. So he prayed all right. He prayed for Logan, but he prayed harder that Erika wasn't involved in any unscrupulous activities. The second prayer was futile, though, because if she was involved seven years ago, no prayer was going to change that. It just made him feel better to pray it. It gave him hope.

The back door opened, and they jumped apart like guilty kids hiding from their parents. When the boys returned, Logan actually had a smile on his face. "If I play tonight, I think I'm gonna do all right," he said.

"How 'bout I trim those bangs from your eyes so you can see?" Erika said while smiling back. That was a lot of words from her son.

"Okay," was his more typical one-word reply.

They disappeared into the bathroom. Tanner said, "I may have told him that he's gonna have a good shooting night tonight."

"Why would you do that?" Clay asked with all the sincerity of a disappointed parent.

"I saw the future, Dad. If they're playing Perry tonight, then he's gonna make several baskets. Who are they playing?"

"Perry." Clay was noticeably curious. "More precognition?"

"Yep. I saw into the future."

"What exactly did you see?"

"Three threes in a row from the corner in front of the Durand bench."

"So you told Logan, and he believes you?"

"I sort of told him to believe me, but it's all good, Dad. It would have happened regardless. I can see into the future."

"Have you seen anything else?"

Tanner hesitated. Finally he said, "I saw that short, stocky cop that I saw the night Adrian's body was recovered. He had a barrel chest, thick neck and arms. Kept staring at Erika."

"That's Dan Duncan. I know him."

Tanner hesitated again. "I saw he had a gun, and he shot it at you."

CHAPTER 25

While the Thomases and Paynes were at Erika's house, Chief Hopper met with an expert in train mechanics. When Hopper and the mechanic arrived at the Depot, Roberto Gomez was just finishing work. Anna had been dropped off by Stacy, and she was pretending to drive the train engine—the brakes of which Roberto was repairing. Brake work was exceptionally difficult but vitally important, and Roberto was good at his job. However, when he saw Hopper leading the mechanic to the train exhibit outside of the Depot, he knew he could be in trouble. He hung up his tools, gathered Anna from the engineer's seat, and left as quickly and inconspicuously as possible.

He was having trouble deciding what to do, but he finally decided to call Erika rather than Stacy. Erika took the call on her cell phone while she was cutting Logan's hair. She could tell that Roberto was distressed, so when he asked if they could talk, she invited him over. Logan would need to leave soon for his game, but no one else would have to go until just before game time.

When Roberto arrived, Logan had already taken Erika's car and left in time to be at the JV game. Anna peeked in the door with her familiar smile and immediately asked for Logan. She was clearly disappointed that he wasn't there, but Tanner came to the rescue. Once they were reintroduced, they were off playing almost immediately. Gomez was clearly nervous. He didn't like that Clay was there, but it wasn't something that he could control, so he sat down in a chair next to the couch and fidgeted momentarily while he worked up his nerve.

"I have something that I need to tell you," he said. "And Stacy doesn't know about some of this."

Erika, as sweet as could be, sat down on the edge of the couch next to Roberto, and reached for his hand. "I can tell something is wrong, Robbie. What is it?"

"I'm sorry, but could we speak privately? I know that Clay is your friend, but he's working with Chief Hopper. I think it's best if I spoke to you alone."

Erika was going to object, but Clay agreed to leave. By the time Clay found the kids in Erika's basement, Tanner had already stood Anna up on a stool at one end of a ping-pong table, and he was teaching her how to play ping-pong. Clay ended up shagging all of the balls she missed. Little Anna was squealing and laughing at each point. She was so cute that Clay couldn't help but smile right along and admire her enthusiasm. After one particular shot in which her return tipped off the net and trickled over for a point, she smiled her crooked, dimpled smile, and all of a sudden Clay realized what made it so familiar. He headed back up the stairs.

Back upstairs, Roberto had already begun. "I'm so sorry, Erika. I have some things to tell you that you might find very disturbing, but I think it's time that you knew the truth. Chief Hopper has someone checking out the train engine that's on display at the Depot. I'm afraid that they're gonna figure something out that I've been hiding for seven long years."

"This has to do with Adrian's death, doesn't it?"

"Yes. Erika, I'm responsible for his death."

"No, Robbie, I know that's not possible. The coroner says he died as a result of the train crash." She didn't know how to tell about Adrian's claim to having a heart attack, so she added, "Or possibly natural causes. Unless you crashed the train, how could you be remotely responsible?"

"Because the train couldn't stop. I messed with the brakes. When that truck was left on the tracks, the train couldn't stop on time, so it was my fault. Adrian was killed in the wreck. It was my fault, Erika."

"Just explain what you're talking about."

"There's so much to say. I went to Lansing that night. Everyone knew that the engineer—Joe Carrollton was his name— would let Adrian drive the train back into Durand. A lot of us knew that Adrian would buy him a good bottle of liquor, and Joe would sit back and let Adrian take charge. Adrian, to show off, always pulled into the station too fast and stopped the train too fast. On that night, I checked the train schedule and discovered that there was to be a crossing northbound freight train at 9:07. When the Amtrak was to pull into the Depot, the northbound freighter would pass through our railroad diamond. My plan was for the train to have a difficult time stopping as Adrian zoomed into the Depot. I didn't ruin the brakes completely, but I fixed it so he wouldn't be able to stop on time. I wanted to humiliate him. I wanted to embarrass him and cause him trouble with the commission. I was so angry with Adrian that I didn't consider the consequences to other people. When I heard about the train wreck at Oak Street, I realized I had killed Joe, and probably Adrian too once his body was found."

Clay appeared in the entryway to the living room. Roberto looked up and made eye contact with him, so Clay simply used mind control to tell him, "*Keep talking.*"

"Why would you do such a thing, Robbie?" Erika asked.

"I don't know. Lots of reasons. He sexually harassed Stacy. He made racist remarks to me. He treated me like a second-class citizen."

"Tell her the truth, Robbie," Clay said. When Robbie looked up and made eye contact, Clay said, "Tell Erika what he did."

Roberto actually had tears in his eyes. "Your husband raped Stacey."

"What? When?" Clay had not told her what he had learned in the interview.

"About a year before the wreck. He was always coming on to her. Told her he hired me just to make her happy. At a party, Stacy drank a little too much, and Adrian took advantage of her. When she resisted, he told her that he'd fire her and me if she didn't let him continue. He said there were lots of people who saw her flirting with him, and they all knew she had come on to him in the past, so no one would believe her. Plus he'd make sure we lost our jobs. After the rape, Stacy found out that even before the rape, he had been telling people that Stacy was after him. He'd *planned* on raping her. After the rape, he treated me worse than ever."

"There's something you're leaving out, isn't there, Robbie?" Clay said. He had figured it out while he was in the basement with Tanner and Anna. Robbie tried to act like he didn't know what Clay was talking about. But he knew it had to come out eventually. It was Clay who said, "Anna is Adrian's daughter, isn't she?"

***

Chief Hopper and Robert Parker, the mechanic who was brought in to investigate the train engine, stepped up into the train and flipped on a couple of powerful flashlights to ward off the darkness that was quickly creeping in. It was cold outside, but there was shelter from the wind inside the train car. In a matter of seconds, Parker noticed that the air gauge instrument that indicates the amount of air pressure in the brake pipes was broken. "Could have happened in the crash," said Parker. "But if it was broken prior to the accident, the engineer wouldn't know how much air was in the reservoirs."

"From all we're hearing, it was a pretty well-known fact that Adrian Payne would have been driving the engine. I checked. He wasn't certified or even trained to drive the train. And the engineer, Joseph Carrollton, had a blood-alcohol content of .17, more than twice the legal limit. He was found at fault after the accident. It's completely possible neither of the men would've noticed the broken instrument. The black box recorded a failed attempt to break the train on time. Is there any way you can identify break trouble?"

After a thorough examination, Parker found two other interesting problems. "First of all, Luke, this here brake cylinder has been tampered with."

"What's the problem?"

"The brake cylinder is a part of the air brake system. There's lots of components to the entire system, but how this here part works is the cylinder contains a piston, which is forced outward by compressed air. The compressed air is what applies the brakes and slows the train. When the air pressure is released, the piston returns to its normal position by a release spring coiled around the piston rod inside the cylinder. This piston rod don't got no release spring."

"Which means what exactly?" Luke prodded.

"It means the piston can't return to its normal position, so the air pressure ain't able to build up for the next application. It means once the brakes are applied once, like when roundin' a bend, for instance, then air'll leak out and not enough pressure is built up to slow down the train properly the next time the brakes are applied."

"Someone removed the spring?"

"Well, it can't just fall out of the cylinder, Chief, even if it *did* somehow break. Now if the air gauge was workin', the engineer would've known for sure there was a problem."

"Isn't there a secondary system if something malfunctions? I mean, surely the engineer has another way to stop the train."

"Sure thing, but that's the other problem I seen. This is the brake shaft." He pointed at the shaft. "A chain is wound around this shaft, and it's because of that chain that the power of a hand brake can be applied to the wheels."

"What chain?"

"Exactly. There ain't no chain. It's been removed. Ain't no way to stop a train quickly when the air brakes aren't buildin' up enough pressure. Given enough time and room, the driver could bring the train to a stop, but if there ain't time and space, an engineer would have to rely on the hand brakes. This engine didn't have no workin' hand brakes."

"So what's your assessment?"

"It's simple. Someone who knew what he was doin'—and had some specialized tools—rigged this train so it wouldn't stop when the driver wanted it to. Someone broke the air gauge and walked away with the spring and the chain. The brakes on this train were messed up somethin' good."

"Wouldn't these things you're telling me have come out in the investigation seven years ago?"

"Could be they weren't lookin' if there wasn't reason to believe the brakes failed. You said the engineer was drunk. Maybe they just blamed it on him and walked away nice and neat. Or maybe they saw it and didn't publicize it, 'cause it woulda been bad pub. Hard to say."

"Well, whatever reason, the guy has gotten away with his crime for seven years. It's time he came to justice."

CHAPTER 26

Erika was shocked. "Anna is *Adrian's* daughter? Did Adrian know?"

"Course he knew. She doesn't look a thing like me."

"I just figured you had some Caucasian blood in your ancestry."

"I'm one hundred percent Mexican, as are both my parents and both their parents. Both sets of grandparents were immigrants from Mexico. While Stacy was pregnant, we didn't know, but as soon as Anna was born, it was clear. When we approached Adrian, he didn't even care. He didn't give any money, didn't take any interest. Didn't even ask what her name was. When Anna was three months old, she got sick and was hospitalized. It was expensive, and my insurance wasn't enough. I asked Adrian for help, and he laughed. Made a few additional racial slurs and told me I was lucky to have a job. He could take it from me anytime he wanted. I wanted to hurt him. When he went to that conference I took things into my own hands. It was predictable that he'd be driving the train. When I saw the train schedule, I figured I could cause an accident, and he would be to blame. I hated him. He violated my wife, the person I love the most in the world. I could find it in myself to love Anna, just because she was Stacy's, but *he* couldn't even love his own child."

Erika was crying. Tears were streaming down her face. Clay went to her and held her while she tried to compose herself. "I was *married* to that monster. I'm so ashamed. I'm so sorry, Robbie.

How could I ever have loved a man who could so easily hurt other people?" She wiped tears from her eyes, spreading mascara onto her reddened face, yet she still looked beautiful. "We can't let Robbie get in trouble, Clay. I don't care what we have to do; please don't let him get in trouble. For seven years they've looked after me and Logan. And their daughter is Logan's sister. Logan loves her. Anna is family. Robbie can't go to prison for this."

"You'd better call your lawyer again," Clay said. "She'll know what to do better than I would. Is a mechanic going to find anything incriminating, Robbie?"

"If he looks closely at all, he'll see that the brakes were ruined, and he'll know it was done by someone who knew what he was doing. Me, for instance."

"What does Stacy know about this?"

"She doesn't know what I did, and she doesn't know what's been happening in the investigation. All she knows is that I wasn't home until just before the train wreck."

"She can't be forced to testify against you. You need to go home and tell Stacy what you did. You need to wait there for the attorney. If Hopper shows before she gets there, don't say a word. Do you understand? Robbie, look at me." When Robbie looked into his eyes, Clay said, "Do not say a word to Chief Hopper."

Just then Tanner and Anna came into the room. Erika rushed over and lovingly hugged Anna. She started crying again, then turned to Robbie. "Does she know?"

"No, how could she understand?"

"I would like Logan to know."

"When the time is right, let's tell them both."

***

Chief Hopper, accompanied by Officer Verne Gilbert, arrived at the Gomez residence a little after 7:00 p.m. He rang the doorbell. When the door opened, it was Andi Nickel who greeted him. Clay and Roberto had already filled her in on all the facts. Hopper was taken aback temporarily. "Hello, Ms. Nickel. I'm here to take Roberto Gomez in for questioning. Would you kindly step aside?"

"On what grounds, Chief Hopper?"

"He is to be questioned in regards to the deaths of Joseph Carrollton and Adrian Payne on Thursday, August 7, 2003."

"And what makes you believe Mr. Gomez has any information in relation to the deaths of those two men?"

"Ms. Nickel, if he has nothing to fear, why would he hire you?"

"Oh, he didn't hire me. I've been employed as counsel by a third party."

"And may I ask who that might be?"

"No, you may not. Or at least I will not be giving you that information. So, again, what makes you believe that Mr. Gomez has information pertaining to two deaths in 2003?"

"We have reason to believe that he may be criminally involved. We are here simply to bring him in for questioning. May I come in now?"

Andi stepped aside. Sitting on their couch, simply watching television, were Roberto and Stacy Gomez. The three Gomez girls were coloring in coloring books on the carpeting in the middle of the room. "Excuse me, Robbie. We're here to take you in for questioning. Would you mind coming with us?"

Roberto never said a word, just as Clay had told him. He simply grabbed a jacket, slipped on his shoes, kissed his girls and wife, and walked out with Andi Nickel and the two policemen. "He'll be riding with me, Chief," Andi informed Luke.

"If you say so, Counselor," Hopper replied.

In the car, Andi explained once again to Roberto to keep quiet. She said that she'd be taking the offensive, which is exactly what she did. Roberto had an alibi for the night of the train wreck. Hopper had no evidence otherwise. Hopper had an eyewitness—a ten-year-old from seven years before who said he *thought* he saw Roberto in Lansing. There were no other corroborating witnesses. There was some damage done to the brakes of the train, something Roberto was capable of doing, but again, there was no physical evidence or eyewitnesses placing him at the scene. When they got to the issue of any kind of motive, all Hopper mentioned was racist remarks and sexual harassment. He was unable to bring up the rape accusation that Clay had read from Roberto's mind. Even if Hopper could persuade a judge to believe Clay read his mind, it would be inadmissible in court, much like a polygraph test would be. As the "interview" continued, Roberto never spoke a word, under the "advice" of his counselor. It took a very short time before Andi Nickel stated, "You barely have *circumstantial* evidence that Mr. Gomez was involved in any wrongdoing. Unless you have any further questions, I believe it would be appropriate for you to excuse us. You've taken up enough of our time."

Hopper had no choice but to agree, so Andi escorted Roberto to her car and drove him back home. Luke Hopper was back to the drawing board. Although, he believed that Roberto Gomez had damaged the train's brakes, it appeared that it would be difficult to get any kind of conviction. Second-degree murder? Manslaughter? Malicious destruction of property? There was still more to the story, so he wasn't giving up yet.

***

Clay, Tanner, and Erika, though they actually weren't in the mood to watch a basketball game, were in the stands at Durand High School watching the Railroaders play Perry High's varsity team. Logan hadn't played a single minute in the first game three days before, but that was after his father's body had been discovered and he had missed school and practices. Erika was hopeful that he'd get in, and was excitedly hoping that Tanner actually did see Logan's future baskets.

It was a close, low-scoring first half, with Perry taking the lead at halftime by a score of 21-18. Durand had six underclassmen on their roster, none of whom played particularly well, yet Logan, a senior, never got off the bench.

Perry extended their lead to 37-25 at the end of the third period and had cruised to a 54-32 lead with three and a half minutes to go in the game. Finally, Logan took off his warm-up jacket and entered the game. He looked up at his mother and gave what looked like a disappointed half-grin, but he was in and his three fans were anxious to see if Tanner actually did see the future.

In the first two and a half minutes, Logan touched the ball, but he looked very tentative. He didn't even look to the basket to score. But with fifty-five seconds on the clock, he found himself wide open in the corner in front of his team's bench. He let fly a three-pointer, and he hit nothing but net. Perry's player stepped on the baseline while inbounding the ball, so the turnover gave the ball right back to Durand. Logan stepped back over to the same corner and received a pass. He shot again and hit another three.

After a Perry player walked the ball back up the court, the team seemed content to run out the clock, but one of the reserves made a bad pass that led to an over-and-back violation. Durand had the ball one last time with nine seconds remaining. The point guard tried to rifle a pass under the basket, but it was deflected and rolled toward the sideline where Logan picked it up and shot another three-pointer from the corner as the buzzer sounded. Once again, the shot snapped the bottom of the net for his ninth point in fifty-five seconds—just as Tanner had seen. Durand lost 54-43, but Erika was jumping up and down and giving hugs like they had won. She was ecstatic. Joyous. Proud. She started laughing and high-fiving everyone within reaching distance.

To Clay, it was like watching Jessie at Tanner's games, and Tanner sensed immediately how his father felt. He put his arm around his dad's shoulders and said, "Mom's up in Heaven watching, Dad. She loves you, so she'd want you to be happy. Zander is right, you know, as hard as that is to admit. It's time for you to move on. Besides, how many men can say they were in love with two women the quality of *your* two?"

Clay had tears in his eyes. Tanner had said just the right thing. How come he was so special? Then he turned to Tanner. "Your mom raised you pretty well, I'll have to admit. Thank you."

Tanner hugged his dad. "God blessed me when he gave me both of you. Thank *you*."

Before Clay went off to give his girlfriend a hug, he had one more thing to say. "It seems you were right about Logan. That's awesome. Your powers keep growing. But do you know what that means?"

Now Tanner had tears in his eyes. "Yeah, it means Dan Duncan is gonna try to shoot you. Promise me, Dad, that you won't let him hurt you."

"One thing I learned when your mother was murdered is that a person's future is in God's hands. I can only hope he's taught me all these things in the past year and has given me renewed faith because he has a plan for my life. I don't know what the future holds, but I promise to be careful."

Clay and Tanner waited around with Erika for Logan to come out of the locker room. They said their congratulations and their goodbyes. Logan thanked them for coming, and Erika gave them both hugs. It had been quite a day.

CHAPTER 27

Tanner had a Saturday night game but because his coach was at a clinic, there was no walk through in the morning, so he spent the night with his dad, and they were on their way to Sports Creek Raceway to find and talk to Lawrence Maloney, the driver of the stolen truck seven years earlier. They arrived at 11:45 a.m. and looked for a truck with Equine En Route, Inc. on the side, or one with license plates from Kentucky. There was nothing, but at 12:05, the truck they were looking for rolled in, drove up to the gate and guard shack, and stopped. A very tall, thin man stepped down from his cab and presented some paperwork. A guard reviewed the papers, had the man sign something, then opened the gate and waved the truck through. The gate closed and Clay was left wondering what to do.

"Tell him to let you in," suggested Tanner.

"Just like that? What if I get the guy in trouble?"

"You have a better idea?"

Because he didn't, Clay drove to the gate and stopped. The guard stepped out of his shack and stood before Clay's door. "Can I help you?"

Clay looked him in the eyes and said, "Yes, sir. I need to speak with Lawrence Maloney, so I'd appreciate it if you'd open that gate for us and let us in."

The guard seemed unsure of himself, but he said, "You'll have to sign in."

"No problem," Clay replied. He signed the sheet and waited for the gate to open. When it did, he waved, smiled, and drove in. Mind control certainly had its advantages. Maloney was dropping his horses off at a paddock. There was a crew of men there waiting—presumably the owners. Maloney was clapping and rubbing his hands together to ward off some of the cold.

Clay parked, and he and Tanner walked up to the man. Clay spoke first. "Excuse me. Are you by chance Lawrence Maloney?"

"I am. But everbody calls me Larry," he said with a heavy Southern accent.

"I'm Clay Thomas, and this is my son, Tanner."

Larry shook hands. "What kin I do for y'all?"

"Larry, we've been investigating the train wreck from August of 2003. Do you think we could ask you a few questions?"

"I reckon so. It's been a mighty long time. I might disremember some thangs, but if'n y'all wanna go inside, I was fixin' to git some coffee afore I freeze to death."

"We might could do that," Tanner smiled and joked in such a way that he wasn't offensive at all.

"A Yankee with a sense of humor. If'n there was more Gol-darned people who could laugh, it wouldn't be so mighty aggervatin visitin' these parts. Why'n tarnation caint people laugh more these days?"

"I reckon we're all a bit too serious, Larry. How 'bout we fetch a seat yonder?" Tanner smiled and pointed, and Larry smiled and headed right over. Clay marveled at his son's personality.

Once they were seated, Clay explained that they were simply interested in what he remembered about that night.

"I came outta the john, fixin' to git a cuppa coffee, but the dad-burned rig was missin' from the lot. Lord a'mercy, and nairy a person seen a thang. If'n someone drove a semi-truck from a dinky gas station, you'da thought someone would hafta seen it, but no, not in Du-rand."

"There was a police car there. Do you remember that?" Clay asked.

"I looked pert' near everwhere fer the guy, but he warnt nowhere to be found. I recollect callin' my boss back home. Spent a few minutes tryin' to figger out what to do next. Boss was havin' a hissy—hootin' an' hollerin'. If'n there's someone who kin kick up a ruckus, it's my boss. Then I seen the no 'count cop joggin' into the lot."

"He was running?"

"Yes, sir. I headed outside agin. He was all outta breath and was fixin' to git in his car and drive away. I hitched my breetches like I use'ta when I was a young'n, and stopped the man. Aggervatin' little man didn't much care 'bout my predicament, but, finally, he got to workin' on a dad-burned police report. I was fixin' to wring his thick neck when he got a call on his radio. A train'd smashed a semi-truck on some tracks purdy close by. We got in his car to see if'n it was my truck seeins how I happened to be missin' one. My rig was on fire. Part of the train was toppled over. That no-count cop got out the car and left me there alone. Went down the tracks like he was lookin' fer someone. Never came back. Warnt nothin' I could do but watch."

"Larry, do you have any idea who could've stolen your truck?"

"Not a clue, Clay."

Hearing the word "clue" gave Tanner an idea. "Did you ever go back through your rig, Larry? I mean were there personal affects in the cab or anything?"

"Yes, sir, I did fetch some thangs from my cab. Course I did."

"Do you remember anything unusual?"

"Unusual? It's been a long time to recollect somethin' like that, Tanner."

"If I could help you remember, would you let me?" Tanner asked.

"How'd ya do somethin' like that?"

"I could hypnotize you."

"Young man, if'n I let you hypnotize me, would y'all do me a favor? I got this gosh-darned pain in my neck—and, no, it ain't my Missus. Do ya thank ya could make the pain go 'way?"

"I've never done anything like that, but I could try. I promise to try, Larry."

"Then let's do 'er. Whatcha got, a watch or somethin'?"

"Just sit back and relax. Count backwards from ten." Tanner focused his powers on Larry's mind.

"Tin, non, eight…"

"You're hypnotized, Larry." He turned to his dad. "I just make 'em count for dramatic effect." Clay laughed.

"Larry, concentrate for a minute on the cab of your rig seven years ago. The one in the train wreck. After the wreck, you went back and took out some personal items. What do you remember? Oh, and if you don't mind, would you speak in English, so I can understand you?"

Larry was in a trance. He started speaking quite clearly for a hillbilly. "I climbed up in the cab. I 'member now. The seat was pulled way forward. I got purdy long legs. No way I could git in the cab without movin' the seat. Someone super-short drove it last. I grabbed things from the glove box—papers and other junk. Had some clothes, bedding, books, food, toothbrush and stuff in the bunk. An atlas, other maps, an' some garbage was under the seat. Sunflower seeds was spilt all on the floor. I don't eat seeds. Where'd they come from?"

"Was there anything else unusual?"

"I caint remember anything else that warnt the way I left it."

"Thanks, Larry. Now, when I snap my fingers you'll wake up, and you'll feel rested, and there'll be no more pain in your neck. If'n you start feelin' pain agin…" Tanner started laughing…"Jist thank of yer Missus, and the pain'll go away." He snapped his fingers and Larry snapped out of his trance.

"Well, I'll be. The pain's gone. How's about if I bought y'all a beer to show my gratitude?"

"No thanks," Clay said. "You helped us plenty in return. That no-count cop friend of yours? He's the one who stole your truck. Thank you very much, Larry."

"Parked it right on the tracks, fixin' to cause a wreck? He ain't no friend of mine. You're gonna make sure that low-down piece of turd ends up in jail, right?"

Clay looked at his watch. "You can count on it, Friend. Now, I need to get Tanner back to college. He has a game tonight."

Clay and Tanner shook hands with Larry, returned to their car, and drove away without incident. "Dan Duncan's definitely the one who stole the truck. His car was in the lot, but *he* wasn't because he was driving the truck to the tracks. He's a former trucker and would have no problem driving the thing. Then he must've run back to the station. It's just a little over a mile. He wasn't there when Larry was first looking for him, but Larry saw him run up later, all winded. Dan is short, chews sunflower seeds, and is dumb enough to leave them on the floor. He as much as admitted to me when I read his mind that he killed two men and that he was at the tracks before and after the wreck. He went back to look for Adrian, just like Larry said when Dan left him at the tracks. I think we have our murderer."

CHAPTER 28

Clay dropped Tanner off to get his car so he could drive back to Ann Arbor. Tanner's game was to be on television, so Clay was hopeful that he could head back to Durand and watch it with Erika. Maybe if he visited Dan Duncan, the whole mystery would be solved before the day was over. Once Tanner left, Clay took care of a few things, called Erika, who invited him over, and then headed back to Durand. On the way, he called Chief Hopper with his news.

"How about if we stop by Dan's today, Luke?" Clay asked. "I'm on my way right now. You could meet me there."

"This is a touchy subject with me," Luke responded. "Dan's one of my men. I'm not gonna just walk in and make accusations. I'm not sure how I wanna handle it yet."

"I'd say that we should present the facts and see what happens from there."

"Okay. I'm on my way. Don't go making accusations before I get there. Wait for me."

Luke put his gun in his shoulder holster, put a light coat on to hide it, and hopped in his car to head to Duncan's house. Clay pulled off the expressway, checked his GPS, and followed the directions to Dan's house.

Chief Hopper was nervous as he reviewed the case in his head. The coroner believed Adrian Payne was killed in the accident. Adrian's ghost mentioned more than once that he had a heart attack. That *could* be true since Marshall Mortonson discovered

Adrian's body apparently passed out on the train. Marshall attempted to save Adrian's life by jumping with his body off the train just before the accident. An overturned train car crushed Adrian. Marshall then decided to hide the body, which he later buried with the horses that were killed in the crash. Someone—most likely Roberto Gomez—had wrecked the brakes on the train. The engineer was drunk and was declared responsible for the wreck. There was a semi-truck parked on the tracks at the Oak Street crossing. Someone had stolen the truck, and apparently that person was Dan Duncan, one of his own police officers. Erika didn't have a good alibi during the wreck, and she had motive for killing Adrian. Roberto Gomez's alibi was his wife. He had a strong motive for murder because Adrian had raped his wife. Dan Duncan was at the gas station during the wreck, and was on duty, but evidence suggests that he stole the truck and parked it on the tracks. Dan had ample reason to hate Adrian, so motive could be established. If the crash actually *did* kill Adrian, then both Dan and Roberto were responsible if Luke could prove it, but what if he was already dead? Could Erika have had something to do with that? However, even if Adrian *was* already dead, Joseph Carrollton also died in the wreck, so someone was responsible for *his* death. According to Clay; Dan, Roberto, and Marshall all believed that they killed Adrian, but Adrian seemed to think not. This was a very confusing case.

While Luke was reviewing the case in his mind, he came to a railroad crossing with an unmoving train. Luke looked as far as he could see to his right and left in hopes of locating the engine so he could determine which direction the train was running, but he couldn't see it. He was nervous about Clay getting to Dan's house before him, so he did a U-turn and made a guess which direction the train was facing. He decided to head north, hoping he could make it to a crossing ahead of the train.

Clay was nearly at Dan's house. He was feeling a bit jumpy because of Tanner's vision. What if Dan tried to shoot him? Would mind control work? Mind control kept Jessie's murderer from killing Clay, but it didn't keep him from killing Jessie. Clay wondered how he could be prepared for all possibilities. What if he didn't see Dan in time? He pulled into the driveway before Chief Hopper arrived. He paused, trying to decide if he should get out of his car or wait.

Luke found the next street farther north and turned down it. The train was crossing that street as well, and it still was not moving. He turned his car around again and headed another street farther north.

A sports quote from Clay's past entered his mind while he was indecisively waiting in Dan Duncan's driveway. "Courage is not the absence of fear, but rather the judgment that something else is more important than fear." Clay was admittedly a bit afraid of Duncan's gun, but as he thought of the quote, he realized that his purpose—to find the truth and help Erika and Logan Payne—was more important than his fear, so he opened his car door and stepped out of his car. Whether Luke was there or not, it was time to confront Dan.

As Luke turned on the next street north, he could finally see the end of the train. The train was still sitting, unmoving, across that set of tracks, as well. Luke was getting anxious. Clay might be at Dan's house already. What Luke could see was the engine, so he knew that he could go one street farther north and cross the tracks ahead of the train. He turned his car around for the third time, and headed for the next crossing.

Clay stepped up on Dan's porch, took a deep breath, and rang his doorbell. There was no answer, but Dan's car was in the driveway, so Clay patiently rang the bell again and waited.

Luke turned down the next street and groaned in dismay. The train had begun moving forward and was now blocking that crossing as well. It was moving incredibly slowly. Luke was already three streets farther north than he needed to be. As he paused a few seconds to think, the train stopped once again. The chief was forced to decide if he wanted to risk driving another street north, hoping the train wouldn't move again, or if he wanted to head back to the south, knowing, at least, which end was the back. He decided to head back to the south.

Dan never answered the door. Clay didn't know if he was being ignored or if Dan was somehow occupied; there was no way to know for sure. So Clay stepped off the porch and headed around the house to the back yard. It was a cold day, but maybe Dan was outside. As he rounded the house, his heart jumped because there was Dan with a gun in his hand. But he wasn't aiming it at Clay; he was aiming it at a squirrel that was sitting on one of his bird feeders. "You know there are bird feeders that are squirrel-proof, Dan," Clay said.

Dan jumped in surprise to hear his name. He looked at Clay, first in surprise and curiosity, but then in anger. "What are you doing here?"

"Waiting for Chief Hopper. We plan on talking to you about the night of the train wreck again. Don't you think shooting your pistol at a squirrel is a bit dangerous?"

"I've earned my certificate as a marksman. I can hit it."

"You've obviously tried and missed in the past. Why don't you just get a different bird feeder?"

"Because I want to kill that stupid squirrel!" Dan yelled. "*Then* I'll get a different feeder." *BOOM! Thunk!* In a crazed state, Dan actually shot his police revolver at the squirrel. He missed and the semi-automatic Glock .22 sent a 9-millimeter slug into the wall of his shed, putting a nice hole into a wooden sideboard. "Crap!" Dan yelled. The squirrel looked up temporarily, but within seconds, it continued attacking the birdseed.

"Listen, Dan. Is it legal for you to be shooting that gun in your yard? There might be another way to get rid of that squirrel, you know?"

"I'm kind of in a killing mood, Clay. What is it again you're here for?"

Chief Hopper turned the car and started heading south again. As he headed back for the street he originally planned to turn on, he got a call on his radio. "There's been a complaint of a gunshot, Chief. It's the same lady who said Dan Duncan shot out her bathroom window. Says he just shot his gun again in his backyard."

"I'm on my way to his place right now."

Luke hung his radio back up, and felt his heartbeat increase noticeably. "*What are you doing, Clay?*"

***

"I talked with Lawrence Maloney yesterday, Dan."

"Who's Lawrence Maloney?"

"He's that tall, thin, Southern truck driver whose truck you stole on the night of the train wreck."

Dan visibly stiffened, but he said, "I don't know where you'd get such a crazy idea as that, 'cause I didn't steal no truck."

"Exactly."

"What? I thought you just accused me."

"I did. And you just confessed. You said you 'didn't steal *no* truck,' so you must have stolen *a* truck. I'm simply suggesting that I have proof that you stole Larry Maloney's."

"You think you're clever, don't you? What proof do you have?"

"Well, first of all, Roger from the gas station explained how your car was parked in the Shell lot, and you weren't there. Explained how long it was before you finally showed up. Then I talked to Larry Maloney. Seems when you finally showed, you were *running* down the road from the direction of the crash. Seems, also, that you were in a hurry to get away and weren't too cooperative concerning his stolen truck. The most damning evidence, though, Dan, is that the truck seat was moved forward considerably, and there were sunflower seeds on the floor of the cab." Clay began to wonder where Hopper was. Cops were never there when they were needed most.

"And you think that proves I stole the truck?"

"That and your motive...*motives* actually. You had feelings for Erika and resented how Adrian treated her and Logan. That's actually quite honorable of you, but not a good enough reason to commit murder. Secondly, Adrian put your father out of business, a business, by the way, that prepared you with the skill to drive a semi-truck. Your father, whose health faded after he lost his business, had passed away just before the wreck, probably motivating you to get your revenge."

"So, Sherlock Holmes, you've put all those simple clues together and came to the logical conclusion that I'm a murderer. Ha! That's funny."

"I don't know if you meant to murder Adrian. But you certainly stole a truck and caused a serious train accident. Two men died, so you'll be put in prison for murder. Second degree, maybe, but murder nonetheless."

Dan was actually staying quite composed, something that surprised Clay, so he decided to push him a little harder. "By the way, Dan, Erika's *my* girl now, so if you have any ideas, forget it."

Anger flashed on Dan's face.

"And, Dan, we have proof that you lied to the chief and me. You were at the train crossing before the accident. You said you weren't." Clay was stretching the truth a bit, but he was getting desperate for a confession.

Duncan was still seething about the comment about Erika, but the "evidence" that Clay just mentioned put him over the edge.

Chief Hopper was back on the correct street and crossed the railroad tracks more than ten minutes behind schedule. He started driving furiously to Dan's house, hoping he wasn't too late.

Dan raised his gun and pointed it at Clay. "I don't know where you're getting your information, but you're not gonna be alive to tell anyone about it."

Clay stepped several deliberate steps into Dan's backyard, trying to establish a viewpoint from which he might see Luke if he showed up before Dan shot at him. "You've been struggling for the last seven years with the guilt of killing two men. We *know* now that it was you. Maybe if you turn yourself in, it'll be easier for you."

"I ain't turnin' myself in, Clay. Yeah, I stole the truck, and yeah, I parked it on the railroad tracks. I knew Payne would be driving the train, and I wanted to hurt him. And if he didn't get hurt, I was gonna try to get back to the tracks and maybe hurt him there. But that stupid hillbilly truck driver got in my way before I could get away from the gas station. When I finally got back to the tracks, Adrian was gone. I never heard from him again, which was okay with me, but it *was* a bit disturbing to not be able to find him. I hear Morty buried him," Dan laughed. "Even his partner wanted him to disappear. He was a swell guy, that Adrian Payne. He got better'n he deserved."

"What about Joseph Carrollton? Did he get what he deserved?"

"That drunk? Who cares about him? And who cares about you, Clay. Not Erika, I bet. She can't be trusted either. Do you think she missed her husband? Not a chance. And she won't miss you either when *you* turn up dead too."

Dan raised his gun to shoot at Clay. He wasn't looking into Clay's eyes. He was staring right into his chest, and Clay began to panic. He could see Dan's finger tightening on the trigger. He really *was* going to get shot. Out of instinct and possibly desperation, Clay raised his hand and using his mind-control telekinesis, he "pushed" Dan's gun to Dan's left just as the trigger was engaged and a shot fired.

"Drop your gun, Dan!" Chief Hopper yelled. "Don't make me shoot! Drop your gun, *now*!"

Dan's eyes never left Clay, but he lowered his gun, and then dropped it onto the grass.

"Now back away! Move away from the gun, Dan, and put your hands on your head."

Dan backed away from the gun, put his hands on his head, and turned to Chief Hopper. "Seven years, Chief. I been sufferin' seven years for what I did. What kind of person am I?"

"A bad person, Dan. What you did? A bad person. I don't know what else to say." Hopper took a pair of handcuffs, snapped one on Duncan's right wrist, and then pulled his arms behind his back and snapped the other cuff on. Hopper glared at Clay, obviously angry about the impatience that almost got him killed. He led Duncan to the front of the house where his car was parked.

As Dan was sliding into the back seat of the car, Clay appeared. He was holding something in his hand. "I just thought you'd like to know, Dan, that the shot that was meant for me hit *this* instead." Dangling from his hand by the tail was a dead animal. Dan had finally killed his squirrel.

CHAPTER 29

As Clay pulled into Erika's driveway, she was just leaving her house. She smiled an awesome smile, though, and gave Clay a hug as soon as he exited his car. It felt good to Clay to have someone to care about and to care about him again. He was phenomenally grateful for Tanner and for a friend like Zander Frauss, but a relationship with a woman was obviously different.

"It is *sooo* nice to see you," Clay said.

"Ditto," Erika said. "I've been wondering when you'd get here."

"It's been quite a day already, and I have lots to tell you. Where're you going?"

"I was gonna run up to the Depot to kill some time. You said that Adrian's still saying 'skeleton key,' so I figured I'd look around again in the attic to see if I can find anything. There's still time before Tanner's game. Why don't you come and we can look together?"

In the car, Clay caught Erika up on the discussion with and hypnosis of Larry Maloney. Then he told about Dan Duncan and Dan's attempt to shoot him. "Dan's been arrested. He confessed to stealing the truck and trying to kill Adrian. He also tried to kill me, so it's my guess he'll be going to prison for quite a long time."

"You say Tanner saw a vision of Dan trying to shoot you, and you went alone anyway? That's not very smart, Clay. I don't want to lose you—again."

"Again?"

"Like in high school. I plan to do my best to keep you around this time."

Clay was so grateful for those words that he grabbed and squeezed Erika's hand and sincerely said, "Thank you."

When they reached the Depot, they walked straight to the attic, opened the vault door, turned on the lights, and began a futile search. "How will we know we've found something when we don't know what we're looking for?" Erika asked.

"Excellent question. One in which I have no answer. I've been looking for another safe or cabinet or anything that needs a key. So far there's nothing."

"Maybe if we look in the safe again, there's a secret compartment or false back or something."

"Good idea. Let's try."

They opened the safe and pried, prodded, and searched every inch of the compartment and the drawer, but there was nothing.

"Maybe we could try asking Adrian again. Who knows? Maybe he'll cooperate."

"It's worth a try," Clay agreed. "Let's go."

They locked the attic back up and walked back down the hallway to Erika's office. Clay walked up to the family picture. Before he spoke, he looked at Adrian and could see little Anna in his features. There were several noticeable similarities. When he spoke, he said, "Adrian? Are you still here? Dan Duncan was arrested for the murder of both you and Joseph Carrollton. Morty cheated the company and buried your body, but it was Dan who tried to kill you. If you can hear me, do we have it right?"

"*What's the point?*"

"What's the point? I don't really know, Adrian. We've kind of just been trying to find answers. We've been hoping to help Logan too."

"*Ease the pain.*"

"What pain, Adrian? I don't…"

"*EASE the pain.*"

The hair on Clay's arms stood on end when it *finally* occurred to him what Adrian was saying. "You did *not* say what I just thought you said, did you?"

"*EASE the pain!*"

"And the 'point' is a clue?"

"*Yes, it is.*"

"Adrian, you didn't die during the train wreck, did you?"

"*A heart attack.*"

"How would I prove that?"

"*Skeleton key.*"

The hair on the back of Clay's neck now rose. A shiver went through his entire body. If what he was thinking was accurate, the truth of what happened on the train still had not been revealed, but Clay was certain he knew what to do next.

***

Clay was visibly upset. That fact alone was upsetting to Erika, but when Clay refused to tell her what he had learned, Erika was even more upset. She thought she had a trusting relationship with Clay, but his behavior made her concerned that he was hiding something from her, and it made her concerned about the consequences. If he wouldn't tell her, it must be something bad, but if he didn't trust her, that would be worse.

Clay dropped her off at her home. He said what appeared to Erika to be a sincere apology, but he still left without confiding in her. He didn't hold her hand, didn't hug her, and left without so much as a peck on the lips. He was distant. She walked into her house in a daze, went into her room, and cried. She hated getting so emotional, but she was falling in love, and what was more emotional than that? She was hurt, confused, and worried, and it would be two days before she would hear from Clay again.

***

Clay's hands were shaking as he tried to call Chief Hopper. He literally had to pull his car off the road to complete the call.

Finally, Hopper answered the phone. "That was a stupid thing for you to do, Clay, confronting Duncan without me."

"Hello, to you too, Dan. And thanks for the concern."

"He could have *killed* you!"

"That's more like it. You really *do* care."

"Heck, I just didn't want to have to do the paperwork. Murder is so much more work than I'm used to. I'm tired, Clay."

"Well, now that we have Dan Duncan safely tucked away, I have something else I need you to do. If you thought the work was done and it was time for your beauty rest, you'll have to think again. I've figured it out, but you're gonna have to investigate—earn those tax dollars, you know?"

"I'm all ears. Whatcha got?"

Clay reviewed his most recent meeting with Adrian Payne. He explained what he had discovered and what needed to be done. "I've got something to drop off to you, then I'm goin' home to pray. Seriously. You can call me when you have the evidence. In the meantime, I may just do some resting myself.

***

Clay couldn't get his mind off Erika. He was worried beyond any worry he'd ever felt before. Erika had taught him to have faith, but when Clay prayed, he found it very difficult to put the situation in God's hands and step back. He knew that the outcome of the whole mystery really wasn't his to control, so it was the *consequences* that were worrying him. He was unsure what that would mean for him, for Erika, and for Logan.

To get his mind from the situation temporarily, he watched Tanner play on television. Clemson from the Atlantic Coast Conference was playing Michigan. As much as Clay's mind was moiled in concern, he felt a temporary reprieve when his son was introduced as a starter, and the game began. Dick Vitale was raving about Tanner being a "diaper dandy," and it sounded good to Clay's ears to hear about his own son's maturity and leadership. What was better, however, was Tanner's performance. From the opening tip, Tanner was directing traffic out on the court like a veteran and hitting shots with regularity. Vitale said he was a "PTCer, a prime time candidate," and twice in the first half, after Tanner hit a "trifecta" with a hand in his face, he proclaimed, "Are you serious? Are you serious?" When he made his fifth shot in a row in the second half, Vitale yelled, "Call the fire chief 'cause he's on fire!"

When Michigan pulled out a close 69-65 victory, Tanner was named the Chevrolet Player of the Game, and Vitale said he was "Awesome baby! Awesome baby with a capital *A!*" Tanner had twenty-five points and nine assists. Clay was as proud as a dad could be, but as soon as the game was over, he was back to his temporary despondency. He was worried about Erika and, selfishly, his relationship with her. It was going to be a long, difficult wait for news from Chief Hopper.

CHAPTER 30

The following Monday at 4:00 in the afternoon, Clay finally got the call he was waiting for. Hopper confirmed that Clay's theory was correct. "I've got a meeting planned for 7:00 at the station. I assume you will be here," he said.

Clay had given this inevitable meeting an enormous amount of thought over the last two days. There were two important people that Clay wanted to attend, so he made a couple of phone calls. Tanner was his first, but he wasn't able to attend. Clay found himself disappointed that he wouldn't have Tanner's moral support. If things didn't go well with Erika, he would have liked for him to be there. He then called Andi Nickel, and she agreed to attend as a legal representative of the Paynes.

He pulled into the police station lot at 6:45. Clay made his way to the chief's office where Luke Hopper and Eric Haynes, a forensic anthropologist whom Hopper brought for the meeting, greeted him. Soon, Andi Nickel arrived. Finally Erika and Logan Payne entered the room. Erika looked at Clay a bit suspiciously, hurt in her eyes. Clay wanted to go to her and hug her, but he knew it wasn't the right time. He turned to Chief Hopper and nodded. It was time.

"I'd like to thank all of you for agreeing to this meeting. Then he turned to Eric Haynes. "This is Dr. Eric Haynes. He's here at my invitation. Dr. Haynes is a forensic anthropologist and he's graciously agreed to tell you about his recent findings.

"As you know, Erika," Hopper continued, "we've been investigating your husband's death. After seven years, his body was finally discovered eleven days ago. I began, with the help of Clay here, investigating first the burial and, eventually, the cause of his death.

"We all know that a truck was parked across the railroad tracks on South Oak Street. Even so, the initial investigation in 2003 placed the blame for the train accident on Joseph Carrollton, the engineer who died in the wreck. He was intoxicated, and it was determined that he didn't respond properly to the emergency he faced. However, once Adrian's body was uncovered, it opened up a mystery. Why was his body hidden? And since it was hidden, it led us to wonder if there was foul play involved. Without question, it was evident that Mr. Carrollton was killed as a result of the crash. And when the forensic pathologist examined Adrian's body, he was convinced that Adrian died in the crash as well. The pathologist was unable to diagnose any foul play, but that wasn't adding up with the information that we were discovering during the investigation.

"We eventually uncovered that Marshall Mortonson hid the body away and eventually buried Adrian at the gravesite where the horses that were killed in the train wreck were buried. As we continued the investigation, we discovered that the brakes of the train were purposely damaged, making it difficult for the train to stop. Also, we discovered that Officer Dan Duncan was responsible for stealing the truck and intentionally leaving it on the tracks in an attempt to cause the wreck.

"All of these disturbing findings still left the question unsettled as to exactly how Adrian actually died. The reason for this meeting is to uncover the mystery of his death. I've invited Dr. Haynes here so he can explain his findings."

"Thanks, Chief Hopper. I'm sorry to be here under these circumstances, but I'm here to present my findings, hopefully in a way that is understandable to each of you." The mood in the room was extremely tense. Clay felt heartache, and it hurt him to see that Erika was afraid of what she was about to hear. "First of all, let me explain that a forensic anthropologist is different than a pathologist. I've been trained specifically to study bones, like the anthropologists on the TV show, *Bones*. During his examination, the forensic pathologist would have naturally overlooked some bone trauma since the train wreck broke so many of Mr. Payne's bones. He reached the obvious conclusion, once the body was identified, that Adrian Payne died as a result of the train wreck. The body was completely skeletonized when it was discovered, so all he could base his judgment upon was the broken bones. There was no way to conclude that the deceased died in any other manner because there was no other forensic evidence.

"However, because of the information that Chief Hopper shared with me, I knew exactly what I was looking for." Haynes pulled out some pictures. "I was able to use my expertise to reach some conclusions that the pathologist was unable to determine."

Erika had her arm around Logan's shoulders in hopes of reassuring him, but her own confusion and uncertainty were obvious. Haynes showed an anatomical picture of the human chest. "This bone here, the sternum or breastbone, is protecting the heart. I found a wound just to the left of this bone," he pointed. He showed another picture of a human heart. "There is a pericardial sac that encloses the heart." Again, he pointed. "A knife wound passed through this bone—yes, it *is* possible for a knife to cut through bone. It would cut into the muscles as well. A wound like this, especially with a small knife and a small puncture, would cause blood to seep out of the heart, but it would get trapped in the sac that protects the heart. The end result is the heart would be constricted and, in a sense, suffocate itself. It would stop beating, much like with a heart attack."

Erika gave a confused and questioning look toward the anthropologist. "With a possible weapon in my possession, I could run tests to see if that *specific* blade cut through the sternum. We believe we have a match to that specific blade—the one that caused the death of Mr. Payne."

***

Clay found that his hands were sweating. He looked over at Erika, who had a lost look on her face. He couldn't tell if she was concerned about the findings or simply hurt about the manner she was finding out. Clay cleared his throat and began to speak. "I've spent the last two days trying to figure out what I might say at this moment. I've spent the majority of my life hiding secrets from people I care about. A little less than a year ago, as a couple of you know, my wife was murdered. I learned a lot of things from that tragic event and from several events leading up to it. But one of the things I learned was to be honest and quit keeping secrets.

"Why I'm telling you this is because there is no way that Chief Hopper and I could have figured this mystery out without clues from Adrian's ghost. As hard as it is to fully comprehend, somehow I can hear him speak when I'm in the train depot. He actually hasn't been fully cooperative. The obscure clues that he gave me have often been *really* difficult to interpret. But his clues *did* lead us to his body, and they also led us directly to the arrest of Marshall Mortonson.

"However, the ghost would continue to repeat the same clues. We would think we had the mystery solved, yet Adrian's ghost didn't seem to agree. Until two days ago, I believe I was either flat out *not* understanding him or I was *mis*understanding him or I was misinterpreting his clues. He kept saying he died of a heart attack, for instance. That was confusing, but it led us to ask questions about the day of the wreck. Evidence about the train brakes and the stolen truck resulted. Because of those discoveries, we began to wonder if Adrian was murdered, but if Adrian was murdered, why did he think he died from a heart attack? The heart attack clue was one that I believe I was, flat out, *not* understanding. He also kept saying "skeleton key." Because of Marshall Mortonson's set of skeleton keys, we were able to find evidence against Morty, but that particular clue, I believe, was one that I was simply *mis*understanding. Also, the ghost kept saying, "ease the pain." Because he was a ghost, and because he was a man who understandably would have many regrets in his life, I completely misinterpreted that clue. We kept thinking he wanted us to solve the case and somehow "ease [his] pain" before he could cross over into the next life, or some such thing.

"A few days ago," Clay said directly to Erika, "Logan took the jackknife that his father gave him and threw it in the wastebasket in your office. Adrian said 'waste not want not' and when I finally figured out that he wanted me to retrieve the knife, he said it would help me figure out 'the point of all of this.' Saturday, he asked me again, 'What's the point?' I asked him if that was a clue, and his response was 'Yes, it is.' Adrian restated all his previous clues— 'heart attack, skeleton key, and ease the pain.' Erika, sometimes when I was talking to Adrian's ghost, I'd look at the family picture on your wall. While I was looking at the picture on Saturday, I realized for the first time that he wasn't saying 'ease the pain.' All along, he'd been saying, "*He's* the Payne.' Not P-A-I-N. P-*A-Y-N-E*. That's when I figured it out. All of a sudden, the other three clues made sense too. I'm so sorry that I abandoned you so suddenly, but I stopped by to see Chief Hopper to tell him what I'd figured out, and he contacted the morgue where Adrian's skeleton was still being stored. Adrian's *skeleton* was the key to the solution of the mystery."

Chief Hopper stepped in at that point. "On the day of the train accident, Adrian had taken Logan with him to East Lansing. Morty went along to watch over Logan while his father was otherwise unavailable. When we asked Logan what he remembered from seven years ago, he explained to us that about a half-hour into the trip home, he went to see his father. He wanted to ride with him in the train engine. A few minutes later, according to Morty, he returned, very upset, and hiding his face against the train seat-cushion. We now know that his father struck him in the face. Minutes later, Morty went to talk to Adrian about Logan. When he reached the train car just behind the engine, he found Adrian apparently passed out on the floor of the train.

"We obviously wondered if he'd had a heart attack. The ghost kept saying 'heart attack' and Morty never mentioned an injury or blood or anything of the sort. When the train was about to crash, Morty picked up Adrian and jumped from the train, but one of the overturned cars after the crash fell on Adrian and crushed him. Morty realized that Adrian was dead and proceeded to hide and later bury the body—a body that was *not* killed in the wreck. Because of what Clay figured out on Saturday, I contacted the pathologist who originally examined Adrian's body. We needed him to take a closer look at the bones. He expressed that I would need a forensic *anthropologist*, an expert in trauma to the bones. Dr. Haynes, then, is the man who re-examined Adrian's body. Clay had given me the jackknife that he had retrieved from the wastebasket. Dr. Haynes was able to identify that it was that knife that sliced Adrian Payne's sternum and entered his heart—the knife 'point' and the 'heart attack' from Adrian's clues. We believe that *Logan* is the 'Payne' that Adrian was talking about. Adrian's skeleton was the key. Logan is responsible for killing his father."

CHAPTER 31

Andi Nickel transitioned immediately from curious bystander to attorney. "Chief Hopper, I'm here to represent Logan Payne on behalf of my client."

"And your client is?" Hopper asked.

"Confidential," she responded, but Hopper looked immediately to Clay and Clay simply smiled a sheepish smile. Erika looked up, tears in her sad, hurting eyes, and looked at Clay.

"You're not leaving this time, are you? You're gonna be here for us, right?" The words were more of a statement than a question. They came from a woman who knew her heart and was determined to have faith in a man she cared about deeply.

Clay replied, "I wouldn't have it any other way."

Andi Nickel started in on Hopper again. "He was ten years old."

"The case will be referred to the county prosecutor, Ms. Nickel. It's my guess that the prosecutor won't even bring the case to court. It's not even conceivable that he'd be tried as an adult, so the case would go to a magistrate, who would rule first in a preliminary hearing. Because of the probability that Logan acted in self-defense, the case would almost certainly be dismissed anyway, but if for some reason it wasn't, and Logan was tried for manslaughter or second degree murder, a conviction by a juvenile court judge would put him into the juvenile system. In five days, Logan is going to be eighteen years old, and at that point, he'll have *already* aged out of the system. He hasn't had any trouble in the past seven years either—he's been a good, clean kid. A prosecutor will almost certainly see any court action as a complete waste of the county's money."

"So I'm free to escort my client from the premises?"

"We've done our job here. We found the answers that we were looking for, Andi. Get him home to be with his mother. He's been through enough already today. The prosecutor will be in touch, but it's my feeling that there's nothing to worry about. It's time for the healing to begin."

***

It was Logan's eighteenth birthday party. Clay and Tanner had arrived early. Logan gave Clay a firm handshake with steady eye contact. Clay had been a steady presence at his home ever since the meeting at the police department, just like he'd promised.

Logan had opened up first to Lydia Frauss and then to his mother and Clay. His father had punched him hard in the face, knocking him to the floor. When Logan cried and told his father that he was going to tell his mother, Adrian had threatened to kill Erika and abandon Logan if he said a word. Logan had flipped open his jackknife and had palmed it in his hand with the blade sticking between his fingers. When his father attempted to strike him again simply because he was crying, Logan punched back, hitting him in the chest. Then he ran back to his seat on the train. He had no idea what had happened to his father. He had lived in fear for seven years that his father would return and hurt him again, or worse yet, hurt his mother. He cried at the gravesite when his father's body was recovered partly out of relief that Adrian would never return and partly out of grief that he would never experience his father's love.

Being rid of the constant fear, and freeing himself to tell the truth had made a remarkable difference in Logan. He was a different kid, and now he was eighteen years old and an adult. He fist-bumped Tanner and explained that at his game the day before, he had started and scored fourteen points. Durand had lost to Lakeville, but the game was close.

The Gomezes also came to the party and so did Logan's woodshop teacher, Mr. Jorgenson. "Everyone gather around. It's time for cake and ice cream," Erika announced. They sang "Happy Birthday," and after his mother made him make a wish, Logan blew out the candles.

"Let's open presents!" Anna squealed. "She had a present in her hands and was bursting with excitement to have Logan open it.

Mr. Jorgenson spoke up. "If you don't mind, I'd like you to open my gift first. I have to get going. Indoor soccer with my daughter."

Logan took a neatly wrapped package, shook it, shrugged his shoulders, and then opened it slowly. It was a complete wood carving knife set. "I was planning on giving you this for your graduation, but I think it's best if you got it now. I've never seen anyone as talented as you, Logan. With this set, you'll do amazing things."

Logan stood, approached his favorite teacher, and literally gave him a hug. "Thank you, Mr. Jorgenson. This means a lot to me."

As Mr. Jorgenson said his goodbyes, Anna cried out, "Mine next!" Stacy told her to be patient. Logan next opened a card from Clay and Tanner. It was four tickets for the Detroit Tigers home opener. "Yes!" Logan shouted. "Thank you. This is something I've always wanted to do." Then he smiled, looked at Clay, and said, "I wonder who I'll take?"

Clay laughed. "Whoever you want." Logan's smile was contagious, just like his mother's.

He opened his gift from Erika next. Tanner helped her pick it out. It was a pair of Jordan XVII's, a pair of basketball shoes that would make every Durand teammate envious. "Oh, man. These are the best! Thank you, Mom."

"I love you, Logan."

"Love you too," he said with not a hint of embarrassment. He meant it and openly shared it.

Finally, Anna was permitted to share her gift. Erika put her arm around Clay's waist in anticipation of what was coming next.

Anna ran to Logan and skidded to her knees on the floor right in front of where Logan was sitting. "This is from me!" Anna announced excitedly.

"Thank you. I can't wait to see what it is, Anna." He tore open the neatly wrapped package. It was a picture frame with a picture of Anna.

"Read the card," she said.

Logan opened it up. He started reading out loud. "Happy Birthday, Logan. Put this picture somewhere that you can see it every day. Love, your sister, Anna Gomez."

Logan paused as what he read slowly sank in. He looked at Anna, who was smiling the biggest dimpled smile imaginable. Then he looked at his mother, who was crying and shaking her head up and down to let Logan know that, yes, it was true. Finally, he looked at Stacy Gomez, who was also crying and nodding affirmation. Then Anna spoke up again. "Momma said that even though our dad isn't here today, he would want you to know that he gave you a gift this year anyway. He gave you a sister."

The enormity of what Anna said sunk in and Logan also started crying. "Come here, you nut." He gave his sister the first of many, many hugs to come. "You're the best birthday present I ever got. I love you, Anna. I'm gonna be the best brother in the world. You just wait and see."

"You already are, Logan."

***

Clay was sitting in a chair in Erika's office while she was on the phone. A knock sounded on her door, so Clay opened it and leaned forward, looking both ways down the hallway, but there was no one there.

"I'm down here, you moron. Jeesch, Clay!"

Clay started laughing. When he looked down, he said, "You're not going to jump me again, are you?" He said it with a sincere smile of friendship on his face. "Just toying with ya, Jasper. I saw you down there. What's up?"

"*Everything's* up compared to me, Dipstick. I've come to see, Erika, if you don't mind." He was smiling too.

Erika had her back to the men, a hand covering her free ear. She was starting to hang up the phone as she spun in her chair. When she saw Jasper, she screamed, and the phone jumped from her hand, landing four feet away in the wastebasket.

"You really have a way with women, Jasper," Clay continued to joke. He retrieved the phone from the wastebasket.

"I'm so sorry," said Erika.

"It's me that needs to apologize. That's one of the reasons I'm here. Maybe someday we'll be friends and you won't scream when you see me." Jasper smiled, and Erika returned his smile with her thousand-watt specialty. She could really light up a room. She walked to the front of her desk and Jasper extended his hand. "Would you accept my apology for being such a rotten person over the years?"

Erika put a knee on the floor and faced him at eye-level. "I've been afraid of you for years and years. I guess I made a bad first impression a long time ago, didn't I? I accept your apology, Jasper, if you'll accept mine, and then we can be friends." Then instead of shaking his hand, she gave him one of her signature hugs. Jasper held on extra-long. Who could blame the guy for enjoying hug perfection?

When he managed to compose himself, he said, "Deal! Now do you mind if I sit down?" He literally jumped into the chair that Clay had been using. His feet were dangling off the floor as he pulled some papers out of a file folder. "Erika, when I talked with Clay about a week ago, I felt ashamed. I've lived a long time as a selfish, bitter man. And then Clay came along, forgave me, and did something nice for me that I didn't deserve. I've been ashamed of myself ever since."

"The moment Clay told me about your talk, I forgave you too, Jasper. Unconditionally. If you will just trust that you're forgiven, you can forgive yourself, and we can have a friendship that we both appreciate. I don't need or want anything else from you."

Jasper smiled. It was a smile that confirmed in his mind that Erika was the person that Clay had said she was. "Your ex-husband was a creep. Don't know if I've ever met a more unlikable person. Except me, at times. He liked me, I think, because I was just as self-centered as he was. We put together a will and a living trust. Because of the contract with Morty, you got half ownership of the Depot, no matter what, unless he could divorce you or convince Morty to write up a new contract. And unless he could get you to sign a different insurance policy, which he never did before he disappeared, you were the beneficiary of his life insurance. I made those things part of the trust for tax purposes. What no one knew was that Adrian had lots of money stashed away for himself. We wrote his will, and in it, he gave it all to me. He said if he died, he wanted to make sure that you and Logan didn't get any of it."

"Why would he do that?" Clay wanted to know.

"Said he hated his wife's spirituality. All her prayers. Going to church. Raising Logan to be kind-hearted and sensitive. Said he cheated on her and used and hurt people—many of them her friends—and she didn't have the guts to stand up to him. Instead she prayed for him. He didn't love her, and he cared less for Logan. In our last meeting, ironically just a short time before the train wreck, he outlined for me that he had more than a million dollars that I could have if he ever passed away. Said that helping me after he passed away was the one good deed he would do. When his body was never discovered after the wreck, he was never declared dead, so I never got his money. That made me bitter too."

Clay began to feel that familiar coolness permeating the room again. He felt certain that Adrian was witnessing the conversation. He bit his tongue in an effort to not say something nasty about Adrian. He was also amazed at Erika's composure as she sat listening, not interrupting.

"Well, I've learned a lot of things the past few days. Erika, the Depot is worth 5.3 million dollars in the latest appraisal. Andi Nickel told me that she calculates that from Marshall's share of the Depot's sale, he will owe you in excess of another million dollars. I know you have a two million dollar life insurance policy to collect as well. In the process of tracking down your money, I also learned some things about Adrian. I now know he blackmailed his partner, cheated on you, abused his son, ran friends out of business, committed at least one known rape, and ignored his illegitimate daughter. I can name other things, but you get the point. He was a rotten man. He seemed to think by giving me some sort of inheritance, he would make up for all his dirty deeds. Well, I can't be party to that, so I'm taking the inheritance and giving it away."

"What!! You can't do that!" Adrian yelled. *"Giving you my inheritance is my one good deed! It's my ticket out of this miserable, lonely existence."*

"Forgive me for saying this, Erika. But you don't need his money. However, there *is* someone who does. I'm going to give the money to Stacy Gomez and to Anna. That way, Adrian will provide for them just like he managed to provide for you."

"Nooooo! You can't do that! I don't care about them! I gave that to you! You'll be rich, and I can move on!" Adrian began to have a temper tantrum. Pictures started flying through the air. Things started flying from Erika's desk. Jasper's eyes got huge as he curled up in a ball on his chair, arms covering his head. Erika backed herself into a corner of the office beside a file cabinet, and Clay ran to her side to protect her from the articles that were flying around the office.

"The office is haunted, Jasper. Let's get out of here!" Clay shouted. He ushered Erika out, then returned and literally scooped the unmoving, terrified Jasper up in his arms and carried him from the room. Several articles smashed into Clay, but he managed the retreat without serious injury.

"You'll still my protector, Clay," Erika said in relief.

"Looks like you're mine too," Jasper said with big, fearful eyes. "But you've also managed to save me from myself."

JEFF LAFERNEY

Epilogue

It was a very warm but overcast spring day. Tanner had picked Clay up at the airport and brought him home to find Erika and Logan waiting on the front porch. A smile lit up Clay's face as he saw the woman in which he was deeply in love. After his baseball team's return from Alabama, Clay was excited to be home and to see his girlfriend and her son. Clay and Erika hugged and gave each other a short but satisfying kiss. Then Clay gave Logan a handshake, which also turned into a hug.

Logan and Tanner began to play catch as Clay and Erika settled into a two-seated swing on the porch to watch and talk. A lot had happened in nearly five months. After Adrian's temper tantrum in the Depot, Erika never went back. Marshall Mortonson ran the Depot until it was sold, and eventually was tried for embezzlement, tax evasion, and money laundering. In a civil suit, headed by Andi Nickel, Morty paid Erika over a million dollars, and with fines, interest, penalties, and back taxes owed, he owed the IRS more than a million more. Then between attorney's fees, realtor fees, and taxes owed for the sale of his business, Morty was left with $25,000. While serving his sentence, he was tried and convicted for a class 5 felony and put in jail for two and a half years for moving, hiding, and abandoning a dead body, and was fined $25,000. When Morty would eventually be released from prison, he would be bankrupt.

Dan Duncan was tried and convicted for his attempted murder of Clay, malicious destruction of property, grand theft auto, and second-degree murder of Joseph Carrollton. He would be in prison for a long, long time.

Roberto Gomez was never tried. The prosecutor determined that there wasn't nearly enough evidence for a conviction, but Chief Hopper was convinced of his guilt, and he let Robbie know how fortunate he was.

Jasper became a new man. He was the realtor who brokered the sale of the Depot. With his six percent commission of over three hundred thousand dollars, he became the most generous man in Durand, showing special generosity for children, and even more special generosity for the Gomez girls. He became the family's closest personal friend. Jasper's co-careers as an attorney and as a realtor both took off, and the more prosperous he became, the more generous he was as well.

Chief Luke Hopper ended up getting an accommodation for the "Adrian Payne Case," but he knew that he could have never solved it without Clay, and Clay knew he could have never solved it without Tanner. Luke and Clay became good friends, and Clay took to calling him Copper. It was the perfect nickname for the copper-headed police officer, and soon Luke gave up and accepted the nickname from all of his friends.

What happened to Adrian, no one knows for sure. There are still stories and rumors of ghosts haunting the Depot, but Clay never went back and neither did Erika. He certainly was instrumental in solving the puzzle of what happened on the train that night. What other purpose he might have in roaming the earth as a ghost was unknown.

The prosecuting attorney reviewed Logan's case and determined that it would simply be a waste of the county's money to try Logan for any crime. Andi Nickel was prepared to argue self-defense, but it was never even necessary. Logan ended up getting honorable mention all-conference in basketball, and was doing very well on the varsity baseball team as well. His new coach loved Logan's attitude, which was becoming more and more outgoing and friendly. He smiled a lot and had put all signs of depression behind him. Every time Clay looked at him, he felt immense pride in the fact that he had used his powers for the good this time. He had helped Logan, the Gomezes, Erika, and Jasper, without hurting any of them.

A light rain began to fall. Tanner looked to his dad and smiled. It had become a tradition for the father and son to sit on the porch and think of Jessie Thomas during a rain. "I love a good spring rain," Erika said. "It smells good. It's so refreshing. I think when I'm sitting here with you, it's kind of romantic."

Tanner and Logan walked over and sat on the porch with their parents. "Mom loved the rain too, Erika. Dad and I always think of her when it rains."

"You know when the sun shines and it's still raining somehow? We like to say that she's smiling down on us."

"I know she was special, Clay and Tanner. I hope she approves of me."

Just then the clouds separated, and though it was still raining, the sun began to shine. A rainbow of colors appeared in the heavens, and the beauty of nature was exposed in a way that was awe inspiring to each of the persons sitting on the porch.

Tanner, who always seemed to know just the right words, said, "It looks to me that she's smiling down on you right now. Mom approves. If you ask me, it was a match made in Heaven."

Erika, with tears misting up her eyes, snuggled just a little closer to Clay. It was as if the line was choreographed when all four people said at the same time, "I love the rain."

Catch the other two books in
The Clay and Tanner Thomas Series:

ABOUT THE AUTHOR

Jeff LaFerney has been a long-time language arts teacher and coach. He and his wife, Jennifer, as well as both of their kids, Torey and Teryn, live in Michigan. Jeff loves sports and exercise as well as reading and writing (his blog is called "The Red Pen"). *Loving the Rain* and *Bulletproof* are suspense/mysteries which also include Clay and Tanner Thomas. Each novel stands alone and can be read in any order. *Jumper* is a science fiction adventure and is the first in his Time Traveler series.

Made in the USA
Middletown, DE
05 June 2015